ITHACA FOUND

Wingspan Edition

KIRSTEN MCKENZIE

SSP

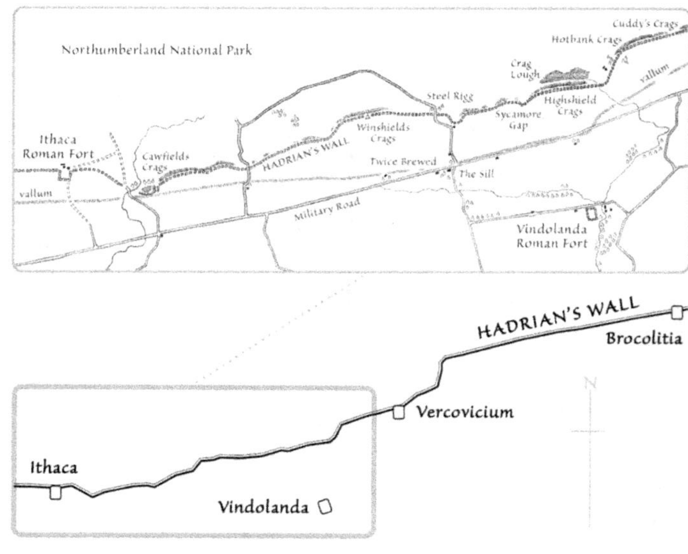

Northumberland National Park
Cuddy's Crags
Hotbank Crags
Crag Lough
vallum
Steel Rigg
Highshield Crags
Sycamore Gap
Winshields Crags
Ithaca Roman Fort
Cawfields Crags
HADRIAN'S WALL
Twice Brewed
The Sill
vallum
Military Road
Vindolanda Roman Fort
HADRIAN'S WALL
Brocolitia
Vercovicium
N
Ithaca
Vindolanda

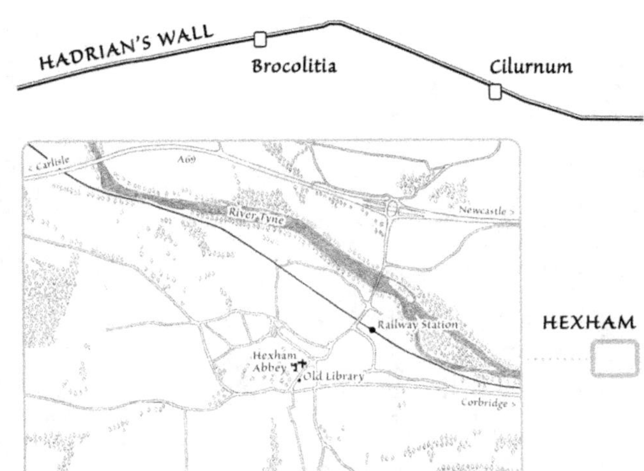

HADRIAN'S WALL
Brocolitia
Cilurnum
< Carlisle
A69
River Tyne
Newcastle >
Railway Station
Hexham Abbey
Old Library
Corbridge >
HEXHAM

This edition published 2025 by Squabbling Sparrows Press

ISBN 978 1 991331 61 8 (Wingspan Paperback Edition)

A catalogue record for this book is available from the National Library of New Zealand.

Cover design: Germancreative

Also by Kirsten McKenzie

The Old Curiosity Shop Time Travel Trilogy
FIFTEEN POSTCARDS
THE LAST LETTER
TELEGRAM HOME

The Ithaca Time Travel Trilogy
ITHACA BOUND
ITHACA LOST
ITHACA FOUND

The Cheviot Hills Time Travel Series
THE DEADLY LIFE OF DIANA PENN

Standalone Paranormal Thrillers
PAINTED
DOCTOR PERRY
THE FORGER AND THE THIEF
THE VAMPIRES OF YORK TOWER

Short Story Anthologies
LANDMARKS
NOIR FROM THE BAR
REMAINS TO BE TOLD

KIRSTEN MCKENZIE

ITHACA FOUND

TIME CONQUERS ALL

For Norman and Graham,
who both provided much
mirth whilst digging in the dirt

Allies

Pierced by the echoes of gunfire and the screams of the fallen, the mist dissipated as Albinus surveyed the scene from atop his horse. The metallic beast had turned the tide against the Iceni. He'd quickly recognised the advantage the stranger had brought.

"By the gods, what is this sorcery?" one of his advisors exclaimed, his hand tugging at the talisman hanging around his neck.

Albinus Clodius kept his composure. "It matters not. She fights against our enemies. We shall deal with the source of this magic later. For now, let us press the advantage she has given us."

With renewed vigour, the Roman soldiers rallied, their disciplined ranks forming a formidable front against the disoriented Iceni. Emboldened by the unexpected intervention of the blonde woman, the Romans fought with a renewed sense of purpose, and it wasn't long until the only sound reverberating around the snow-clad hills were the cries of the wounded. Cries cut short by the slicing of a sword to the throat, or a spear through the eye.

"Bring her to me," Albinus directed, his eyes shining with the same ambition he'd witnessed in the woman's eyes from across the battlefield. "Bring her so that I may thank her in person. And her iron beast. Bring that too. I may have need of that in Rome."

A Drink Between Friends

Jane Badrick emerged from behind the wheel of the battered but serviceable VW, her eyes shining, and her blonde bob in complete disarray. She stood with one hand on the door and held a cocked flare gun in the other, and waited for the Romans to come to her. Deploying the emergency flare had been a stroke of genius. Almost without exception, every man on the battlefield had frozen at the sight of the flaming red star hanging above them. The Roman soldiers had been the first to recover, redoubling their routing of the Iceni warriors. Jane almost felt sorry for the barbarians. A small part of her had wanted them to win. That wouldn't have suited her needs, but there was always room in life for the underdog to have a moment of glory. But that wasn't to be today. Today was about her power, and consolidating that power within the Roman Empire.

Jane stiffened as an advance guard of Roman soldiers approached on horseback, the horses skittish in such close proximity to the car, whose engine she had left running, in case she needed to beat a hasty retreat.

"Hail," cried one soldier as he approached, his scarred face barely concealing his trepidation.

"Hello," she called back, enunciating every vowel and syllable.

"The commander wishes to speak with you."

"Then let the commander approach."

Navigating these waters was no different from the council chamber, or any local body committee. You had to show strength as soon as you could to gain the upper hand. There would be no point diminishing herself to the role of a weak woman. No. She had to be in control from the start. It was the only way to push her agenda.

The soldier wheeled around, cantering back to the man she presumed was at the commander. It was interesting that he appeared to be an albino, and somewhere in the dark recesses of her memory, she struggled to remember why that seemed familiar. It would come to her.

Jane watched and waited, and wondered about fuel consumption. She quickly leaned into the car and turned the key. The engine fell silent, causing every Roman head to swivel back towards her. Perhaps that had been what they were waiting for, as the commander urged his mount forward, and her welcoming committee advanced. Perfect.

"Hail," called the statuesque albino man from atop of his chestnut horse.

"Hello," Jane replied. "Commander."

"We thank you for your service today. Your name?"

Shakespeare once said, *what is in a name*. Jane pondered how best to answer that question. Would they understand the title of mayor? Would the road to power be any the sweeter?

Through Different Eyes

Lillian's hands shook as she watched Jane's stolen VW Polo tear through the Iceni warriors like they were nothing more than training dummies. The sound of gunfire echoed across the battlefield, punctuated by screams that would haunt her dreams forever. This wasn't how history was supposed to play out. None of this should be happening.

"What manner of beast is that?" Julius whispered beside her. They were crouched in the scribe's chamber, peering through the narrow window that overlooked the killing field below. His presence should have been comforting, but it only amplified her guilt. She knew what was coming — or at least, what was supposed to come — and she couldn't tell him.

"It's..." she started, but what could she say? That it was a second-hand Volkswagen being driven by a corrupt small-town mayor with delusions of becoming a Roman empress? "It's not important. What matters is that woman. She's dangerous."

The red flare Jane had fired still hung in the sky, casting an otherworldly glow over the carnage below. Lillian watched as Albinus approached the car, his pale form unmistakable even at this distance. She could almost feel the timelines shifting, like threads being pulled from a tapestry.

"Apple," she breathed, scanning the battlefield for any sign of her friend. "She has to stop this."

"The pale girl?" Julius asked, his hand moving to his sword

hilt. "Marcus claims she's a spy, but I'm not so sure. There's something about her…"

A commotion in the courtyard below drew their attention. Marcus was gathering men, preparing to ride out to join Albinus. His face portrayed determination, but Lillian caught something else in his expression — calculation. He was planning something.

"We need to move," she said, pulling away from the window. "Now."

"Where?" Julius asked, but the sound of approaching footsteps in the corridor outside cut his question short.

Glass shattered across the stone floor as Julius yanked Lillian down beneath the window. Her heart hammering in her chest, she pressed herself against the icy wall. She counted the seconds between each of Julius' breaths, those shallow intakes of air that would give them away to the person in the corridor.

But just as quickly as the footsteps had approached, they retreated. Whoever it was must have had somewhere else more important to be. Like outside with Marcus and Jane and her weapons. Marcus had not been obvious in his plans as he gathered his trusted men, but Lillian had seen betrayal brewing in plenty of faces around her in Hexham. She knew the look well. Jane had worn it on her face for weeks before the Saturnalia Festival.

The footsteps returned. But this time, they were not alone. A muffled conversation snaked under the gap beneath the door.

"It has to be now," a voice said.

"She's in the fort somewhere. Up in one of the towers, most likely. We can gain access through the—" Lillian missed the rest of the words as heavier footsteps echoed past.

Her skin crawled as the fort's bells began ringing, once again announcing imminent salvation, or perhaps destruction.

Until this moment Lillian hadn't realised there were still men left with enough breath to ring the bells. She would never know if it was a warning that the governor was arriving, or if it was signalling Marcus's betrayal had begun. Again, Neumegen's dire warnings about the dangers of changing time haunted her.

"You should not be here," Julius said, his voice low against her ear.

She knew that meant he had worked out that she was a spy, but not who she spied for. No one would believe her if she admitted her connection to the governor, and nothing she could say would convince Julius that she was from two thousand years in his future. She barely believed it herself most days. But maybe there was something else she could say to make him understand?

"Apple is a friend. She means you no harm."

"The pale girl has strange eyes, and she is not one of us. Just like you, with your cloak and your talk of portents."

She knew he wasn't wrong. She and Apple were outsiders. They didn't blend in, didn't understand the correct protocols, and couldn't even communicate with any of the local people. They were more dangerous to the timeline than Jane was with her guns and her stupid car. Jane at least knew what she was doing.

But something else bothered her.

"You used to trust me," she started. "And now..." But he silenced her with his hand, his rough, calloused fingers on her lips. She should have stayed by the altar in the snow, waiting for Neumegen. Right now she could be at home in the present day, with the radiators cranked up, instead of being crouched down under a window in a cold stone tower, waiting to see if she would live or die.

"They're breaking cover. They want something," Julius breathed, already on the move, his sword drawn and his shield at the ready.

"Who?" she whispered, darting to the window to peer out, ignoring his sharp intake of breath.

Several long figures raced out of the cover of a sprawling copse, darting between shadows and snow drifts like wraiths.

So much blood stained the ground that the snow had long since lost its pristine whiteness, and it would take several storms before any evidence of today's betrayals would fade.

She watched as Marcus made his way down the tower stairs ahead of his band of soldiers, only to disappear into God knew where. It didn't matter which side Marcus was on, Lillian had no intention of dying in the past. History would have to be changed, rules be damned.

JANE EMERGED FROM BEHIND THE VW POLO, PLAYING HER role to perfection, standing beside the still-smoking car like she was posing for the Hexham Gazette. The surrounding battlefield transformed by gunfire and the red flare that still hung in the sky like a bloody star. Iceni warriors lay scattered across the snow-covered ground, their bodies testament to the devastating power of her intervention.

Decimus Clodius Albinus approached on horseback, his pale form stark against the winter landscape. The governor surveyed the scene with a mixture of calculation and wonder.

"By the gods," one of his advisors muttered, "what sorcery is this?"

Albinus remained composed. "A weapon," he said, his eyes fixed on Jane and the smoking car. "One that has turned the tide of battle in our favour."

Gar, the Iceni chieftain, stood at a distance, his face a mask of fury and disbelief. The druid Iolo beside him muttered incantations, his bony fingers clutching a staff adorned with what looked like human bones.

"I am the Mayor Jane Badrick," she announced, her voice cutting through the chaos. "And I bring a warning."

Ripples in Time

Loretta's fingers worked their magic as the knitting needles moved with practiced ease across her latest creation until they didn't. The needles fell from her grasp, clattering against the worn floorboards of Pramod's secret library as the figure she had been working on — the emperor Septimius Severus — changed before her eyes. The woven features melted and reformed, like wax held too close to a flame.

"Henry," she called out, her voice tight. "It's happening again."

Neumegen looked up from the stack of ancient documents spread across Pramod's desk. The temperature in the library had dropped, their breath now visible in the air.

"Show me," he said, abandoning his research.

Loretta held up her work. Where there had been an emperor's face crowned with laurel leaves, there was now something else. Someone else. A woman's face, her blonde hair woven through with gold thread.

"Jane Badrick," Neumegen breathed. "She's actually doing it. She's changing time."

A stack of newspapers on the desk behind them rustled, their headlines morphing and changing like mercury.

Neumegen snatched up the topmost copy of the Hexham Herald.

The masthead remained the same, but the text beneath it shifted and blurred.

"We're running out of time," he said, scanning the changing words.

Outside the library's frosted windows, the Hexham skyline flickered like a faulty television signal. The lights dimmed, and somewhere in the distance, church bells tolled at the wrong hour.

"There's more," Loretta said, pulling another piece from her bag. This one showed a pyre, flames licking towards a figure with skin as white as sun-bleached bone.

Neumegen's face paled. "Apple."

"History is being rewritten as we speak," Loretta said, her needles lying abandoned on the table beside her. "Is there anything we can do to stop it?"

"There will be a way," Neumegen insisted. "The portal—"

"Is closed. You know that."

"Then we find another way." Neumegen's fingers drummed against the ancient oak table. "There's always another way."

The bells tolled again, their formerly rich tones replaced by something hollower, something wrong. Like time itself was being stretched too thin.

JASPER FLETCHER STARED AT HIS COMPUTER SCREEN IN THE Hexham Herald office, his fingers hovering over the keyboard. The words he'd written moments ago were changing, the letters rearranging themselves like ants on the march. Names had changed. Events had shifted. The story about Jane Badrick's weapons cache now mentioned Roman coins and ancient altars.

"Rhema, is your computer playing up too?"

"Did you see this?" Rhema asked from her desk. The intern's face was lit by the sickly glow of her monitor. "The mayor's staff photo. Does it look a little weird to you? I haven't seen this before."

Jasper crossed to her desk, ignoring the flickering of the

fluorescent lights above them. The photo on the council website showed Jane Badrick as he remembered her, but somehow not.

She wore something straight from the pages of a history book.

"She looks like she's a Roman matron or something," he muttered.

"A what?"

"Straight out of my Cambridge Latin course."

The lights went out, plunging the newsroom into darkness. When they sputtered back on, John Revell stood in his office doorway, his face a picture of anger.

"Who signed off on this?" the editor said, holding up the next day's morning edition of the paper. The front-page story about Jane's disappearance was gone. In its place was a feature about the council's plans to demolish the Bellingham Tea Rooms. The byline bore Jasper's name.

"That's an old story," Jasper stuttered. He vaguely remembered it. It had never gone to print because a new owner had been found, and the demolition plans never saw the light of day again. "How did that get in there?"

"I'm asking the same thing," Revell said. "Get it fixed and stop wasting my time."

The bells of Hexham Abbey tolled, their familiar rhythm distorted. Like they were being rung from very, very far away.

Historical Relics

Pramod leaned against a marble column in Publius Aper's private garden, his walking stick propped beside him as he watched Metella tend to her father's prized sculpture. The Pantheon Boxer, as Aper called it, dominated the central courtyard — a bronze masterpiece that history had somehow forgotten. In Pramod's time, no record of this statue existed. Another treasure lost to the mists of time.

The boxer's face looked skyward, its bronze features caught in an eternal moment of triumph or perhaps pain. Blood - rendered in copper — streamed from cuts on the fighter's face. The details were extraordinary: leather hand wraps, broken nose, cauliflower ears. Even the spatters of blood seemed to glisten in the Roman sunlight.

"He unnerves me," Metella said, sprinkling water around the statue's base where winter flowers struggled to bloom. "The way he stares at the heavens, as if begging the gods for mercy."

Or warning them, Pramod thought. He had seen that same look on the faces of time travellers who had witnessed too much. Who had seen history changing around them like water flowing upstream.

"Your father seems fond of him," Pramod offered. Every word here had to be measured, considered. Aper had eyes and ears everywhere.

"Father is fond of anything that shows suffering," Metella replied, her voice bitter. "He says it builds character to be reminded of pain."

Pramod's fingers brushed the leather pouch that should have been hanging around his neck. Its absence felt like a missing limb. Without it, and the keys to time locked inside, he was just as frozen as the boxer.

"He will call for you soon," Metella said, her eyes darting towards the house. "Another round of questions about Albinus."

Pramod shifted his weight, testing his weakened leg. The stroke had left him diminished, but not as helpless as he let Aper believe. Every day he felt a little stronger, even as he played the invalid for Metella's father.

"And what shall I tell him this time?"

"The truth," Metella's hand rested on the boxer's bronze foot. "Or enough of it to keep him satisfied."

A shadow fell across the garden. Silas. The man moved like a ghost, appearing and disappearing at will. His presence meant Aper required their attendance.

"Your father wishes to speak with you both," Silas said, his face unreadable. But something in his eyes made Pramod uneasy.

"News from Britannia?" Metella asked.

Silas's silence was answer enough.

As they followed him inside, Pramod cast one last look at the forgotten boxer. In his time, no record of this statue existed. It was lost like so many other treasures. But something about its anguished face haunted him. As if it knew what was coming. As if it had seen the future being rewritten by Jane Badrick's hands.

Aper's study felt different. The busts of emperors that had lined the walls had shifted somehow — faces altered, names changed on their plinths. Pramod noticed one was missing, leaving only a shadow on the rich crimson wall where Severus had once stood.

"Interesting times," Aper said, not looking up from the despatch in his hands. A leather pouch — Pramod's pouch, sat on the desk beside him like a trophy. "Our friends in Britannia send word of a most unusual development."

Metella remained standing, her back straight as a gladius. Only Pramod saw how her fingers twisted in the folds of her dress.

"A woman has appeared," Aper continued. "One who commands an iron beast and wields the power of the gods themselves. She stands at Albinus's side even now." He looked up then, his dark eyes fixing on Pramod. "Unless you'd care to explain how such things are possible?"

"I wouldn't know anything about—" Pramod started, but Aper cut him off with a laugh.

"No? Then perhaps you can explain why my agents report she bears a striking resemblance to your companion at Ithaca Fort. The one who disappeared so mysteriously?"

Silas shifted in the shadows by the door. Something clinked beneath his cloak — metal on metal. A warning?

"The gods work in mysterious ways," Pramod offered carefully.

"The gods?" Aper's smile didn't reach his eyes. "No, this is something else. Something that might explain your own mysterious origins, friend." He lifted the leather pouch. "And perhaps what secrets this contains."

The air in the room felt thin, as if reality itself was struggling to maintain its shape. Through the window, Pramod could see the boxer statue — forever threatened with a blow that would never come.

"What do you want?" Metella asked, hand clenched at her side.

"Want? My dear daughter, want what I've always wanted." Aper stood, moving to the window. "The future. And it seems the gods have finally provided the means to secure it."

Pramod felt the weight of Aper's gaze. The leather pouch was everything — his only key back to his own time, to safety. He had to protect its secrets while revealing just enough to keep Aper satisfied.

"The woman you speak of," Pramod said, "is not from the gods. She is from a place far from here. A place of iron and stone, where machines move faster than horses and men fly like birds."

Aper's eyes glinted with humour and a modicum of interest. "And Albinus? What role does she play in his plans?"

Pramod chose his words with surgical precision. "She brings knowledge. Warnings. About those who would challenge his rise to power."

"Severus," Metella whispered.

Aper nodded, a predatory smile spreading across his face. "Tell me more about these challenges."

Before Pramod could respond, Silas stepped forward. "My lord, the dispatches from Britannia suggest more than just a warning. The woman commands weapons that could change everything."

Pramod's mind raced. He knew Jane Badrick's arrival could fundamentally alter the timeline, but he couldn't reveal too much. "The woman seeks to protect Albinus," he offered. "But her methods, and the weapons she commands, are... unpredictable."

The Puppet Master

Publius Septimius Aper spread the dispatches across his massive wooden desk, each document a thread in the complex tapestry of power he was weaving. The bronze bust of Augustus watched from a nearby pedestal, its stone eyes seeming to follow his every move.

Severus was climbing in power, but his distance made him vulnerable. The brief reign of Pertinax had created a moment of extraordinary opportunity. Aper understood what others did not — emperors were not born, they were made. And he would be the architect of Rome's next transformation.

Pramod's information was tantalisingly incomplete, but useful. A woman from another time? Ludicrous. One who brought warnings about challenges to Albinus's rise? That he could believe. Aper's fingers traced the edge of a despatch detailing troop movements in Britannia. Metella's Indian man was in the grips of a madness, but he knew things that had since come to pass.

Decimus Clodius Albinus. A governor with ambition, but lacking the last ingredient for true power — a strategic ally who understood the intricate dance of Roman politics.

Silas entered, a scroll tucked beneath his arm.

"The latest intelligence from the border," he said, laying the document before Aper.

Aper's eyes scanned the report. Albinus was gathering his

legions, preparing to move. But move where? And to what purpose?

"We need to ensure Albinus understands the true nature of power," Aper mused. "Not through military might alone, but through careful manipulation."

The coin Pramod had mentioned — the one featuring Albinus — suddenly seemed more than a mere trinket. It was the key to something larger. Albinus's delusions of his own importance. That would have to be cut down to size before Aper progressed his plans any further.

"Prepare a message," Aper instructed Silas. "We will offer Albinus more than military support. We will offer him a path to the throne that circumvents Severus entirely."

Silas nodded, his face impassive. But Aper knew the man was more than a simple servant. He was a weapon, carefully honed and waiting to be deployed.

The woman from the future — this Jane Badrick — intrigued Aper most of all. A harbinger of change, bringing knowledge of events yet to unfold. Her appearance was no accident. She was a message, both a warning and an opportunity.

Aper pulled his map of the empire closer, his fingers tracing the routes between Rome, Britannia, and the outer provinces. The pieces were moving. And he would ensure they moved exactly where he wanted them to go.

"We will need to act," he told Silas. "Pertinax's grip on power is tenuous. The Praetorian Guard can be... persuaded, with the right incentives."

A smile played at the corner of his mouth. The game of emperors was about to change. And Publius Septimius Aper intended to be the one holding the dice.

Aper's interest shifted, his keen mind finding a moment of respite from political calculations. "Do you play games where you come from?" he asked Pramod, as he moved to a beautifully carved wooden chest inlaid with mother-of-pearl.

He withdrew an exquisite set of gaming pieces crafted with meticulous care. The dice were precision-carved from polished bone, their surfaces smooth and unmarked. But it was the gaming counters that caught the light most dramatically: jet-black pieces alternating with brilliant white bone, each carved with intricate miniature scenes.

"Black and white," Aper mused, holding up a jet counter depicting a battle scene, then its bone counterpart showing a peaceful harvest. "Good and evil. Light and darkness. Order and chaos."

Pramod watched as Aper set up a game board — a chequered marble surface that shimmered with possibilities.

"*Ludus latrunculorum*," Aper explained. "A game of strategy. Of war and cunning." His fingers traced the board's surface. "Did you know the divine Emperor Claudius wrote an entire treatise on dice and gaming? *De arte aleae, 'On the Art of Dice'.* Tragically lost to time, like so many treasures."

He caught Pramod's eye. "Would you care to play? I find games reveal more about a man than a thousand conversations."

The jet and bone pieces glinted in the room's soft light, each counter a potential weapon, each move a potential betrayal. Aper's smile suggested this was far more than a simple game of chance.

The Price of Victory

Apple pressed herself against the cold stone wall of the fort's upper gallery, her heart thundering in her chest as she watched the scene unfold below. The great hall of Ithaca Fort buzzed with the energy of victory and something else—something wrong. Through gaps in the wooden railings, she could see her ancestor, Decimus Clodius Albinus, seated at the head table beside Jane Badrick, their heads bent close in conversation.

The sight made Apple's stomach churn. This wasn't how history was supposed to play out. She'd memorised every detail about her ancestor's life that she could find, and nowhere did it mention an alliance with the Iceni or their defeat at Ithaca Fort. Jane had already changed too much.

Below, servants scurried about with platters of food and amphorae of wine. Celebrating their victory over the Iceni had been going on for hours, but Apple couldn't tear herself away. She needed to understand what Jane was planning, even as dread settled like lead in her stomach.

The defeated Iceni chief, knelt in chains before the head table. Gar's once-proud bearing was bent but his eyes burnt with a hatred that made Apple shiver from her hidden vantage point.

JANE HAD SOMEHOW TURNED THE TIDE OF BATTLE WITH HER modern weapons and knowledge of history. The timeline was unravelling before Apple's eyes.

"To victory!" Jane's voice carried to Apple's hiding place. "To Rome, and to you, Governor Albinus—future emperor of Rome!"

Apple's breath caught. Whispers of ascending to emperor? Already? This was happening too fast. Her ancestor wasn't supposed to declare himself emperor for years yet. Jane was accelerating events, reshaping history with every word she spoke.

The gathered soldiers roared their approval, the sound echoing off the stone walls. Apple watched as Jane leaned in closer to Albinus, her words lost in the din, but her influence clear in the way he nodded at whatever she was saying. The sight of their easy familiarity made Apple's skin crawl.

She touched her pale hair—so like her ancestor's—and fought back tears of frustration. She had come back to save him, to preserve the timeline, but she was too late. Jane had arrived here first, had already begun weaving her web of manipulation and modern knowledge.

A soldier passed beneath her, and Apple pressed further into the shadows. She was powerless here—a girl out of time, watching history being rewritten by someone who didn't care about the consequences. What would this mean for the future? For her own existence?

The sound of Gar's chains rattling drew her attention back to the scene below. The Iceni chief was being dragged away, but not before Jane stood and approached him. Apple couldn't hear what was said, but she saw Gar's face contort with rage and something else—fear. Whatever Jane had told him, it had shaken even this fierce warrior.

Apple's fingers curled against the rough stone. She had to stop this and preserve the timeline as she knew it. But how? Jane had weapons, influence, and the ear of the governor. Apple had nothing but her knowledge of history. And history was becoming less reliable with every passing moment.

As she watched Jane return to her seat beside Albinus, Apple felt the weight of time itself pressing down on her. She could almost feel the future changing, reality shifting around her like sand in an hourglass. Would she even notice when her own existence unravelled?

"I won't let you destroy everything," she whispered, although her words were lost in the continuing celebrations below. "I'll find a way to stop you."

But even as she made the promise, Apple knew she was running out of time. The feast below wasn't just a celebration of victory over the Iceni—it was a celebration of Jane's growing power, of her ability to reshape history to her will. And somewhere in the future, the consequences of these changes were already beginning to ripple outward, unseen but unstoppable.

Apple took one last look at her ancestor, memorising his face in case... in case what? In case she ceased to exist? In case the timeline changed and she never came back here at all. The possibilities were too terrifying to contemplate.

With silent steps, she retreated from her hiding place. She needed to find Lillian — their only hope lay in working together. The fort's shadows seemed to shift and dance in the flickering torchlight as Apple made her way through the maze-like corridors, every sense straining for signs of her friend.

A sound behind her made her freeze. Footsteps echoed off the stone walls. Apple pressed herself into an alcove, hardly daring to breathe. The footsteps stopped.

"I knew I'd find you eventually." Marcus's voice cut through the darkness. "Although I must admit, you've led me on quite a chase."

Apple's heart stopped, and she bolted from her hiding place, but Marcus was faster. His iron grip closed around her arm before she'd taken three steps.

"Let me go!" she hissed, struggling against his hold.

"I think not. The Commander will want to see you." His voice held a note of satisfaction that made Apple's blood run cold.

Apple's attempts to break free proved futile as Marcus marched her through the fort's corridors, his grip never loosening. Her mind raced, searching for a way out, but each passing step brought her closer to what she knew would be a devastating confrontation.

The sounds of celebration grew louder as they approached the great hall. Marcus paused at the entrance.

Apple's stomach lurched as she saw Jane's eyes lock onto her from across the room, and a predatory smile spread across the mayor's face.

"Well, well," Jane's voice carried across the suddenly quiet hall as Marcus forced Apple forward. "Look who we have here."

Apple lifted her chin, determined not to show fear as she approached the head table. Her ancestor, Albinus, studied her with clear curiosity, no doubt noting their shared colouring.

"This is the spy you mentioned?" Albinus asked, his pale eyes—so like Apple's own—narrowing as he examined her.

"Oh, she's much more than that," Jane replied, rising from her seat. She circled Apple like a wolf sizing up its prey. "She's a threat to everything you've built. To your future."

"I'm trying to protect his future," Apple spat, unable to contain herself. "You're the one destroying everything!"

Jane's laugh was cold and sharp as a blade. "Protecting his future?" She turned to Albinus. "This girl claims she can read the future, where your bid for the empire ends in defeat and death. To earn her coin, she's here to ensure that happens."

Apple watched horror spread across Albinus's face, quickly replaced by anger. "Is this true?" he demanded.

"She's lying. This is—," Apple pleaded. "History isn't meant to be changed like this!"

"History is written by the victors," Jane said softly. "And I intend to ensure that we are victorious." She turned to Albinus. "She is not right in her mind. Imagine the damage her words could do to morale? Her madness is dangerous."

Albinus's expression hardened as he looked at Apple. Despite their shared blood, she saw no recognition, no sympathy in his eyes. Jane had poisoned him against her.

"What would you suggest?" he asked Jane.

Jane's smile was terrible to behold. "There's only one way to deal with threats to the empire." She turned to the guards. "Take her to the execution yard. Death is the only answer."

The blood drained from Apple's face as the guards seized her arms. This couldn't be happening. She looked desperately at her ancestor, but Albinus had already turned away, dismissing her to her fate.

As they dragged her from the hall, Apple caught one last glimpse of Jane raising a wine cup in mock salute. The mayor's voice followed her into the corridor: "To the future. Our future!"

Behind her, the celebrations resumed, drowning out Apple's protests as the soldiers led away to await her death.

The Hours Before Dawn

Apple's cell was little more than a storage room converted into a prison cell — a narrow space tucked beneath the granary stairs where sacks of grain had left permanent indentations in the packed earth floor. The only light came from a guttering torch in the corridor outside, its flames casting writhing shadows through the iron grate.

She huddled in the corner furthest from the door, knees pulled tight to her chest. The borrowed army cloak did little to ward off the bone-deep chill that seeped through the stone walls. Each breath formed a pale cloud in the frigid air.

Time moved strangely here, marked only by the gradual shortening of the torch and the distant sounds of the victory celebration continuing above. Snatches of drunken singing filtered down, interspersed with bursts of laughter that made her flinch. Somewhere up there, Jane was spinning her web of lies, reshaping history with every carefully chosen word.

Apple's fingers traced absent patterns on the dirt floor as memories surfaced unbidden. Her father's study back home, warm lamplight spilling across his desk as he shared stories of their famous ancestor. The pride in his voice when he spoke of Decimus Clodius Albinus. "We carry his blood," he would say, touching her pale hair so like his own. "Never forget that."

But Albinus hadn't recognised that shared blood when she stood before him. Jane had thoroughly poisoned his mind, twisting Apple's desperate warnings into threats. Now her own ancestor had condemned her to death.

The sound of approaching footsteps snapped her back to the present. Multiple sets, moving with purpose. Apple pressed herself further into the shadows as they drew closer.

"The prisoner stays under guard until dawn," a familiar voice ordered. Marcus. "No one enters without my direct permission."

"Yes, sir," the reply came from at least two others — new guards being posted.

"Anyone caught helping her escape answers to me."

Apple's heart sank. Marcus was too thorough, too calculating to leave any obvious routes for rescue. She could almost admire his efficiency if it wasn't currently working against her.

The footsteps retreated, leaving only the shuffle of the guards taking up their positions. Apple closed her eyes. There had to be a way out of this. She just had to think.

More memories surfaced of her father's lessons about their ancestor, but this time tinged with new understanding. He had never expanded upon Albinus's eventual fate, she realised. Had he known how the governor's bid for power ended?

A quiet scraping sound from somewhere above made her look up. Through gaps in the wooden ceiling, she caught glimpses of movement. Someone in the granary? Her pulse quickened. A rescue attempt, already?

No, just rats scurrying through the stored grain. The victory feast would keep them well-fed tonight. Apple's own stomach growled, reminding her that her last meal had been... when? She couldn't remember.

The torch in the corridor sputtered, threatening to go out. A guard cursed softly and moved to replace it. In that moment of deeper darkness, Apple heard something else — a whisper of movement in the shadows, so faint she might have imagined it.

Her eyes strained to pierce the gloom. There. A darker patch of shadow near the far wall. Was someone there? She opened her mouth to call out, but thought better of it. If someone was attempting a rescue, drawing attention would only endanger them both.

The new torch flared to life, driving the shadows back. Whatever, whoever she thought she'd seen, was gone. Apple's shoulders slumped. Just her imagination playing tricks, desperate for any sign of hope.

From far away came the sound of breaking pottery, followed by raucous laughter. The celebration showed no signs of winding down. How many hours until dawn? Until her scheduled execution? She had no way to mark the passing time except the gradual burning of the torch and the slow creep of cold through her limbs.

The guards changed once during her vigil, the new pair just as alert as their predecessors. They spoke little, but their presence was constant — a reminder that escape would not come easily.

Apple's thoughts turned to Lillian. Was her friend even now planning some desperate rescue? Had they captured her friend, too? The fort was crawling with soldiers, all of them celebrating their victory over the Iceni. A victory that should never have happened, that existed now only because of Jane's interference.

More memories surfaced — of the day she'd first met Lillian at the *Mooreeffoc* cafe, neither of them knowing then how their lives would intertwine. The frantic preparations for Saturnalia that seemed so long ago now. As too did Neumegen's warnings about the dangers of changing time.

She should have listened more carefully to those warnings. Should have being the operative word...

Shadows of Rome

Pramod traced his fingers along the edge of Aper's desk — a masterpiece of citrus wood imported from Mauritania, its surface inlaid with ivory and tortoiseshell in intricate geometric patterns. In two thousand years, he knew similar pieces would sell for millions at Christie's or Sotheby's, fought over by museums and collectors.

"The dispatches from Britannia are concerning," Aper said, arranging scrolls across the desk's polished surface. A silver inkwell sat nearby, shaped like a sleeping lion with garnets for eyes. The sort of personal item that rarely survived intact, though Pramod had seen fragments of similar pieces in museum collections.

"Tell me again what you know of this woman," Aper demanded.

Pramod chose his words carefully. Through the study window, he could see Metella in the garden, pretending to tend the roses while staying within earshot. "She is dangerous," he said simply. "More dangerous than you know."

Aper's fingers drummed against a wooden writing tablet, its wax surface covered in his precise handwriting. "She commands weapons we've never seen. Brings knowledge that seems impossible." He fixed Pramod with a penetrating stare. "Rather like you, wouldn't you say?"

Before Pramod could respond, a slave appeared in the

doorway — one of the many who kept Aper's household running. "My lord, the merchant has arrived with the items you requested."

Aper waved the man in. Two more slaves followed, carrying a large chest between them. They set it down with exaggerated care, as if it contained something extraordinarily valuable or dangerously fragile.

"Leave us," Aper commanded. Once they were alone, he opened the chest, revealing nested layers of cloth-wrapped objects.

Pramod watched as Aper unwrapped them one by one: a bronze mirror polished to a mirror shine, its handle shaped like intertwined serpents; a delicate glass perfume bottle in swirling shades of blue and gold; a set of gaming pieces carved from ivory and jet.

"Beautiful, aren't they?" Aper lifted a small bronze figure — a dancer frozen mid-spin, her dress appearing to flow despite the solidity of the metal. "The merchant claims they came from Alexandria. What do you think?"

Pramod examined the figure. The patina and styling suggested Egyptian manufacture, but something about the pose felt wrong for the period. A forgery then, though an excellent one. Even in this era, fakes plagued the trade in antiquities.

"The workmanship is impressive," he said diplomatically.

Aper's lips twitched. "But not genuine Alexandrian work, is it? Your eye is keener than you let on." He set the dancer aside and removed something else from the chest — a small wooden box inlaid with mother-of-pearl.

The box's surface was decorated with scenes from the Odyssey, each tiny figure rendered in incredible detail. Pramod's breath caught. He'd seen this box before — or rather, he'd seen photographs of its remains in a museum catalog. It would be discovered centuries later in a tomb outside Rome, its delicate inlays mostly intact though the wood had largely rotted away.

"This, however, is genuine," Aper said, opening the box to reveal several glass bottles nestled in purple silk. "The contents come from the personal physician of Cleopatra herself."

"Cleopatra's physician?" Pramod kept his tone neutral.

In his own time, any proven connection to Cleopatra would make an artefact priceless. He'd seen lesser pieces sell for millions.

Aper selected one of the bottles, holding it up to catch the light. The glass was impossibly thin, with a faint iridescent sheen that spoke of its age. "Each contains a different remedy. This one," he uncorked the bottle, releasing a faint herbal scent, "will cure any poison."

Pramod's eyes narrowed. Was that a threat? He'd come to learn that with Aper, every conversation had layers of meaning.

A commotion in the atrium interrupted them, and Metella appeared in the doorway, her face flushed. "Father, another messenger from Britannia."

Aper slid the cork back into the bottle and returned it to its silken nest. "Show him in."

The messenger was young and travel-worn, his official courier's cloak stained with mud from the road. He carried a scroll case made of tooled leather — the kind that would survive centuries buried in the right conditions, though its contents would be lost to time and decay.

"Speak," Aper commanded.

"My lord," the messenger bowed. "News from Ithaca Fort. The governor's forces have routed the Iceni rebels completely. They say..." he hesitated.

"Go on."

"They say a woman wielding divine powers led the attack. That she commands a beast of metal and fire that no Roman weapon can harm."

Pramod watched Aper's reaction, noting that the senator's face betrayed nothing, although his fingers strayed to the box of poison remedies.

"And what of this woman now?"

"She sits at the governor's right hand, advising him. There are whispers..." The messenger glanced nervously towards Metella and Pramod.

"You may speak."

"Whispers that she has knowledge of the future. That she's warned the governor about threats to his power." The messenger swallowed hard. "They say she's named Severus as a traitor who would see himself named emperor without the support of Rome."

Aper's hand closed around one of the glass bottles. "Indeed? How interesting." He turned to the chest of antiquities, selecting another object — a small bronze seal matrix, its surface engraved with a complex design. "Take this to my scribe. Have him prepare letters to be sent to all my allies in the Senate. Mark them with this seal only."

The messenger bowed and retreated. Pramod studied the seal as it passed — another item he recognised from museum collections. Dozens of impressions of that distinctive design survived in various archives, though the matrix itself had been lost to history. Until now.

When they were alone again, Aper returned to the chest. "Strange times we live in," he mused, lifting out a clay oil lamp shaped like a sleeping dog. "A woman appears from nowhere, bearing impossible weapons and knowledge of things yet to come." He glanced at Pramod. "Rather like that coin you carried. The one featuring Albinus as emperor. A coin I dismissed as a folly."

Pramod said nothing. The coin was safely hidden now, though he suspected Aper knew more about its location than he let on.

"The question is," Aper continued, "what game is she really playing? And how might it align with our own interests?"

He removed something else from the chest — a small bronze figurine of a seated scribe, his tablet eternally poised to record history. The workmanship was exquisite, every detail perfect from the folds of his toga to the stylus in his raised hand.

"Do you know what this is?" Aper asked.

Pramod nodded. The piece was famous, or would be one day. "A votive offering found in temples dedicated to Minerva."

"Very good. But this one is special." Aper turned the figure over, revealing tiny letters engraved on its base. "It belonged to a man who recorded the great events of his time. The rise and fall of emperors. The secrets that shaped the empire." He set the scribe down on his desk, positioned as if ready to take dictation. "History," Aper continued, "is a delicate thing. Like these treasures, it can be broken, or lost, or changed. Unless someone makes sure that it follows a suitable path. The correct path."

A Winter's Tale

Snow continued falling on Hexham, coating the ancient market square in layers of white that grew deeper by the hour. The town felt wrong somehow — buildings appearing and disappearing like mirages.

Neumegen stood at the library window, his pocket watch ticking with reassuring regularity even as time itself seemed to unravel around them. Behind him, Loretta's crochet needles clicked as she worked on another piece - this one showing the Roman walls of their town, though the pattern kept shifting under her fingers.

"The records are changing again," Loretta said, her needles falling still. She nodded toward the shelf of local history books, their spines shifting and reforming like mercury. "Look."

Neumegen crossed to examine a volume of the definitive history of Hexham Abbey. The pages flickered between different versions of events, as if history itself couldn't decide which version was true. One moment the text described the original Roman stones used in the Abbey's foundation, the next those same stones became part of a grand villa built by a woman named Julia Badrix.

"It's accelerating," Loretta continued, abandoning her work. "The changes are coming faster now."

Thunder crackled overhead. Through the windows, they watched as the outline of Hexham Abbey blurred and reformed. The familiar towers remained, but now appeared with Roman-style additions that had never existed.

Loretta pulled a handwritten diary from the shelf, which detailed archaeological finds along Hadrian's Wall. "The documents are changing, too. Look at this."

The diary fell open to a page filled with careful ink drawings. Neumegen's breath caught. Among the usual Roman finds of pottery shards, coins, and fibulae, was something impossible: a detailed sketch of what appeared to be modern bullet casings, labelled as 'metal tubes, possible ritual objects'.

"This isn't right," Neumegen said, his fingers tracing the neat copperplate handwriting beneath the sketch. The date given for the find was 1849; the location listed as Ithaca Fort.

"The past is bleeding into itself," Loretta said, standing at his shoulder. "Items from different times mixing." She touched the diary page. "If this continues..."

A faint sound like breaking glass echoed through the library. They rushed to the window to see part of the market square... shift. The Victorian drinking fountain at its centre blurred and reformed as an ancient Roman altar, then back again, as if reality couldn't decide which version was correct. To ordinary passersby, nothing had changed. They walked past what had always been there — a Roman altar that had stood in that spot for centuries. But Neumegen could see both versions simultaneously — the Victorian fountain and the ancient altar occupying the same space, like a double exposure in an old photograph. Only his time traveller's senses allowed him to perceive the alteration in the timeline.

"Do you see it?" he asked Loretta.

"The timelines are collapsing," Loretta said, her needles clicking faster. "Past and present bleeding together." She held up her work, showing how the yarn seemed to twist in impossible ways. "The changes are invisible to most people. Their memories adjust to match the new reality."

LORETTA GESTURED TO THE PEOPLE WALKING PAST THE library windows. "To them, Hexham has always been this way. Only we can see what's being lost, what's being... overwritten."

Neumegen moved to Pramod's desk, rifling through the papers there. "There has to be something, some reference to how to stabilise time when it starts to..." He stopped, staring at a document that hadn't been there moments before. The paper was both centuries old and yet covered in fresh script, the ink still wet despite its obvious age.

"What is it?" Loretta asked.

"A letter. From Pramod." Neumegen's fingers traced the words, careful not to smudge the fresh ink. "He's warning us about a plot in Rome. The Senate..." He leaned closer, studying the shifting text. "There's a faction moving to support Albinus's bid for the throne."

"Is he in danger?" Loretta asked.

"He doesn't say. He couldn't risk being too explicit. But he's discovered documents in Aper's study, correspondence between senators. They plan to remove anyone standing between Albinus and the throne." Neumegen looked up. "Including Septimius Severus."

Through the window, another shimmer caught their attention as reality continued its subtle shifts. To ordinary people walking past, nothing had changed, but their time travellers' senses showed them the truth. That the fabric of history had frayed.

"There's more," Neumegen continued reading. "Aper has received intelligence about unusual military movements in Britannia. The Sixth Legion gathering at Eboracum. Supply lines are being established. They're preparing for something big."

"A march on Rome?" Loretta's needles resumed their clicking as she worked, recording the original timeline before it was overwritten.

"That's what Pramod suspects. But it's happening too soon. The historical timeline..." Neumegen stopped, remembering that Pramod knew nothing about Jane or her interference. Whatever had accelerated events in Rome was happening separately to her actions, or at least, appeared to be.

"Two separate threats to the timeline," Loretta mused. "Working independently but affecting the same events. No wonder reality is becoming unstable."

The Sealed Testimony

The late afternoon sun cast long shadows across the muddy field near Hadrian's Wall, where the metal detecting team from Hadrian's Heroes worked with methodical precision. Graham Ryan adjusted his headphones, sweeping the detector in careful arcs across the rich Cumbrian soil. Beside him, Clifton Beaufort watched, his weathered hands clasped behind his back.

A sharp, high-pitched beep cut through the ambient sounds of the countryside. Graham stopped, raised his hand, and called out, "Got something!"

Clifton hurried over, his excitement palpable. They'd been working this site for weeks, a location that had already yielded scattered Roman coins and the occasional piece of military equipment. But this signal was deeper and far more substantial.

Graham began digging. The soil was damp and clingy, reluctant to give up its secrets. After several minutes of careful excavation, a glint of metal caught the light. A remarkably well preserved lead-lined box emerged from the earth.

"Just like the tablets from Vindolanda," Clifton murmured, his archaeological expertise shining through. "Lead's remarkable for preservation."

Back at their base, Graham and Clifton broke the ancient seal. The box opened with a soft, almost reverent creak.

Inside lay several wooden writing tablets, their surfaces covered in faded ink—delicate, fragile, and potentially of enormous historical significance.

"We'll have to report this," Graham said, his professional integrity clear. "We can't risk damaging these before they're properly examined."

Clifton nodded, carefully closing the box. "To the Finds Liaison Officer. Though I suspect she'll be more interested in the gold coins."

When they arrived at the Portable Antiquities Scheme office, their suspicions proved correct. Ayla Raposo was deep in conversation about the spectacular gold coin find from their previous excavation. The lead-lined box was set aside and almost forgotten in the excitement of the more glamorous discovery.

That evening, Neumegen and Loretta sat in their living room, half-watching a Netflix documentary about the hidden power brokers of the Roman Empire. The narrator's voice caught their attention.

"Perhaps the most intriguing figure of this period was Publius Septimius Aper," the documentarian intoned, "a Roman official with an unusual advisor — an Indian scholar. While Roman archaeological sites are found on the periphery of India, it was rare to find an Indian intellectual at the heart of Roman political intrigue."

Loretta leaned forward. "Did you hear that? An Indian advisor to a Roman political figure?"

Neumegen's eyes narrowed. "Pramod," he whispered.

The documentary continued, detailing the complex political machinations surrounding Decimus Clodius Albinus and his rise to power. But Neumegen and Loretta were no longer listening. Their minds were racing with possibilities.

The Governor's Feast

The bronze lamp flickered, casting dancing shadows across the rough-hewn walls of the commander's quarters. Decimus Clodius Albinus swirled the wine in his cup, the deep red liquid catching the lamplight like liquid garnet. Beyond the window, the stone walls of Ithaca Fort rose against the twilight, a testament to Roman engineering and imperial expansion.

Jane sat across from him, impossibly confident, her movements a strange blend of deference and challenge. Albinus was both irritated and intrigued as she spoke of things no provincial woman should know, with knowledge that cut through the usual political posturing like a sharp blade.

The missing soldiers' pay weighed on his mind. Castus had reported the vault empty, the theft blamed on the Iceni warriors. Another complication in a growing list of problems that threatened to undermine his plans.

And then there was the iron beast — the machine Jane had brought, which defied every understanding of transportation Albinus possessed. Its metallic hide gleamed with an unnatural perfection, its wheels precision-crafted beyond anything Roman artisans could conceive.

"You seem troubled," Jane said, her voice cutting through his thoughts. She leaned forward, the lamplight catching the emerald brooch at her shoulder.

Albinus studied her. When she first arrived, her clothing had been an abomination—tight-fitting garments of strange materials that shocked the fort's inhabitants. The commander's wife, Claudia, had taken pity on her, producing a stola of the finest dyed wool from her own wardrobe. Claudia had expertly pinned and draped the deep green fabric, transforming Jane from an exotic curiosity into something resembling a proper Roman matron. The brooch at her shoulder—an intricate piece of gold and emerald—completed the transformation, though something in Jane's bearing suggested she was anything but a typical Roman woman.

She wore the stola with a confidence that belied its recent acquisition. But her eyes—her eyes held something familiar to him — blatant calculation.

"The Iceni," Albinus said abruptly, "Are becoming a persistent problem."

Jane's laugh was sharp. "Problems have a way of resolving themselves," she replied, "if one knows how and where to apply the right pressure."

The lamplight guttered. Outside, the first stars pierced the evening sky. Somewhere in the fort, Gar remained in chains—another complication in a night full of them. The prisoner's rage burned hot and uncontrolled. When Jane had passed his cell earlier, he had unleashed a torrent of abuse that would have made even the most hardened legionary blanch. "Witch!" he had screamed, his voice raw with hatred. "Demon! Liar!" Every foul name in Latin and Celtic poured from his lips, accusations of sorcery and deception mixing with base insults that spoke to his fear and desperation. Jane had walked past without a glance, her indifference more cutting than any response could have been. But Gar's hatred remained, a festering wound of impotent anger.

Albinus refilled his wine cup, watching Jane over the rim. She returned his gaze without flinching, a smile of invitation playing at the corners of her mouth.

THE CHAMBER WAS DARK SAVE FOR A SINGLE OIL LAMP, ITS flame casting Jane's shadow against the stone walls. She was half-dressed, her modern undergarments hidden beneath the Roman stola. The soft sound of fabric shifting was the only noise until the door opened.

Clodius Albinus entered with a predatory grace that made Jane's breath catch. This was her moment. She had chosen her target carefully — the man who could elevate her beyond the mundane life of a small-town mayor. Her husband in Hexham was but a distant memory, replaced by the burning ambition that coursed through her veins.

"Governor," she said, letting the fabric slip to reveal her shoulder.

Clodius's eyes were unreadable. "Tell me about where you are from," he said without preamble.

Jane laughed, a sound meant to be seductive. "And what makes you think I would share such secrets?"

"Your iron beast," Clodius said, "will return to Rome with me. Thus, I require you to show me its workings."

Jane's smile faltered. "Let me show you the magic," she offered, "In exchange for you taking me with you." She let her stola drop to the ground, and he moved closer. Jane smiled, like a cat with the cream.

Her smile soon faded as Clodius bent to retrieve the delicate fabric, his eyes never leaving hers. As he placed the stola back over her shoulder, she realised her mistake. This was not a man interested in seduction. This was a man interested only in power, and how to obtain it. He gestured to the semi-automatic rifle leaning in the corner. "The magic stick," he said. "will also come with me."

His voice held no room for negotiation and Jane knew, with a sudden chill, that she was not in control. Not anymore.

Whispers and Shadows

The Hexham police station buzzed with a tension that had nothing to do with standard law enforcement. Spread across a makeshift evidence table were the artefacts Graham Ryan and Clifton Beaufort had unearthed from the frozen ground—a collection already sending tremors through the archaeological community.

Matthew Badrick leaned over the items, his breath catching. These weren't just Roman artefacts. The armour segments told a far more complex story—a mixture of Roman and local tribal craftsmanship that defied everything they thought they knew about the region'.

"Look at this," he muttered to Dr Elena Rodriguez, his colleague from Newcastle University. His fingers hovered just above a segment of armour, tracing the unusual pattern of damage. "These crush marks. They're not from typical battlefield trauma."

Elena adjusted her glasses, leaning closer. "It's almost like… compressed impact. But that doesn't make sense."

At the front desk, Jasper Fletcher from the local newspaper pressed forward, his persistence wearing down the reception staff. "Come on," he cajoled, "everyone's going to know about this in an hour, anyway. This is Hexham—nothing stays secret for long."

Sergeant Gavin Bishop watched the growing crowd with increasing concern. His small station wasn't big enough to host an impromptu archaeological conference. Clifton and Graham stood to one side, a mixture of pride and bewilderment on their faces.

"We need to secure the entire site," Matthew announced, turning to the Finds Liaison Officer. "No one can know the exact location. We can't risk nighthawks descending before we can document everything."

The FLO nodded, understanding the stakes. These artefacts represented something unprecedented—there was no historical record of a significant battle in this area. The mixture of Roman and local tribal armour suggested a narrative that could rewrite local history.

"How did we never know about this before?" Graham muttered, breaking the intense silence.

Clifton shook his head. "Forty years of detecting these fields and finding nothing. And now this?"

Matthew's fingers hovered over an intricate piece of armour. The craftsmanship was exquisite—a blend of Roman precision and local tribal artistry that spoke of a far more complex cultural interaction than anyone had previously imagined.

Jasper Fletcher had perfected the art of persistence. The young constable manning the desk was no match for a reporter who knew every trick of local journalism. A flash of his press badge, a confident stride, and he was through— standing now at the edge of the makeshift evidence room, notebook in hand.

His eyes swept the scene. Archaeological finds were good. But secrets? Secrets were better.

Matthew Badrick looked like a man dragged backwards from hell. Something that might have been coffee, or blood, stained his rumpled tweed jacket. Three days of stubble covered his jaw, and his eyes were red-rimmed, sunken. The recent Herald article about Jane's disappearance hung between them like an accusation.

The headline screamed:

MAYOR'S MYSTERIOUS VANISHING:
PEOPLE SMUGGLING SUSPECTED?

Matthew's hands shook with barely contained rage. His knuckles were white, fingernails pressing into his palms.

"After everything my wife has done for your paper," Matthew shouted.

Razor-sharp silence followed.

Jasper's response came measured, almost soft. "After everything about your wife we have covered up..."

The room seemed to hold its breath.

Sergeant Bishop moved quickly, his hand firm on Jasper's shoulder. "You need to leave. Now."

But Jasper's eyes landed on something incongruous among the finds. "Funny," he said, pointing, "that you bothered to pick that up too."

A tube of Dior lipstick. *Rouge.* Jane's signature colour.

And with that, the hope drained from Matthew's face.

Bishop shoved Jasper out of the room as pandemonium erupted around the table. And outside, a lone wolf howled, carrying with it the secrets of centuries. A wolf long extinct from modern day Britain...

THE COLD BIT AT JASPER'S FACE AS SERGEANT BISHOP shoved him through the station's front door. The crisp winter air made his ears sting, but his mind was already racing.

"That lipstick could have belonged to anyone," Bishop muttered, more to himself than to Jasper.

Jasper scoffed. "You know as well as I do what shade the mayor wears. It's been on enough collars..." He let the implication hang in the air.

Bishop's jaw tightened. "That's enough. I'm warning you— keep this find out of the press. Nothing gets published."

"Warnings are just suggestions in Hexham," Jasper replied, pulling his coat tighter.

They stood in uneasy proximity, their breath visible in the freezing air. Jasper's next question came casual, almost offhand. "By the way, what's the story with Darby's skull?"

Bishop paled.

"I can confirm that it belongs to Darby," Bishop said,

almost involuntarily. Then, catching himself, "We haven't notified his family yet."

Jasper smiled. He'd got exactly what he came for.

"And how did his skull get to be…" Jasper prompted, leaning in.

Bishop's hand came up, a warning gesture. "I've said too much already. And I've just eaten."

"You can't just drop something like that and walk away," Jasper pressed.

Bishop's response was curt. "I can and I will. Stay away from this, Fletcher. For your own good."

The sergeant turned, moving back towards the station's entrance. Jasper called after him, "Small towns have long memories, Bishop. And short secrets."

Bishop paused, just for a moment, and then the door closed behind him.

Jasper pulled out his phone. He owed Charley Scott a favour, and this would well and truly make them even.

The number rang twice before she picked up. "I've got a story for you," he said, before she could speak. "And trust me, it's going to be bigger than anything you've ever chased."

Barnstorming

The barn was a cathedral of shadows when the man returned. Twilight had long surrendered to night, leaving only the faintest suggestion of moonlight through the wooden slats.

Nicole stirred at the sound of footsteps. Her body was a collection of bruises, each movement a negotiation with pain. Dehydration had rendered her almost weightless, her muscles weak and uncooperative.

The metal detector hung from his hand—an anachronistic companion in this timeless space. Its electronic display cast a sickly green glow across his gloved fingers, creating shadows that moved differently to his body.

She lifted her head.

He stood motionless, a silhouette more shadow than man. His gaze fixed on her, unreadable. Was he her salvation or something else? The barn creaked. Mice skittered in the darkness.

"Water," Nicole pleaded.

The man didn't move or speak. He just watched.

Then movement. The rope around her wrists loosened, then fell away and Nicole's arms dropped like lead.

He scooped her up in his arms and carried her outside, where the night was alive with impossible sounds.

Distant war cries carried on the wind—the clash of metal on leather, the screams of warriors echoing through centuries.

Nicole blinked. Were those real? Or was this another hallucination born of dehydration and fear?

Mel's face swam before her eyes. Home. Stonehenge. Those massive stones she loved to walk among, touching history with her fingertips. Smooth, ancient rock warmed by sunlight, the wind whispering secrets older than memory.

The sounds of battle faded. Or perhaps they were never there? She couldn't decide. Then cool leather pressed against her back and she was moving somewhere. Or nowhere. The world dissolved into darkness.

White. Everything was white. The ceiling. The walls. The harsh fluorescent light that seemed to cut through her consciousness.

Nicole blinked, her eyelids like sandpaper. A plastic tube ran into her arm, connecting her to a clear bag of fluid hanging beside her bed. Someone had wrapper her wrists in clean white gauze, the edges stained with what might have been antiseptic.

A nurse approached, her sensible shoes making a soft squeaking sound against the linoleum floor.

"You're awake?" the nurse asked.

Nicole tried to speak, but her lips were too cracked, the movement painful. The nurse noticed and reached for a small jar of petroleum jelly. As she applied it to Nicole's lips, her gentle touch still sent a sharp stab of pain through Nicole's cracked skin.

"Where am I? How did I..." Nicole croaked, her voice barely more than a whisper.

The nurse stared at her. "Someone dropped you off last night. No one saw it happen," she said. "The police were hoping you'd be able to fill in the rest?"

Nicole's eyes filled with tears. The last thing she remembered was being tied up in the barn. A flashing metal detector, and the man who'd stood over her. Now she was here. Alone and confused and worried that Darby would return to finish the job he'd started.

Nothing On The Bow Street Runners

Gavin Bishop had long since passed the point of believing his day could get any worse. Yet here he was, standing in the sterile corridor of Hexham General Hospital, a folder of increasingly complicated case notes tucked under his arm, waiting to interview a woman who had been found barely alive on the front steps of the hospital.

So he had this recent development and the medical examiner's report on Darby's skull, which sat like a fresh lead weight in his mind and stomach. He didn't think he'd eaten a proper meal in days.

Bishop pushed open the door to the woman's hospital room, his movements heavy with accumulated stress. The fluorescent lights drained the colour from everything—the walls, the medical equipment, and the woman's face.

"Ms Pilcher," he said, pulling a chair closer to her bed. "I'm Sergeant Gavin Bishop. I need to ask you some questions about what happened to you."

Nicole's bandaged wrists told their own story of her captivity, according to the doctors who'd reported her arrival to the emergency services. Bishop knew what those marks meant. They weren't a sign of hours of restraint. They showed days of being held against her will.

"Darby," she croaked, her voice little more than a whisper. "It was Darby."

"Anson Darby?"

The woman nodded, the movement sending a grimace across her face.

Bishop's hand tightened on his pen. The same Darby whose skull was being examined by the pathologist? The same Darby who was supposed to be dead?

"Tell me everything," he said, his voice carefully neutral.

Nicole's story emerged in fragments. Tied up in the barn at Ithaca Farm. Left alone. Terrified. A mysterious rescue by a man with a metal detector. No details. No description beyond "he was just... there."

Bishop's mind was in full overdrive. The missing mayor, Darby's skull, the surplus of Roman artefacts. And now this woman, who should by all rights be dead, talking about a man who was supposed to be dead.

"I did not sign up for this," he muttered, more to himself than to the patient.

Outside the hospital window, a winter crow landed on the bare branch of an oak tree. Its black feathers stood in stark contrast to the grey Northumberland sky. An omen, Bishop thought, although he wasn't sure of what. Weren't crows omens of death?

"Ms Pilcher," he said again, "I need you to be very clear. Are you certain it was Anson Darby, the archaeologist?"

Her response was immediate. "Absolutely."

Bishop's phone buzzed. A text from the team. More complications.

This was going to be a very long day.

BISHOP'S OFFICE WAS NEVER MEANT FOR THIS LEVEL OF complexity. Three mobile phones lay scattered across his desk, each one connected to a different level of law enforcement.

"I'm telling you," he said to his local superintendent, "we're looking at something beyond a simple missing person or an archaeological find. The mayor, the Roman stuff, Darby's skull, the woman in the hospital—it's all connected."

He paused, listening to the skeptical response.

"Mark my words," Bishop continued, his voice dropping, "we'll find the mayor's body before this is over. And it won't be pretty. The public will be screaming conspiracies."

The call to the National Crime Agency was less confrontational but no less urgent. Bishop detailed the Roman artefacts, the circumstances of Darby's skull, and the other ones, and the potential of a major archaeological crime being committed right under their noses.

"We need more resources," he concluded. "And we needed them yesterday."

The North East Regional Special Operations Unit representative was more pragmatic. They'd seen their share of unusual cases, but this one was pushing boundaries.

As he hung up the final call, Bishop rubbed his temples. The weight of the investigation pressed down on him like a physical force.

Then his computer pinged.

Newcastle Chronicle
Breaking News
MASSIVE ROMAN HOARD DISCOVERED IN
HEXHAM
By Charley Scott

Bishop's blood pressure skyrocketed.

He'd known Charley since she was a bright-eyed intern at the Hexham Herald, always with a notebook in hand and fire in her eyes. Now she was plastering their sensitive investigation across the internet.

He stabbed at his phone. His call was answered immediately.

"You," Bishop growled before Jasper Fletcher could speak, "leaked this to Scott."

It wasn't a question. It was an accusation.

THE HEXHAM HERALD NEWSROOM BUZZED LIKE A HORNET'S nest. Phones rang with a cacophony that would have been deafening in any other era, but now felt like a symphony composed by a musical savant.

Jasper and Charley hunched over a corner desk, their heads almost touching. Scattered papers, half-empty coffee cups, and a forest of Post-it notes surrounded them like a protective barrier.

"Look at this," Jasper muttered, pointing to a line of text on his screen. "We need to tie in the Roman artefacts with Jane's disappearance."

Charley's fingers flew across the keyboard, her eyes sharp with journalistic hunger.

John Revell sat like a king in the centre of the room. His considerable paunch pressed against a shirt that had seen better days, straining buttons that looked ready to surrender. But Revell was smiling—a rare occurrence that transformed his usually dour expression into something more benevolent.

Jane Badrick was gone. And with her absence, the Hexham Herald was experiencing a renaissance.

Advertisers were calling. Readers were buying. For the first time in years, the paper might actually break even. Revell had even skipped his religiously observed Thursday golf game, which was something that hadn't happened since Thatcher was in Number 10.

His intern scurried past, dropping a stack of press releases. Another staffer juggled three phones, her headset creating a comic halo around her head.

"Bishop's going to lose his mind," Charley whispered to Jasper, a mischievous glint in her eye.

Revell overheard. His smile widened. The weight of Jane's past blackmail—those carefully documented indiscretions she'd held over him—had lifted. And so, for the first time in years, he felt free.

The phones continued to ring and the breaking news. And under his leadership, the Hexham Herald was riding the wave.

This Little Piggy Went To Market

The Forum Boarium erupted with life. Pramod limped beside Metella, his senses overwhelmed by the cacophony of Roman commerce. Beneath their sandalled feet, a carpet of discarded vegetable leaves, fish scales, and crushed nutshells created a slippery, organic mosaic. The air was a complex tapestry of smells—sharp vinegar from nearby pickling stalls, the rich musk of livestock, fresh blood from the butcher's sections, and the sweet undertone of honey and spices.

Merchants called out their wares, their voices rising and falling with that peculiar rhythm still used today. "Fresh sardines from Ostia!" "Olive oil from Hispania!" Chickens squawked in woven baskets. Dogs darted between stallholders' legs, scavenging for scraps.

"A writing box," Pramod had explained to Metella that morning when he asked to go to the market. "I need writing materials."

"My father has some you can use?" she responded.

"I need my own," Pramod replied. "He can't know what I'm doing. There will be too many questions."

She'd agreed, and here they were. To Pramod, the market was an experience he would never forget.

IT OVERWHELMED HIS SENSES, AND HE ITCHED TO TOUCH and taste everything they encountered. If only the future of the world wasn't weighing on his slight shoulders.

At a stall specialising in scribal supplies, Pramod examined the wooden box. Cedar-lined, the brass fittings caught the midday light. The merchant, sensing a potential sale, began extolling its virtues.

"Fine craftsmanship," the merchant said. "Perfect for a scholar. See how the lid fits? Keeps papyrus dry, protected from moisture."

Pramod selected several papyrus scrolls and several beech-wood ink tablets, a set of reed pens, and a small inkwell of fired clay. Metella watched, her money pouch heavy at her side.

Unbeknownst to them, Silas too formed part of the market crowd. Dispatched by Aper, Silas's eyes watched every purchase or interaction, regardless of how innocuous. The spy moved like liquid through the throng—a fish swimming through a sea of humanity, observing, recording, waiting.

"I need a blacksmith," Pramod explained to Metella.

She cocked her head in question.

"I need some alterations to this," he said, lifting the box.

The blacksmith's workshop was a cacophony of heat and sound. Flames roared in the forge, casting dancing shadows on the stone walls. The rhythmic beating of a hammer on metal created a percussive soundtrack to their arrival. Sweat glistened on the muscular arms of the smith, who paused his work and looked up.

Pramod approached with the wooden box cradled in his hands. Metella hung back, away from the intense heat and noise.

"I need a lead sheath for this box," Pramod explained. "Which I can seal. It must also be watertight."

The blacksmith's eyes narrowed as he considered Pramod's request and the obvious wealth of Metella. Pramod wished for a moment he had come alone, but that would have been impossible. Aper had him on a very short leash.

"Lead work is delicate. For what purpose do you need this

thing?" the smith asked, wiping sweat from his brow with a soot-covered forearm.

Pramod hesitated. "Protection for important documents."

That the blacksmith understood. And Pramod kicked himself as he watched the blacksmith adjust his price skyward.

With minimal haggling, they agreed the price, and he left the wooded box with a boy lingering beside the great hulk of a man who'd agreed to take on the job.

"I'm hungry," Metella announced, breaking the silence that had followed their transaction with the blacksmith.

Pramod looked at her, surprised by the declaration. She had been quiet since leaving the blacksmith's workshop, her eyes darting about the bustling street with a mixture of caution and excitement.

"We could return home," he suggested.

A flash of defiance crossed Metella's face. "No," she said, standing her ground. "I want to eat out and I want to choose where."

The market surged around them, a living entity of commerce and conversation.

"There," she said, pointing to a taberna that looked both familiar and timeless. "I know this place."

Nestled between a pottery shop and a cloth merchant's stall, the taberna's wooden facade weathered by years of Roman summers and winters. Wooden shutters framed a small window, and the door stood propped open to catch any afternoon breeze.

Entering from the bright, chaotic market, they stepped into a world of shadow and muted sound. The interior was lit by oil lamps that cast warm, flickering light across wooden tables and clay-tiled floors. The air was thick with competing aromas—wine's sharp bite, roasted meats, fresh bread, with an underlying scent of wood smoke.

An older man looked up from behind a small counter. One eye—a startling, milky blue and permanently fixed in a distant gaze, while the other burned with an intensity that seemed to look deep into Pramod's soul. A deep, jagged scar ran from his left temple down to his weathered jaw, testament to some long-forgotten battle.

When he smiled—as he did the moment he recognised Metella—the scars came alive, shifting like a map of hidden stories. Quintus Valerius was not a man easily forgotten.

"Metella?" he called out, his voice a mixture of surprise and genuine warmth. "Is that you?"

The innkeeper was Quintus Valerius, a man who had known Metella since she was a child. His family had run this taberna for generations, a landmark in this part of Rome that had survived changes of emperors, political upheavals, and countless market days.

"Uncle Quintus," Metella said, using the familiar term of respect for an older family friend. "My hunger forced me here! And my desire to see your handsome face once more."

Quintus laughed, a sound that filled the entire space. "Sit, sit!" He gestured to a table near the back, secluded but with a clear view of the main room. "Marcus!" he called to a younger man who appeared to be his son or apprentice. "Bring wine. And food!"

Pramod watched, fascinated, as Metella shed her usual cautious demeanour. Here, in this familiar space, she was more relaxed. Almost playful.

Marcus arrived with a broad clay platter. Roasted lamb, its edges crisp and slightly charred, sat alongside fresh bread still steaming from the oven. Olives glistened with olive oil, their dark surfaces reflecting the lamplight. A small dish of garum —the fermented fish sauce Romans loved—accompanied the meat.

The wine came in a broad-bellied amphora, its contents a deep red that caught the light like a ruby. Quintus poured with the practiced hand of someone who had been serving drinks for decades.

"Tell me," Quintus said, pulling up a stool, "what brings you home? Your father—"

Metella's hand shot out, touching his arm. A silent warning. Quintus understood. Some conversations weren't intended for public spaces.

Around them, other patrons ate and drank. Merchants

discussing the day's trades. Labourers sharing stories of their work. Sailors speaking of distant lands. The taberna was a microcosm of Roman life, and for this moment, Metella and Pramod were part of its living narrative.

Quintus leaned closer, his good eye fixed on Metella. "Your father's man is outside," he breathed, almost conversationally.

Metella's hand, which had been reaching for a piece of bread, froze. And across the table, Pramod stilled, his body coiled with sudden tension.

"Silas?" Metalla asked. "Why?"

The tavern's background noise—the clinking of cups, distant conversations, the shuffle of feet—receded as Quintus explained that had known Silas's reputation for years. A man who moved like smoke, who collected information the way others collected slaves. "I assume he's here to watch out for you? No father wants to see his daughter defiled on the streets of Rome."

Metella sipped for wine. Pramod didn't think she'd bought the explanation, especially given what they'd both experienced from Silas during the journey to Rome. He was spying on them, pure and simple.

"I will not press you," Quintus said, pushing a cup of wine towards Metella. "But rumours abound your father is reentering the political arena. Just when we thought he'd retreated to his villa, content with his past glories."

Metella's fingers tightened around the wine cup. "What rumours?"

Quintus' milky eye looked into a distant memory. "Your father's not a man who stays quiet for long. Some are saying he's positioning himself for a greater glory..."

Pramod watched the exchange, saying nothing.

"He's been meeting with people," Quintus continued. "Whispering in ears that most would consider... unexpected."

Metella looked at her reflection wavering in the wine's dark surface. "I know nothing of his plans," she said. But her voice carried a weight that suggested otherwise.

"Be careful," Quintus warned. "Your father's ambitions have always complicated things for your family. You don't want to get wrapped up in them now. Times are not the same as they were when you were a child. And given that you have your own child to think of..."

A server passed nearby, and the warning about Julius hung unchallenged in the air.

Quintus's good eye missed nothing, including when Pramod's hand brushed against Metella's.

You Won't Believe Your Eyes

The hospital room felt like a prison. Sterile white walls, the constant beep of machines, the smell of disinfectant—everything screamed of confinement. But Nicole's mind was anywhere but here. Her thoughts were fixed on one person: the metal detectorist who had saved her life.

If he hadn't found her in that barn, she would have died a slow and painful death. Tied to that splintered wooden post, surrounded by the musty smell of ancient hay and her own growing desperation.

A nurse entered, bringing a tray of food Nicole had no intention of eating. Accompanying the bland hospital meal was a newspaper. The headline caught her eye:

ARCHAEOLOGIST'S SEVERED SKULL DISCOVERED

Darby. The man who had tied her up. Had he left her to die, or had he planned on returning?

Nicole's hands trembled as she reached for the newspaper. It was short on details and long on speculation. The pathologist suggested that it was a recent death. A chill ran down her spine. How recent? How many days had she been tied up? Everything was a blur.

Her mind wandered back to the barn and to the metal detectorist. The quiet way he'd opened the door and then the way he'd looked at her. Had she imagined pity in his eyes or something else? Was he the man who'd murdered Darby? The man who had beheaded her captor?

"I need to be discharged," Nicole said to the nurse, her voice raspy but determined.

The nurse looked skeptical. "Ms Pilcher, you're severely dehydrated. You're not going anywhere."

But Nicole knew differently. She wasn't returning to her job at The Old Curiosity Shop. Not yet. Not until she found her saviour.

Her fingers traced the bruises on her wrists, still tender from the ropes. Darby was dead. But his murderer was out there. Would they come for her?

"I'm feeling fine now," she reiterated.

The nurse protested, but Nicole had already decided. Darby might be dead, but something about her rescue didn't add up. People don't just vanish, and their heads don't just fall off.

She needed answers. And she knew where to look.

Nicole's fingers fumbled with the buttons of her shirt. Her hands shook—whether from the aftermath of her ordeal or from pure determination. She couldn't tell.

A knock at the door. Two police officers stood watching her, their expressions a mixture of concern and official detachment.

"Ms Pilcher," the older officer began, "are you certain you're fit to leave?"

Nicole fixed them with a look she'd nurtured during her years in hospitality. "Either I'm calling a taxi, or you're about to offer to drive me back to Ithaca Farm? Either way, I'm leaving. So which is it?"

It was a tense drive for all three occupants. The police car's heater struggled against the winter chill, creating a fog on the windows that matched the murky uncertainty of Nicole's mind. What would Lillian say when they reached the farm? And why hadn't Lillian come to see her at the hospital?

Had the police actually informed Lillian about Nicole's incarceration in the barn?

The farm appeared through a veil of winter mist. Bare trees stood like skeletal sentinels, their branches etched against the grey sky. The police radio crackled with static, cutting through a half-heard report about the missing mayor and Darby's decapitated head. The young constable reached to increase the volume, but Bishop's hand stopped him.

"Why aren't the streets crawling with police?" Nicole asked. "If the mayor of London went missing, you wouldn't be able to move through these lanes for police officers."

Bishop shifted in his seat, exchanging a look with the young constable. "There has been a lot going on, that's for sure. And, ah... there's one other thing. No one has seen Ms Arlosh since the night of the Bellingham's Saturnalia party," he explained. "The same night the medical examiner suspects Darby died, and the mayor disappeared. And around when you were tied up in the barn. The timeline is a little confusing, though, to be honest..."

Nicole's breath caught. "Lillian?"

The young constable—Robson, his name tag read—spoke up. "We've been trying to piece together the timeline. Nothing like this happens in Hexham. It's almost as exciting as that time the BBC interviewed my gran over the werewolf she saw in our house, after they dug up two Celtic stone heads down the road. Gran used to be study all that stuff—"

"Cut it out, Robson," Bishop instructed, a pained look on his face. "Werewolves. Next you'll be talking about vampires, or the Lock Ness Monster."

They pulled up to the farmhouse, and Nicole was out of the car before it stopped.

"Lillian!" she called, bursting through the front door. "Lillian!"

Her voice echoed through the house despite the atmosphere inside screaming empty back.

Bishop and Robson followed, the floorboards creaking beneath their weight. Nicole moved from room to room, desperation mounting with each empty space.

"She's not here," Bishop said, his voice gentle.

Nicole whirled around. "Well, that's pretty obvious."

Robson looked uncomfortable. "Sergeant," he said, "shall I make some tea?"

Bishop nodded. "Good idea."

The kitchen was a scene of mild chaos. Broken glass still littered one corner. A chair lay overturned. Evidence of the struggle the officers had mentioned.

As Robson busied himself with the kettle, Bishop guided Nicole to a chair. His notebook lay open, but he made no move to write.

"Help us make was headway on the timeline. Can you start from the beginning?" he asked.

Nicole took a deep breath and her story came out in fragments. The collection of Roman altars. Darby's obsession with them. His violence on the night of the Saturnalia party.

"He was trying to move the altars," she said. "I guess to sell?"

Bishop's eyebrows lifted. "To sell where?"

Nicole shrugged. Not to her, she answered. She didn't have the knowledge, or the financial means, to buy antiquities.

Robson returned with tea. The china cups looked incongruously delicate against the backdrop of the violence which had already occurred.

"Show us these altars," Bishop said. "They've gotta be replicas. There's no way they would have been kept under wraps for so long without someone spilling the beans. Hexham's too small for that. Heck, England's too small for that."

BISHOP PUSHED THE SHED DOOR OPEN. DUST MOTES DANCED in the weak winter light as Robson pulled back the first drop cloth.

The Roman altars gleamed in ancient glory. They were all impossibly perfect.

The young constable's intake of breath was the only sound before a whispered prayer escaped his open lips.

Bishop said nothing. His eyes never left the altars. And his jaw never left the floor.

Threads of Time

The leather-bound journal lay open on the table, its pages covered in Neumegen's precise, almost architectural handwriting. Loretta watched him from across the room, her own cup of tea growing cold.

"He's out there," Neumegen muttered, tracing a line on an annotated map of Roman Britain. "And he's in more danger than he realises."

Without asking, Loretta knew he was talking about Pramod Sharma—who'd chosen to insert himself into the most dangerous political moment of the early Roman Empire.

"The lead box they found," Neumegen said, looking up. His dark eyes, fathomless and intense, seemed to look through rather than at Loretta. "It's not just a container. It's a message. He knew the box would survive. What's in it doesn't matter. It's the box itself. We have to see it."

"Pramod would never risk the timeline without a failsafe," Neumegen continued. "He's too careful. Too methodical."

Loretta moved closer, her fingers brushing the edge of the map. "So you don't think he's written something for us on the writing tablets?" she asked. "The ones in the box?"

Neumegen shook his head. "There was no guarantee that they'd survive. But the box, of course, that would survive. Easy to store. Designed to withstand floods and other calamities."

The pocket watch, made by Russells of Liverpool, sat on the table, its steady tick-tock a counterpoint to his thoughts.

"During Saturnalia, the fabric of time becomes... malleable," Neumegen continued. "That's how the box came to light. He forced it through time somehow."

Saturnalia—the Roman festival of misrule. A time when traditional hierarchies dissolved. When the impossible became possible.

Neumegen pulled the map closer. His finger traced a line around Ithaca Farm. "The tablets," he whispered. "They're not the message. They take too long to decipher. It's the box. The box is a clue to a precise moment in time. Where are you, Pramod?"

The pocket watch continued its relentless rhythm. Marking seconds, minutes, hours and centuries. Marking a moment when everything might change.

A memory of Auckland washed over Neumegen like the caress of an old friend.

February 1863. The night Queen Street became an inferno. Neumegen had been standing outside his tiny rented room when the first wisps of smoke appeared. Morrin's store was ablaze, and within moments, the fire became a living, ravenous beast consuming everything in its path.

Time travel whispered its familiar temptation. He could slip away, find another moment. No one would notice. No one would care.

But Pramod was there.

A sudden appearance, as time travellers were prone to make. One moment the street was chaos—burning timbers, screaming people, sparks flying like angry fireflies—and the next, Pramod materialised beside him.

"Watch out!" Pramod had yelled, as a massive burning beam collapsed toward Neumegen.

His friend's hands pulled him back just as the timber crashed where he had been standing moments before.

The heat was extraordinary. Waves of scorching air pushed against their bodies, making breathing difficult.

Lieutenant-General Cameron arrived, mobilising the

military men. Sailors from the French ship *Bonite* climbed onto roofs, beating out flames. Neumegen worked in tandem with Pramod, grabbing buckets and passing water. The smell of burning wood mixed with spirits created a toxic perfume around them.

"You could have died," Pramod said later, as they watched wooden buildings collapse like matchsticks.

Neumegen remembered the powder magazine near the Albert Barracks. One shift of wind, one errant spark, and half of Auckland would disappear in a thunderous explosion.

By dawn, they viewed the charred city. Blackened chimneys stood like memorial stones. The ground was a landscape of burnt timber and scattered belongings. Hundreds had lost everything.

But not Neumegen.

His life—his future—remained intact. Saved by a friend who understood the delicate threads of time better than anyone.

"Some fires," he would later tell Loretta, "burn away the unnecessary and leave only what truly matters."

The pawnshop became his salvation in the aftermath. A cramped space between a butcher and a milliner's. Pramod had suggested it—"Rebuild," he'd said. "Create something for yourself here."

Broken pocket watches became his first acquisition. Worthless to most people, but to Neumegen they had potential. He spent weeks learning their intricate mechanics, repairing what others had abandoned.

He learned to arrange the cabinets just so, creating an illusion of abundance from minimal stock. Each piece told a story. Each item had potential.

More than a business, it was a lifeline. A way of creating stability in a world that could shift beneath your feet at any moment.

Loretta watched him, understanding the weight of his memories. Time travel was not always a gift. Sometimes the constant negotiation with possibility was a burden.

"You could have stayed there," she said. "Then none of

this would matter. Pramod would be nothing more to you than a stranger on the street."

Neumegen's laugh was unexpected. "Oh, I'll return to Auckland, certainly. This time does not suit me one bit," he replied. "I wish Pramod had the same views. But love conquers all, doesn't it?"

Coins and Complications

The *Bellingham Tea Rooms* presented two different worlds. Downstairs, the restoration was immaculate —heritage colours, preserved original woodwork, plush velvet chairs that whispered of old-world elegance. Gleaming brass fixtures and curated historical photographs adorning walls painted in soft greens.

Their assigned bedroom told a different story.

Straight out of 1974, the room was a time capsule of mustard-yellow wallpaper with brown geometric patterns. A brown and orange plaid carpet, worn thin in patches, covered uneven floorboards. A synthetic bedspread looked like it had survived a nuclear war with its garish paisley pattern faded but still aggressively present.

"Good lord," Emma muttered, dropping her bag on a chair that creaked ominously.

A musty combination of old carpet, decades of accumulated dust, and something indefinably stale hit them with as much force as an American cyclone. It was the precise opposite of the meticulously restored rooms downstairs.

"I'm picking no one has touched this room since 1974," Ryan observed, running a finger along a windowsill.

"And that includes the cleaning staff, as well as the interior decorators."

An ancient radiator sat beneath the single paned window

which overlooked a narrow alleyway. The prospect of any future heat from the radiator seemed decidedly unlikely.

"We'll manage," Emma said, her professional demeanour a shield against the room's overwhelming dated aesthetic.

Ryan's hopes of a romantic reconciliation—a tiny flame he'd been nursing since their journey began—dimmed in the musty atmosphere.

"I'll take the floor," he offered.

"You'll do no such thing," Emma replied. "They said they'd bring up a cot, but we're adults. We can share a bed again, professionally."

Their luggage, as well as Emma's Royal Mint documentation and Ryan's investigative files, added a layer of modernity to the room's dated decor.

"I'm going to call my contact at the local station," Ryan said, pulling out his mobile. "We need to see the latest coins."

Emma raised an eyebrow. "Good luck with that. I heard from the proprietor that the local police are overwhelmed. Something about their mayor being missing? I don't think they're going to pause that investigation to talk about some old coins."

"They will," Ryan replied with fake confidence. Being so close to the woman he still loved, and the prospect of sharing a bed, even if it was only in a 'professional' way, had made him giddy with joy.

The phone connection was poor and Sergeant Bishop answered with a tone that suggested he was moments away from a complete breakdown.

"Stolen gold coins?" Bishop said, his voice a mix of exhaustion and irritation. "We've got coins coming out of our arseholes here. Which ones are you referring to?"

Ryan explained their purpose—the coins from Ithaca Farm, the potential connection to the Caernarfon Castle theft, their professional interest in authentication. "You said you had more coins? Can we come in and examine them?" Ryan concluded.

A long pause.

"Tomorrow. One o'clock," Bishop finally responded. "And not a moment earlier."

Emma had emerged from the tiny bathroom, already in her pyjamas.

"Don't get any ideas," she said without looking Ryan. "Keeping it professional, remember?"

Ryan smiled. Some things never changed.

THE *MOOREEFFOC* CAFE BUZZED WITH A NERVOUS ENERGY that had nothing to do with morning caffeine. The coffee machine hissed and gurgled, its steam rising like a persistent ghost, cutting through the rich smell of bacon and eggs that hung heavy in the air.

Ryan attacked his full English breakfast with an enthusiasm that belied the gruesome front page of the Hexham Herald spread between him and Emma. An artist's sketch dominated the page—a fanciful reconstruction of Darby's decapitated head, rendered in stark black and white.

"I just lost my appetite," Emma muttered, pushing aside her plate.

Ryan didn't seem to notice. He forked another mouthful of eggs, his eyes never leaving the newspaper. He'd already clocked the packed room, although they weren't all tourists eager to walk Hadrian's Wall. It was a distinctly local crowd, and a smattering of what appeared to be journalists, all hunched over coffee. Then there was a group he suspected to be police officers. You could spot them a mile off. Same haircuts, similar footwear, and clothing which could have all come from the one shop.

"This is delicious," he said with a mouthful of bacon. "You sure you don't want any?"

Emma's head shook. "You'll die eating all that," she replied.

A blonde waitress approached their table. The name tag on her faded red shirt read "Pauline" in glittery letters. Far too disco for Hexham.

"Are you here to walk the wall?" Pauline asked, refilling their water glasses. "or are you part of the investigation?" It seemed that gossip was Pauline's stock in trade.

Emma remained silent, her eyes fixed on the newspaper.

Ryan opened his mouth, then caught Emma's slight shake of her head. Professional. They needed to remain professional.

"Just here on... business," he managed, cutting himself off before mentioning the Art Loss Register. "It's not the weather to be walking the wall."

Pauline seemed unimpressed. "You'd be surprised at how many do. Idiots, all of them. God invented roads for a reason, you know, and cars. So we don't have to walk miles to get anywhere." Her eyes were already scanning the room, dismissing them from her mind as she moved off, picking up empty plates, and tidying errant chairs.

"Did you see this?" Ryan pushed the newspaper toward Emma, pointing to a paragraph near the bottom. "Unnamed sources suggesting the mayor's abduction might be connected to the horde of gold Roman coins found by local metal detectorists."

"I didn't think metal detecting was allowed along Hadrian's Wall?" Emma said.

"It's what the article says."

"And do you always believe everything you read in the papers?" Emma asked, her eyebrows raised.

"It's not like it's the *Daily Mail*. It's the *Hexham Herald*. Surely the local papers would have said if it was illegal?"

Emma laughed.

Despite the grisly headlines, Ryan felt buoyant. Something had shifted between him and Emma today. There had been a softening, and a hint of something else—not quite warmth, but something close to it.

Outside the cafe, the morning was sharp with winter's bite. Ryan pulled on his gloves.

"We've got two hours before meeting Bishop," he said. "What's our next move?"

Emma was already scrolling through her phone, her brow furrowed. "The metal detecting club," she muttered. "Hadrian's Heroes. They're the ones who found the coins?"

The name caught Ryan's attention. "Heroes? Sounds like they're trying too hard."

"It's a play on Hogan's Heroes, the TV show from the early 1970s about Allied POWs running a secret resistance operation right under the noses of their clueless German captors. People still quote it—especially 'I know nothing!'" She tapped her screen. "And I'd bet the name isn't just a TV reference. If they're metal detectorists, they're probably digging up remnants of wars from throughout history. Very clever."

Ryan felt bloody stupid for missing the reference, but there was no way he was going to admit that. Instead, he shrugged and hoped she wouldn't pick up on his silence—or the fact that he was already trying to remember if he'd ever watched an episode.

A text pinged on Emma's phone. She showed Ryan the screen—a message from a contact at the Royal Mint. Something about preliminary analysis of the coin samples.

"Interesting," she said, her professional mask slipping to reveal genuine excitement.

"We should visit their clubhouse," Ryan suggested. "See if we can get more information about the find."

Emma raised an eyebrow. "Subtle, I like your style."

"I'm always subtle," Ryan replied, a hint of his old charm surfacing.

Whispers and Leads

The second cup of coffee sat half-empty beside Jasper Fletcher, its surface filmed with a thin layer of cooling cream. Charley Scott picked at the remnants of a bacon sandwich, her eyes never leaving the table where the other couple had sat moments before.

"Royal Mint folder," she said, tapping her notes. "Definitely official. Not just tourists then."

Jasper leaned back, his journalistic instincts already spinning possibilities. "The guy looked like a cop to me."

"No," Charley disagreed, sharp and immediate. "Too... polished. Not local law enforcement. Something else."

Pauline approached their table, her glittery name tag catching the cafe's overhead light. She'd been cleaning nearby, her ears attuned to their conversation.

"Them?" she said, jerking her head toward the now-empty table. "Bloody Londoners."

Jasper raised an eyebrow. "Always a joy to have you watching over the place. Better than MI5 every single day. Tell us more."

Pauline leaned in. "The bloke's well keen on her. Proper desperate.

But she's not having any of it. Although there's something else there. Maybe they had a thing once upon a time."

Charley rolled her eyes. "Anything useful?"

"Posh as you like," Pauline continued, wiping down the

table with more force than necessary. "Both of them, but they only left me a two quid tip. Two quid! How can I buy chicken feed with that? My girls need proper feed, not some measly tip from high and mighty Londoners." Pauline moved away, summoned by someone who was a wall walker, as evidenced by their backpack, muddied boots, and complete unpreparedness for the English weather.

"They were really interested in the article," Jasper mused. "More than most people."

"Well, you included a giant picture of a decapitated head..."

"That was a stroke of genius. I thought Revell would have a complete coronary then and there when I first suggested it. Used the intern. She's an amazing artist. Wasted at the newspaper."

Charley was already texting. Her boss at the *Chronicle* wanted constant updates. The national press would be descending on Hexham soon, and he had declared that she'd lose her job if she didn't ensure that the Newcastle paper had first dibs on anything newsworthy about the missing mayor and the bodiless head. First dibs alongside the *Hexham Herald* she'd texted. After all, Jasper had given her access to everything he knew. And he didn't have to.

"We need to decide," she said, "are they a lead or just a distraction? Maybe they're here for a different reason?"

The cafe hummed around them. Gossip hung in the air like steam from the coffee machine.

"We follow them," Jasper said.

Charley nodded. "I was going to say the same thing."

Charley and Jasper exchanged a glance before springing into action. Chairs scraped against the floor as they hurried to gather their things. Jasper fumbled in his pocket and slapped a crumpled five-pound note onto the table. "Put the rest on my tab, Pauline!" he called over his shoulder. "I'll be back later to settle up."

Without waiting for a reply, he bolted for the door.

Charley was right behind him.

Outside, the air hit them like a slap. Charley sucked in a breath, and it felt like ice scraping down her throat. Jasper tugged his scarf higher over his face, muttering a curse as he scanned the street.

"Where'd they go?" Charley asked, her breath curling in the air.

Jasper squinted against the wind, then nudged her elbow. "There," he said, jerking his chin toward two figures moving down Market Place, their heads bent against the chill.

"Come on," Charley said through clenched teeth, pulling her scarf tighter. They hurried forward, boots thudding against the snow-dusted footpath as their prey turned down Beaumont Street, the adrenaline quickening their pace. If they lost sight of them now, they'd have no chance of picking up the trail again.

Jasper and Charley trailed behind the couple, trying to maintain a discreet distance.

"Where are they going? There's nothing down there?" Charley asked, her voice muffled by her scarf.

They followed the pair, watching as the woman consulted what looked like a map on her phone, before they veered off into a car park behind one of the town's older buildings.

"Shit," Jasper whispered. "They've got a car."

With the woman in the driver's seat, and the man in the passenger side, Jasper watched them pull out of the car park and disappear into Hexham's maze-like streets.

Charley and Jasper stood frozen.

"We lost them," Charley said.

The street where the car had been was now empty. No trace of the mysterious couple. And no clue about their destination.

R YAN WATCHED EMMA NAVIGATE THE WINDING Northumberland roads. Her hands gripping the steering wheel, her concentration absolute. He loved—no, he corrected himself—he appreciated how focused she could be.

The landscape outside was pure Northumberland. Bare trees lined the Military Road, their branches like arthritic fingers reaching into a grey sky. Stone walls divided fields bleached of colour.

"We're looking for evidence of provenance," Emma said, breaking the silence. "Those coins aren't just historical artefacts. They're potentially connected to a major theft."

Ryan nodded. The Caernarfon Castle coin theft had been a cold case for decades. If they could prove a connection, it would be a career-defining moment.

"The metal detecting club might have information they don't even realise is important," he said.

Emma raised her eyebrows slightly. A micro expression he'd learned to read years ago. Approval, mixed with a hint of challenge.

St. Oswald's Church emerged against the landscape—a small, historic building that looked like it had grown directly from the Northumberland earth. The church stood on the site of the Battle of Heavenfield, where King Oswald had defeated the Britons and established Christianity in the region. A historical artefact in its own right.

Emma pulled into the small parking area beside the church hall. The building looked unassuming—a typical rural community space with peeling white paint and an askew sign declaring it as the meeting place of *Hadrian's Heroes Metal Detecting Club*.

They sat for a moment after Emma killed the engine.

"We need to be careful," she said. "These aren't professional archaeologists. They're hobbyists, and they've done nothing wrong. We're just after more information about the context of where they found the coins."

Ryan felt a familiar flutter as memories of their time together flickered at the edges of his consciousness.

"I'll follow your lead," he said.

They stepped out of the car and were met with complete silence. The winter air cut through their coats. Ryan couldn't imagine living out here with only the bare bones of the Northumberland landscape to entertain—hills, stone walls, the occasional sheep.

He was about to pass judgment on the countryside when a van pulled up. Emblazoned with brightly coloured flowers and the words *Harley Garden Centre* in bold letters, it looked incongruous against the historic setting.

A man in red overalls with a chin covered in white whiskers emerged. He looked well puzzled by their presence, his gaze moving between Emma and Ryan.

"Can I help you?" he called out, his Northumberland accent thick and unmistakable.

Emma briefly explained who they were and what they were after, pulling her Royal Mint ID out of her handbag.

"Might as well come in and warm up. Bit of a chill today," Clifton said, ushering them into the church hall. The interior was a shrine to metal detecting. Display cases lined the walls, filled with finds from various excavations. Roman coins sat beside Victorian buttons, fragments of pottery, and what looked like a completely intact medieval belt buckle.

"Tea?" Clifton called over his shoulder, already filling an ancient electric kettle that looked like it had seen more decades than most of their finds. "My wife usually does the honours, but I'm not half bad with a kettle myself."

Ryan and Emma exchanged a glance. Emma nodded.

"Please," Ryan said.

Clifton chuckled. "Been making tea since my wife had her hip replacement. Learned quickly that if I wanted a cuppa, I'd have to do it myself." He pulled down three mismatched mugs. "Milk? Sugar?"

"You're allowed to keep all this here? Why isn't it in a museum?" Ryan called through to the kitchen.

Clifton emerged from the kitchen, tea in hand, a look of mild frustration on his face. "Most of this?" He gestured to the display cases. "Worthless, from a monetary perspective. Anything truly valuable goes straight to the museums. Newcastle, mostly. But here's the thing—half the time they don't even bother putting it on display!" His voice rose with indignation. "We find these incredible pieces of local history, and they get tucked away in some storage room. These artefacts tell the story of our region. But the museums? They treat them like we've handed them a bag of dog shite." He set the mugs down with a bit more force than necessary.

"LOCAL MUSEUMS SHOULD BE MORE GRATEFUL. THESE FINDS are our shared heritage. Not just something to be archived and ignored. Which is why we stopped giving them anything other than what the FLO tells us to."

The tea was strong—the kind of brew that you could stand a spoon upright in. Clifton settled into a chair, his metal detecting club jacket hanging on a nearby coat rack.

"FLO?" Ryan asked.

"Finds Liaison Officer," Clifton explained, "the unsung heroes of amateur archaeology. They document everything we find—photograph it, log it, add it to this massive national database. Not just cataloguing, mind you. Museums rely on them to acquire important finds. But more than that, they educate us. Teach responsible detecting. Make sure our discoveries contribute to historical knowledge instead of just disappearing into someone's private collection." He paused to drink his tea, forehead creased, before he shook himself clear of his introspection.

"Now, these coins you're asking about," he began, "first thing I'll say is that they weren't like anything we've found before. Deep burial. Unusual preservation."

Ryan leaned forward. "How different?"

"Most hoards we find are scattered," Clifton explained. "These were carefully placed. Protected. Almost like someone wanted them to survive." He paused, taking a long swig of tea. "The loose coins near where the mayor went missing? Those were surface finds. But the main hoard? Deep. Really deep. I don't think they're connected, although that dead archaeologist did."

Emma leaned forward. "How deep?"

Clifton's eyes lit up. "Want me to show you?"

He retrieved a metal detector from a corner—a top-of-the-line XP Deus, its sleek design contrasting with the cluttered hall. "Most people don't understand these machines," he said. "It's not just about waving something over the ground."

Ryan's interest was genuine. "Would you mind demonstrating?"

Clifton's chest puffed with pride.

"Happy to. But first, let me tell you about the regulations. Hadrian's Wall? It's not just any old patch of ground. It's a UNESCO World Heritage Site. Scheduled Monument."

His tone turned serious. "You can't just go detecting anywhere. It's illegal under the Ancient Monuments and Archaeological Areas Act 1979. Nighthawking—that's unauthorised metal detecting—it's a criminal offence. Fines or prosecution. They can even confiscate your equipment."

Emma nodded. "Historic England takes this seriously."

"Damn right they do," Clifton continued. "Most detectorists are responsible. We're preserving history, not destroying it."

He demonstrated the metal detector's sensitivity, showing how different depths and ground conditions affected the signal. Ryan watched, fascinated.

"These machines can detect objects up to five feet underground," Clifton explained. "But that doesn't mean you have the right to dig. Permission is everything. From landowners. From Historic England. Everything must be documented."

The Prisoner's Dawn

As the early morning light filtered under the door of her cell, Apple stirred, her body aching from a night on the hard bench that served as her bed. Prisoners weren't afforded luxuries.

A guard approached, his sandals scuffing against the stone floor. He carried a wooden bowl—her morning meal—a simple porridge of wheat, known as *puls*, a coarse wheat mixture, thick and filling. Mixed with a little salt and perhaps a drizzle of olive oil, it was the standard breakfast for soldiers and prisoners alike.

Apple sat up, her muscles protesting. The porridge steamed, a reminder of how little she had eaten in recent days. She ate mechanically, each spoonful a battle against her own despair.

"Help!" she called out, her voice echoing off the stone walls. "Please!"

Silence answered her.

The bowl was nearly empty when the second guard arrived. Younger with a well developed sneer. His hand rested on the short sword at his belt, as if she were a dangerous criminal.

"You're to prepare yourself," he said, his voice oozing with officialness.

"Prepare? For what?"

"A journey," the guard responded. "To Londinium first. Then to Rome."

"Rome?" The word escaped her before she could stop herself. "Why?"

The guard's smile stiffened. "To meet your fate. You and that filthy heathen. They should have strung you both up straight away." He spat on the rush-covered floor.

A chill ran down Apple's spine. She thought of Gar—the Iceni warrior who shared her captivity. Were they to be transported together? Executed? Displayed? The Romans were nothing if not theatrical in their punishments.

Her mind flickered to everything she knew about Roman travel. The cursus publicus—the imperial postal system. Prisoners were often transported using this network of relay stations. Horses. Changing horses at way stations. A journey that could take weeks at this time of year.

"When?" she asked.

"Soon," the guard said. And then he was gone.

The cell closed in around her. Apple closed her eyes and prayed that she'd at least live to see Rome. What an adventure, even if it meant she'd die at the end.

THE PREPARATIONS WERE BRUTAL IN THEIR EFFICIENCY.

Two guards dragged Gar from his cell first. Apple could hear the sounds of struggle—chains clanking, a muffled grunt of pain. Her own preparations were no less humiliating.

They fastened heavy iron manacles around her wrists, the metal cold against her skin. A length of chain connected the manacles, limiting her movements to short, shuffling steps. Another chain ran from her waist to the wagon's edge, ensuring she couldn't stray.

The enclosed cart was a wooden prison on wheels. Covered with a heavy canvas top, it offered protection from the elements, but no comfort. Wooden slats formed a crude bench along each side, and the interior smelled of old leather, urine, sweat, and fear.

Gar was already inside when they pushed Apple in. The Iceni warrior looked far worse than she did—bruises marked his face, and his own chains seemed unnecessarily heavy. His eyes met hers. No words. Just a shared understanding of their desperate situation.

"Sit," a soldier commanded, shoving her onto the bench.

The cart's interior was dark save for thin slivers of light filtering through tiny gaps in the wooden construction. The walls pressed in, the smell of damp wood and recent rain permeating everything.

Apple listened to the preparations outside. Horses being hitched with final instructions called out. The jangle of more chains. More prisoners, perhaps?

Gar remained silent.

The first movement of the cart was a jolt, followed by wheels creaking and the sound of hooves on stone. They were moving. To Londinium first, and then to Rome.

"Why are we being taken to Rome?" Apple whispered, breaking the silence.

Gar's response was low, barely audible. "To die, I imagine."

The cart continued its journey. Outside, the landscape of Roman Britain passed by.

The journey was miserable. Periodic stops for basic necessities had been brief and brutal. Snow had fallen constantly, turning the world into a landscape of white and grey. Apple had found herself pressed against Gar, their mutual survival more important than any previous animosity. He was warm, solid, silent, and safe.

Now, the city spread before her. And it was nothing like the London she once knew.

In some areas, the city's rebuilding told a story of survival. Apple noticed sections where newer stone met older, scorched foundations. These were living scars of Boudica's rebellion—the Iceni queen's devastating attack that had burned Londinium to the ground over a century earlier. Some stone walls still bore faint discolorations, darker patches that spoke of intense fire. Older residents, she imagined, would tell stories passed down through generations—tales of the Celtic revolt that had nearly destroyed the Roman presence in Britain.

A monument nearby commemorated the rebuilding, a

testament to Roman resilience. Gar, catching her gaze, seemed to stiffen. The memory of Boudica—another Iceni warrior who had challenged Roman rule—hung unspoken between them.

The River Thames cut through the landscape like a living artery. Wooden structures dominated, with occasional stone buildings advertising the prowess of Roman engineering. Smoke rose from countless chimneys, creating a haze that hung over the city. The smell was overwhelming—wood smoke, animal dung, unwashed bodies, fresh bread, raw sewage, exotic perfumes, fish.

Merchants filled the streets. Carts. Animals. People in various states of dress and undress. No uniform modern clothing here—instead, a riot of fabrics. Wool. Linen. Rough-spun materials. The occasional flash of imported silk that spoke of wealth.

The sounds were cacophonous. Merchants calling out. Animals braying. The clank of metal—blacksmiths, soldiers, traders. Children's voices. The constant background noise of a living city.

Gar remained silent, but she felt his body tense as they were herded through the streets. His warrior's eyes constantly scanned their surroundings—searching, she wondered, for an escape route? Apple was acutely aware of their physical connection. Chained together, she would be dragged along if he chose to make a desperate bid for freedom. Her survival literally depended on his next move. Would he use her as a shield? Leave her behind? Her modern sensibilities warred with the brutal reality of their situation. In these moments, she was at his mercy, her fate determined by the whims of an Iceni warrior who had every reason to hate the Romans—and, by extension, her.

The temperature was brutal. Snow turned to slush beneath their feet, seeping through the worn leather of her boots. Her modern clothing—once a marvel of thermal technology—now revealed its limitations. Those high-tech layers that had seemed so effective for a quick winter walk or a short commute were woefully inadequate for prolonged exposure to Roman winter conditions. The thermal wear was perfect for a brisk walk to the pub or a dash from car to office, offered little protection against the relentless cold.

Each gust of wind cut through her like a knife, making her question whether she'd survive the journey to Rome. The guards kept them close, chains ensuring no possibility of escape, while the cold became her most persistent interrogator.

Wooden buildings pressed close together. No wide streets like modern London. These were narrow passages, some barely wide enough for a cart to pass. The smell of humanity intense—sweat, smoke, cooking food, animal waste. And an all pervasive scent of rotting seafood.

She saw glimpses of wealth. A marble column; a mosaic. Hints of an ability to create beauty even in this frontier town. But mostly, it was raw and functional with survival the primary consideration.

"I see nothing much has changed," she muttered, thinking of the vibrant, multicultural London she knew. Dark-skinned traders from Africa competed alongside pale-skinned merchants from Germania. Arabs from the east, and locals from across Britannia made up the same rich tapestry of humanity that defined her modern city. It was alive here, centuries earlier. A testament to the enduring nature of human migration and connection.

Gar, surprisingly, responded. A grunt. A slight nod.

And still they continued onward. Their journey was not over. Rome awaited whilst Londinium continued—indifferent to the prisoners moving through its streets.

Echoes of Conflict

Ithaca Fort was a chaos of aftermath. Smoke still rose from where the Iron Beast had torn through their defences. Bodies of fallen soldiers and Iceni warriors littered the ground. Julius moved through the bodies with the weight of survival on his shoulders. As well as his concern for the woman he'd left hidden inside the fort's walls.

His men took priority.

The burial detail was grim work.

Roman military protocol was clear, even in winter. They couldn't leave their dead unburied, but the frozen ground made traditional burial impossible. Julius ordered the pyres prepared. Wood was scarce, but they would honour their dead with fire.

The bodies of Roman soldiers were carefully arranged. Those who could be identified were wrapped in their best clothing, personal items placed with them. Those unknown would be burned together, their names whispered to the gods. The funeral pyre was both a practical solution and a sacred ritual.

He watched as the bodies were stacked. Young men and seasoned soldiers alike. Men, he had trained and lead. The smoke would carry their spirits to the afterlife.

The Iceni bodies presented a unique challenge. Yes they were enemies, but they had died as warriors. Some would argue they deserved no honourable treatment. Julius disagreed, and so ordered them placed in a separate pyre, away from the Roman dead, but still with a measure of respect.

His mind kept drifting to Lillian. To Apple. To the impossible *Iron Beast* that had torn through their defences.

From a distance, he could see the vehicle being prepared for transport. Iceni captives—those who survived—were harnessed like oxen, ready to pull the strange machine. The woman stood nearby, her posture rigid with purpose.

Julius approached close enough to overhear.

"I'll demonstrate this to the new emperor in Rome," Jane Badrick was saying to Albinus. "Not a drop of fuel wasted on the journey. Let them see how it can be moved. How it can be controlled."

The Iron Beast looked incongruous. A machine of impossible design, now reduced to being pulled like a common cart. Its metallic hide gleamed in the winter light. Julius remembered the terror it had brought—how it had moved faster than any horse, how it had crushed them as if they were made of paper.

Albinus seemed more interested in the political implications. Julius could see the calculation in the governor's eyes. This was more than a machine. This was a potential weapon. A tool of control.

The captives pulling the Iron Beast were a mixture of defeat and defiance. Some stumbled. Some walked with a warrior's pride. Julius recognised several faces from the battle —survivors who would now become slaves, their fate determined by Roman law.

His loyalty warred within him. To Rome. To his men. To this woman who seemed to know things no one else could understand.

Seeing that Marcus was occupied with the departing contingent, Julius seized his moment.

The safe room was small, barely more than a storage alcove with thick stone walls. When Julius entered, he could see Lillian's eyes darting to the door, then back again. Julius recognised that look. He'd seen it in soldiers awaiting judgment after a failed mission. The look of someone waiting for inevitable punishment.

"Marcus?" she whispered, the name hanging like a threat.

"He's gone. You don't need to worry about him."

Lillian's hands were clenched so tightly her knuckles had gone white. "He accused me of being a spy," she said, her voice catching. "He was going to—" She stopped.

Julius could fill in the blanks. Accusations of treachery in a Roman fort weren't taken lightly. Spies were executed brutally and publicly. To set an example.

"His attention is elsewhere now. His ambitions have moved beyond you. Trust me."

"What about Apple?" Lillian pleaded. "Where did he take her?"

The question caught Julius off guard. Not a plea for her own safety. But concern for another.

"She's gone with Albinus and his contingent, and Marcus," Julius said. "They've taken her to Londinium, and from there to Rome."

Lillian's face changed.

"Rome? We have to save her," she said, her voice rising. Not a request, a command. "She can't go to Rome. How would she ever get home?"

Julius watched her. This woman who seemed to know things she shouldn't. Who had warned him of an attack that had seemed impossible. Who now spoke with such absolute certainty about saving someone he barely knew.

"Apple," she screamed. "We have to save Apple!"

Julius slammed his hand against her mouth, feeling the warmth of her breath against his palm. The touch was both a necessity and a violation—protecting her, protecting himself. His mind raced between the need for absolute secrecy and a growing desire to understand this woman who seemed to know impossibilities.

"You must be quiet," he told her frantic eyes before removing his hand.

"We have to follow them," Lillian whispered, grabbing his arm. "We can't let her leave—"

But her words dissolved into something between a plea

and a command. Julius knew nothing of Apple beyond the brief glimpses he'd caught. Yet Lillian's desperation was absolute.

"I can't just leave," he said, his voice low. The wound on his scalp throbbed—a constant reminder of the battle's brutality.

Lillian's eyes met his. For a moment, something passed between them. A connection deeper than the moment. Deeper than the chaos surrounding them.

"You have to," she said. "Everything depends on it."

And for the first time, Julius realised he believed her. Completely.

As the night deepened, Julius found himself considering Lillian differently. She was no longer just the mysterious woman who had warned him of the attack. Something had shifted. Her complexity intrigued him, and not simply as a source of information. The way she moved, the intensity of her concern for Apple, the absolute certainty in her voice. All of these drew him closer to understanding something beyond his rigid world of Roman military life.

As the night deepened, he took his place on the wall. The funeral pyres cast flickering shadows across the fort. Smoke rose in thick, acrid columns—the smell of burning wood and flesh mixing with the winter air. The flames cast a bronze light across Julius's face, illuminating the moment of transformation where Julius knew he was crossing a line. But in this moment, that didn't seem to matter.

A Woman's Wiles

Lillian knew she had moments to convince Julius. One wrong word, one hint of desperation that seemed too calculated, and he would dismiss her.

"We have to follow them," she said, her voice calm.

Julius's expression was a mixture of confusion and reluctance. A Roman centurion doesn't abandon his post. The very thought is a betrayal of the highest order.

"Apple," she continued, "cannot go to Rome."

She could see the questions forming in his eyes. Why her? Why this specific prisoner? Why now? Lillian chose her words carefully. Too much truth would sound like madness. Too little would fail to convince him.

"She doesn't belong there," Lillian said. "If she goes to Rome, everything changes."

The practical concerns would matter to him. Romans were nothing if not pragmatic. She outlined the challenges of pursuit. The distance and the supplies they would need.

He outlined the risk of discovery.

"We'll need horses," she said. "To move quickly without drawing attention."

Julius's hand touched the wound on his scalp—a reminder of the recent battle. His hesitation was palpable. Leaving Ithaca Fort was more than a simple journey. It was a complete abandonment of duty, and a death sentence.

"They will notice I'm gone," Julius said.

Lillian knew that was the real obstacle.

"By the time they realise," she said, "we'll be well ahead."

"But I can't go back."

She could see the conflict in his eyes. Duty and honour. The rigid structure of Roman military life warring against something else. Curiosity and a sense that something extraordinary was happening.

"I know things," Lillian said softly. "Things that would sound impossible."

Julius's laugh was bitter. "You speak like a seer. Like those Celtic women the legions fear."

The comparison was not entirely wrong. Time travellers were, in their own way, prophets. Carriers of knowledge from impossible distances.

"Apple cannot go to Rome," she repeated. "Her presence there will change everything for us."

She didn't elaborate. Couldn't. The web of time was delicate. One misplaced word could unravel everything.

Lillian watched Julius's military mind assess the risks and the potential outcomes. The likelihood of success versus the certainty of punishment.

"We'll need to move before first light," he said finally.

Lillian allowed herself a small smile. A small victory.

The first light of dawn had barely touched the horizon when Lillian spoke the words that would change everything.

"Albinus cannot leave Britain either," she said, her voice cutting through the morning mist. "Not yet, anyway."

Julius's hand went to his sword. Not a threat of violence, but a gesture of protection—against what, he wasn't certain. Against her words.

"What madness is this?" he demanded.

Lillian's gaze was unflinching. "He can't travel to Rome. He must stay here so he can die... elsewhere. Later."

The words hung between them like a curse. Julius had seen enough of the Celtic lands to know the power of prophecy. The legions spoke in hushed tones of druids and seers, of women who could read the future in entrails and smoke. But this was different. This was a declaration so bold it bordered on treason.

"You speak of the Governor of Britannia," Julius hissed, "as if he were nothing more than a lamb being led to slaughter."

Her calm was infuriating. "Not slaughter," Lillian corrected. "Fate."

Julius's mind reeled. To suggest the death of the Roman governor was more than mere speculation. It was a declaration of intent. A spell. A curse. And treason.

"You seek to bewitch the governor?" The accusation came out as a whisper, but it carried the weight of the Roman's ancient fears.

Romans understood supernatural power. They feared it and respected it. The line between prophecy and witchcraft was thin, and Julius had seen enough in the Celtic lands to know that some words carried their own dark magic.

"I'm telling you what must happen," Lillian said. "Albinus cannot leave Britain yet. It's his destiny."

Julius took a step back from the absolute certainty in her voice. "You speak treason," he said.

Lillian's laugh was sad. "I speak the truth."

"How?" he whispered. "How could you know such a thing?"

"The world doesn't move in a single line," Lillian began. "Time is... more complicated than you understand." Noting that Julius's hand had not left the hilt of his sword. "I come from a time far beyond yours," she continued, "from a world you cannot imagine. Where machines fly through the sky and where information travels faster than a messenger could ride. Where the Roman Empire is nothing more than a chapter in a history book."

"You speak nonsense," he interrupted. "No one travels through time."

"You came to me, remember? You crossed time. It seems like a lifetime ago, but you saved me. Surely you remember?"

Julius felt something shift inside him. A memory that had

haunted the edges of his consciousness since that impossible moment.

He remembered fragments. Flashes of a moment that made no sense. A woman. Darkness. A journey that shouldn't have been possible. He had convinced himself it was a fever dream. A hallucination born of battle fatigue. Something his rational mind had constructed to make sense of an inexplicable experience.

But Lillian's words brought it rushing back.

He had crossed time. He knew he had. And yet, every fibre of his training demanded he reject the impossible.

"That was nothing," he said, the words sounding empty even to his own ears. "A trick of the mind. A moment of weakness." But as he spoke, he felt the memory pressing against the walls of his denial. His hand trembled on his sword hilt.

"It wasn't a dream," she whispered. "And you know it." Lillian smiled as she began explaining the way historical events connect. And how a single misstep, the tiniest of changes, could alter the course of history.

"Albinus cannot go to Rome," she repeated. "If he leaves Britain now, a chain of events will unfold that will destroy everything. Empires will fall differently. People who should live will die. Those who should die will live."

Julius's mind struggled. He was a military man. He understood strategy and tactics. The careful planning of campaigns. But this? This was beyond strategy. This was something else.

"Apple cannot go to Rome, any more than Albinus can, or Jane Badrick," Lillian continued. "Their presence there would be like dropping a stone into the middle of a still pond. The ripples would change everything." Lillian's hand—surprisingly gentle—touched his arm. "Some risks are worth taking. You must believe me," she said.

Julius looked at her. Really looked at her. And for a moment—just a moment—he almost did.

The journey to Londinium would take weeks. Seventeen days at best. Twenty if winter's cruelty prevailed.

Julius knew they were playing a dangerous game. Roman

scouts moved with the contingent, their eyes constantly scanning the landscape. Worse, the remaining Iceni warriors were likely shadowing Albinus's train, waiting for an opportunity to attack guerrilla style, as was their way.

Their provisions were limited. They had no luxurious baggage train. A few strips of dried meat. Some hardtack. And what little they could forage from a winter landscape that offered almost nothing.

Their fires were ghosts—small, carefully managed, more smoke than flame. Each night was a negotiation between warmth and survival. Too large a fire would attract attention from the military contingent ahead or the potential Iceni warriors behind.

"We'll be lucky to make fifteen miles a day," Julius muttered, studying the landscape. The Roman road—Watling Street—stretched before them, a thin line of possibility through a harsh winter terrain.

Foraging was brutal. Frozen ground. Bare trees. The occasional rabbit or bird that might provide sustenance. Julius's military training served them well—he knew how to find food where others saw only desolation. But it was never enough.

Their horses suffered the most. Each day became a test of endurance. They couldn't push too hard—exhausted horses would be worse than no horses at all. Water was a constant concern, with streams often frozen over and rivers requiring careful navigation.

Winter stripped the landscape of mercy. Every mile was a battle against cold, hunger, and the constant threat of discovery. Their mission balanced on a knife's edge—close enough to track, far enough to remain unseen.

Something shifted between them with each passing mile.

The harsh journey stripped away everything unnecessary. Badger. Ithaca Farm. Her plans back home. All of it became distant, with the modern world dissolving like mist, leaving only Julius.

During daylight hours, Lillian watched Julius navigate the winter landscape. The way he could find sustenance out of desolation. How his hand moved when he pointed out a potential food source. The subtle shifts in his expression when he spoke of men he'd lost. The moments of vulnerability that crept through his Roman discipline. And at night, they huddled together for extra warmth, their conversations becoming something more than survival.

Lillian almost forgot about returning to the life she had left behind. The rewilding of Ithaca Farm, and her carefully constructed existence. None of it mattered in the relentless cold and the gnawing hunger. Despite the constant threat of discovery, there was only two souls finding each other in the most impossible of circumstances.

Julius and Lillian. Lillian and Julius.

And for the first time since inheriting Ithaca Farm, Lillian felt at peace.

Shadows of Ambition

The messenger arrived at the worst possible moment.

Aper was reviewing correspondence from his political allies. His fingers, stained with ink, paused over a delicate piece of correspondence from a senator in Lyon.

The scroll was delivered by a courier whose travel-worn appearance spoke of urgency. Dust clung to his sandals. Sweat marked his brow despite the winter chill.

"From Britannia," the messenger said, bowing.

Aper's first emotion was curiosity. Then, as he read, curiosity transformed into a rage so pure it threatened to consume the room.

Albinus was returning to Rome.

But it was not Albinus's return that ignited Aper's fury. It was the details. The whispers of something impossible.

Albinus was bringing a weapon. A machine unlike anything Rome had ever seen.

The courier described an iron beast pulled by captives. A metal contraption that could move faster than any horse. Crush defences like paper. A weapon that could change everything.

And worse. Albinus brought with him a prophet. A woman who spoke of futures that should not be known.

A Cassandra-like figure who carried knowledge that could unravel everything Aper had planned.

"No," Aper muttered, the word a blade of pure hatred.

This was not part of his design. Albinus was not supposed to return. Not now. Not with this... weapon. Not with this woman who seemed to know things no mortal should know. It threatened to upset the delicate balance of power he had been cultivating.

The scroll crumpled in his fist. Outside, Rome continued its endless dance of power and ambition, unaware that everything was about to change.

Pramod knew something was wrong the moment Aper summoned him without Metella.

"Close the door," Aper commanded.

Pramod complied. The click of the door a seal of isolation.

Aper's eyes were predatory. Gone was the careful politician. This was a man cornered, and therefore most dangerous.

"Albinus returns," Aper declared.

Pramod had already heard through the household slaves. "I've heard rumours."

"Rumours?" Aper's laugh was sharp as a blade. "And he brings with him a weapon. A machine that moves without horses. And a prophet who speaks of futures that should not be known. A prophet like you."

Then the interrogation began. Not with shouting, but with a calculated precision that would impress any professional interrogator.

"What do you know?" Aper leaned forward. "And do not think to protect Metella's interests. She is not here. You are alone with me."

The threat was unspoken, but absolute.

Pramod understood the game. Aper wanted predictions. He wanted a way to manipulate Albinus's return so that it favoured Aper. But revealing too much could derail time itself.

"The future is not a simple path," Pramod began.

Aper's hand slammed against the marble table. "I do not want philosophy. I want a way to control Albinus and this new weapon.

The Roman political landscape was a treacherous terrain, more dangerous than any battlefield.

With his historical perspective, Pramod understood what Aper could not—that power in Rome was a delicate ecosystem and the military was restless.

"Explain," Aper demanded, "how Albinus's return threatens Rome, and my position."

Pramod chose his words with surgical precision. If he revealed too much about the future, he risked altering the timeline. If he revealed too little, then Aper would see him as disposable.

The machine Albinus brought with him, the Iron Beast, was more than a weapon. It was a demonstration of technological power that would shift the entire balance of military might. In a world where military strength determined imperial succession, such a device could be more valuable than legions of soldiers. As long as the beast had fuel...

No, the greater threat was the woman. The prophet. Someone who carried knowledge beyond mortal understanding.

"Information is power," Pramod said carefully. "And Albinus brings with him information that goes beyond traditional intelligence."

Aper leaned forward, his eyes narrowing. "But I have that too, in you?"

Pramod's position was razor thin. Every word he uttered was a negotiation, and every breath a potential betrayal. His gift of prophecy hung between them, more dangerous than any weapon.

A Woman Scorned

The cold in Londinium was a living thing. Not the crisp, clean cold of modern winters, but a damp, penetrating chill that seeped deep into bone and spirit alike.

Apple's imprisonment was a study in discomfort. The makeshift cell offered little protection from the winter. Wooden walls had gaps that let in drafts, and the packed earth floor was damp, despite the scattered straw. She'd bundled that up to use for bedding, but it did little to soften the hard ground.

Food was sparse. A bowl of porridge in the morning and something that might charitably be called soup in the evening. Enough to survive. Not enough to feel comfortable.

The soldiers replaced her modern clothing with a rough wool tunic that scratched against her skin. And the single thin blanket they'd provided did little to ward off the ice.

Apple traced patterns in the dirt, remembering the warmth of home and of the comfortable life she'd left behind and thought about survival. And about Lillian. She chided herself for living in the past. Or was it the future? It seemed to crazy now that she'd wanted this experience. That she'd decided that living in the past was better than being treated as a circus freak for what she looked like.

And she'd been right. Here in Roman Britain, no one

seemed to consider her albino features anything more curious than a cloud crossing the sun. Perhaps bullying was a modern invention?

Outside, Londinium moved with the rhythm of a winter-locked city. The sounds filtered through—cart wheels on cobblestones. Occasional shouts. The constant background noise of a city that didn't stop, even in the depths of winter, two millennia ago.

Apple closed her eyes and tried to remember the warnings Neumegen had given Lillian, including the importance of not changing anything. And although Apple shouldn't have travelled back in time with Lillian, here she was. And she knew that just by being here, she was changing everything.

THE MILITARY QUARTERS HUMMED WITH AN UNSPOKEN tension, which felt more dangerous than any battlefield. Soldiers' voices carried through the thin walls; fragments of conversation that spoke of ambition, fear, and the balance of power. Apple pressed herself closer to the wall, listening.

"Britannia is our strength," a sharp voice argued."Our legions here are loyal to Albinus. Every man would die for him."

Another voice—more measured—carried a different tone. "Loyalty means nothing in Rome. Political power is everything."

"Severus is gathering support in the east," another voice continued. "His connections in the Senate grow. I tell you, our position in Rome is precarious."

A third voice joined, rasping like a nicotine addicted chain smoker. "The Iron Beast changes everything. It's a demonstration of power unlike anything I've seen."

Silence followed. A pause that spoke volumes.

"Pertinax's legacy is fragile," someone muttered as a statement of fact.

Apple understood now what Neumegen had meant about the delicate threads of history. Whilst these conversations appeared to be nothing more than idle chatter, they were the reshaped whispers that could transform an empire.

The political landscape was a treacherous terrain. Britannia offered military might—legions loyal to Albinus, strong and battle-tested. Rome offered political legitimacy—the senate, the imperial networks, the ability to claim the throne.

"We cannot stay here forever," the older advisor said. "Our ambitions require Rome."

But the hesitation was palpable. Everyone understood the risk. Severus was not a man to be underestimated. His political cunning was legendary. Where Albinus had military strength, Severus had political chess masters working tirelessly on his behalf.

"The legions of Britannia would follow Albinus into the fires of the underworld," Marcus—Apple recognised his voice from Ithaca Fort—declared. "Severus cannot compete with our Iron Beast. We must go to Rome."

The response was immediate. "Political games win thrones, not military bravado."

Apple felt the weight of change pressing against her. These conversations would determine the fate of emperors, and entire empires.

"We must move," Albinus's commanding voice added. "The prophet has spoken. Rome awaits."

Jane understood power in a way most politicians only dreamed of.

Her knowledge of Roman history was not just academic, it was a carefully honed weapon designed to slice through the most intricate political defences. Where others saw a moment in time, she saw a chess board, with every move calculated centuries in advance.

Her goal was simple yet audacious: influence the imperial succession. Not directly. Not crudely. But with the precision of a surgeon, reshaping the very fabric of Roman political destiny. History declared that Severus would triumph. She knew this with the certainty of someone who had read the history books. But from where she stood, his victory was no longer guaranteed.

That was the trouble with history. It assumed inevitability. Jane intended to prove otherwise. She would adjust the timeline to suit her ambitions, and she didn't care how far the ripples extended.

If, under her guidance, Clodius Albinus crushed Septimius Severus, the Empire might take a drastically different course. Backed by the western provinces, if Albinus also seized Rome, power would shift toward a looser, more provincial rule, rather than the iron grip of Severus' future militarised autocracy. The Severan dynasty would never take root. No Caracalla, no bloody purges, no Antonine Constitution handing citizenship to every free man in the empire. Rome would remain exclusive, its power centred in the hands of the worthy. Perfect.

Of course, there was always the possibility that civil war would drag on, fracturing the empire, weakening it just enough for the Germanic tribes and the Parthians to tear it apart. But that was the beauty of it. Either way, history would be hers to shape.

She studied Albinus. His ambition was a flame—bright, all-consuming, and ultimately destructive. The kind of character she could manipulate. Someone after her own heart.

"The gods have spoken," she had whispered to Albinus earlier. Not a lie, but also not the truth. Something in between. The most dangerous ground of all.

Her modern sensibilities were both a hindrance and an advantage. She understood bureaucracy and power structures, and the art of political manoeuvring in ways the Romans could never comprehend.

Albinus thought he was using her knowledge and strange insights. Her connection to the Iron Beast. But Jane was already three moves ahead. Albinus's future imperial succession would not just be a political event, but a moment of historical transformation. And she intended to be its architect.

Power was never about grand gestures, it was about invisible influence.

She thought of Hexham, and of the small-town politics she had left behind. This moment in time was her true calling. She would not remain a footnote in local body politics. Albinus was a means to an end. The Iron Beast, a tool of demonstration. And her? She would reshape history.

Chains of Vengeance

The chains were an insult. Not just to him, but to everything the Iceni represented.

Gar studied the pale woman beside him with the same calculated intensity he would assess an enemy warrior. She was different. Silver like moonlight. Marked by something beyond the Romans or Iceni's understanding. But she was still just a prisoner. Like him.

His thoughts burned with a hatred that ran deeper than the cold of Londinium. Jane Badrick. The woman who had promised victory. Magic weapons. An "iron horse" that would crush Roman defences. Instead, here he was. Chained. Transported like cattle.

Betrayal sat heavy in his gut.

"They will pay," he muttered, more to himself than to Apple.

Apple turned. Her albino features caught what little light filtered into their makeshift prison. "Pay for what?"

Gar's laugh was brutal. "Everything."

He had been a chieftain. A leader of warriors. Now reduced to this—a captive, pulled along in the wake of Roman political manoeuvring. The druids would interpret this as an omen. As a challenge for the gods.

"The Romans think they can break me," he said, testing Apple's response.

"And can they?"

Gar tested the chains. Studied the room. Memorised every detail. A warrior never stopped planning. Never stopped looking for an opportunity.

"That woman promised us victory," he continued, his voice low. "Promised weapons that would crush the Romans. Instead, we are here. Chained. Humiliated."

Apple listened. Something in her understood not just the words, but the deeper meaning. That survival and revenge were a long game.

"We could escape," she blurted.

In that moment, an unspoken alliance was born.

As darkness fell that first night in Londinium, Gar began chanting an ancient Iceni prayer.

The chains could bind his body, but not his spirit. Not the connection to the gods his people had honoured for generations. Apple watched, silent and curious, as he closed his eyes and murmured.

First, he called to Andraste—the war goddess of the Iceni. His breath formed prayers like sacrificial smoke. Andraste, who had guided Boudica's fury against the Romans. Andraste, who understood the language of blood and resistance.

His fingers traced invisible symbols in the air. Patterns learned from the druids. Sacred geometries that connected the physical world to the spiritual realm. Each movement was a prayer. Each breath a communion.

"Hear me," he commanded.

The gods of the Iceni were not gentle gods. They were gods of survival. Of resistance and transformation. Gar called to the earth spirits. To the wind spirits. To the ancient powers that existed before Rome. Before conquest. Before chains.

Apple watched, fascinated. The prayer was unlike anything she had ever witnessed. Part invocation, part strategy, and part raw, unbridled fury.

Gar spoke of the betrayal. Of Jane Badrick's broken promises. Of the Romans who thought they could break an

Iceni warrior. Each word was an offering, and every breath a weapon.

He spoke of the Iron Beast. Of magic from another time. Of the prophecies the druids had whispered. His connection to the spiritual world was as real to him as the chains that bound him.

"I am not defeated," he muttered. "I am waiting."

The gods would hear and would understand. The gods would provide a way. Gar's prayer was a promised declaration of war.

Apple dismissed Gar's prayer as complete nonsense.

In her mind, it was nothing more than superstitious mumbo jumbo. She'd grown up in a world of rational explanations which followed the science. A world where mysterious rituals were something to be explained away, not respected.

Her initial reaction was pure skepticism. A mental eye-roll that would have made her friends back home proud. Druids. Ancient gods. Spiritual connections. Something you'd expect from late-night US cable TV, with a wild-eyed preacher promising miracles, whilst simultaneously asking for your bankcard details.

But then she remembered she had travelled through time. The irony was not lost on her.

Who was she to dismiss something as impossible? She, who had quite literally stepped out of her own time and place? Who had experienced something that would sound completely insane to anyone back home? Time travel. That was real. And if that was possible, then what else might exist beyond her limited understanding? The druids' gods seemed far less impossible than her own journey.

The makeshift cell felt smaller now. Winter's cold seeped through gaps in the wooden walls, carrying with it the damp smell of decay and stone. Frost traced delicate patterns on the single small window, its crystalline edges sharp. She watched Gar with new eyes. The way his fingers traced patterns in the air and the intensity of his connection. He possessed the absolute certainty that something beyond the physical world was listening.

Who was to say they weren't real? Some prosperity gospel televangelist from Alabama promising miracles for a donation? Apple had seen impossible things. She was an impossible thing.

"They will come," Gar said with absolute certainty, interrupting her thoughts.

The chains binding them clinked as he moved, a constant reminder of their captivity. A rat scurried in the corner, just visible in the dim light filtering through the frost-covered window.

"Who?" One minute ago he'd been praying to his gods, and now he said they were coming. Apple hadn't realised that the gods worked that fast.

"My men."

Apple studied him. That same unshakeable belief that had powered his prayer now fuelled his confidence in his warriors. The Iceni were not a people who abandoned their leaders. Especially not a chieftain like Gar.

"How can you be so sure?" she asked.

Gar's laugh was brutal. "Bricius will track us. My most trusted warrior. He understands strategy better than most Romans understand their own battle plans."

Rome. The ultimate destination. And a potential death sentence. Apple was sure that Jane would ensure her elimination. An albino woman from the future? A potential witness to impossible events? No. Jane would see her as a threat to be removed.

But if Albinus went to Rome, where would he then meet his ultimate fate? He was meant to be trampled underfoot in Lyon by Severus's horse—the ultimate desecration for a Roman warrior. A moment of historical inevitability. Jane's interference would change everything.

"We have to destroy the car," Apple muttered.

Gar looked at her. Curious. "*Car?*"

"The Iron Beast. Jane's weapon," she clarified. "If we can disable it, we might change something. Might prevent something."

The car represented more than a technological marvel. It

was a potential point of intervention. A moment where the future might be nudged.

"Your people," Apple asked Gar, "they'll come for you? Even if it means fighting the Romans here in Londinium?"

His smile was predatory. "Fighting Romans is what we do best. And we destroyed this town once already. We can do it again."

A flicker of memory passed through his eyes. Boudica's revolt—a moment of legendary resistance. In CE 60 or 61, the Iceni had unleashed a fury that nearly drove the Romans from Britain. Londinium—then a newly established Roman settlement—had been destroyed. Burnt to the ground, with thousands massacred.

"My mother told me the stories," Gar continued, his voice taking on a rhythmic quality of oral tradition. "How Boudica led our people. How we burned Londinium. Colchester. St. Albans. We killed everything. That stinking river ran red with Roman blood."

It wasn't just a historical fact. It was a living memory. A generational wound. A promise of vengeance passed down through Iceni bloodlines.

"They thought they could break us," he said. "Rape our daughters. Steal our lands. But we showed them the true meaning of resistance."

Apple listened, understanding now that for Gar, this wasn't just history. It was a continuing story of survival and defiance.

Apple understood that sometimes survival was about more than just staying alive. It was about creating possibilities and changing trajectories.

Destroy the car. Prevent Albinus's return. Keep the timeline in check.

These thoughts became her new mission. Her reason for living.

Shadows of Pursuit

The world snapped back into focus with a dizzying lurch. Bricius stumbled, his sword arm dropping as he fought to maintain his balance. The familiar weight of his blade felt alien after the disorienting journey through time. He blinked, struggling to process the abrupt shift from the bewildering modern world back to his own time.

Gone were the strange, smooth surfaces and incomprehensible objects. The air no longer carried the acrid scent of Jane's Iron Beast. Instead, the rich scent of damp earth and wild herbs filled his nostrils. The gentle rustling of leaves in the breeze replaced the cacophony of unfamiliar noises that had assaulted his ears in that other world.

Bricius's chest heaved as he fought to calm his racing heart. He had witnessed impossible things — objects that moved on their own, buildings that gleamed like polished metal, people dressed in fabrics and styles he couldn't comprehend. Now, standing in the familiar field near the altar at Ithaca Farm, those memories felt like wisps of a fading dream.

But they weren't a dream. The lingering taste of fear on his tongue and the trembling in his sword arm were all too real.

Forcing himself to focus, Bricius took stock of his surroundings. The altar stone stood silent and unremarkable, betraying nothing of its incredible power. The field stretched out before him, bathed in the golden light of late afternoon. In the distance, he could make out the outlines of the Roman fort, its presence a constant reminder of the enemy that sought to crush his people.

There was no sign of Jane or her strange conveyance. They had vanished as abruptly as they had appeared, leaving Bricius alone with the weight of his experiences and the pressing urgency of his mission.

Gar.

The thought of his chieftain snapped Bricius back to the present. How long had he been gone? Minutes? Hours? The sun's position suggested it hadn't been long, but every moment counted when pursuing Romans.

Bricius's mind raced, piecing together what he knew. Albinus, the treacherous governor, had taken Gar captive. They would head for Londinium – that cesspit of Roman corruption that had once burned under Boudica's righteous fury. The Iceni warrior's lips curled into a snarl at the thought. History might repeat itself soon enough.

But first, he needed information. Bricius crouched low, his keen eyes scanning the ground. There, the telltale signs of many booted feet, the disturbed earth where horses had pawed the ground. The Romans had passed this way, and recently.

As he studied the tracks, Bricius's thoughts turned to Jane and her cryptic warnings. She had spoken of great danger, of a threat not just to Gar but to the very fabric of time itself. He didn't pretend to understand her ramblings about the future, but he recognised the gravity in her voice. Whatever game the witch played, the stakes were higher than he could fathom.

For a moment, doubt gnawed at him. Should he wait to speak with Jane? She possessed a power beyond his understanding. Perhaps she had a plan, a strategy that his limited perspective couldn't grasp?

Bricius shook his head, banishing the thought. He was Iceni, a warrior of a proud and fierce tribe. He would not cower in the shadows, waiting for aid from strange magic he didn't trust. Gar needed him now, and every moment of hesitation put his chieftain in greater danger.

Decision made, Bricius allowed himself a grim smile. Let Jane play her games with time. He would do what he did best — hunt, track, and when the moment was right, strike with deadly precision.

With practiced ease, Bricius gathered what he needed for the journey ahead. His sword, of course, never left his side. A small pack of dried meat and hard bread to sustain him, and a water skin filled from a nearby stream. He needed nothing more. Anything else would only slow him down.

As he prepared to set out, Bricius cast one last glance at the altar stone. Whatever power it held remained a mystery to him, but he couldn't shake the feeling that it hadn't finished playing its role in this unfolding drama. For now, though, his path was clear.

With silent determination, Bricius melted into the lengthening shadows of the forest's edge. The hunt had begun.

THE FOREST EMBRACED BRICIUS LIKE AN OLD FRIEND, ITS shadows offering concealment as he moved with practiced stealth and heightened senses, attuned to the subtle signs of his quarry. The Romans, for all their military discipline, left a trail as clear as a merchant road to his trained eye.

Broken twigs, disturbed undergrowth, the occasional glint of discarded metal — each clue wove a narrative of Albinus's journey. Bricius moved like a ghost, his feet finding purchase on silent paths parallel to the Roman column. He was close enough now to catch snatches of conversation carried on the wind, the Latin words grating against his ears.

As dusk settled over the land, Bricius caught his first glimpse of Gar. His imposing figure was unmistakable, even in chains. The Iceni chieftain's head remained unbowed, his stride defiant despite his captivity. Pride swelled in Bricius's chest at the sight, tempered by a fierce rage at seeing his leader so degraded.

Beside Gar walked a woman with skin as pale as

moonlight, her hair a shock of white. He had never seen her like before. She moved with a strange mix of fear and determination, her eyes darting about as if searching for something. Or someone.

Bricius's hand tightened on his sword hilt. The desire to charge forth, to cut down the Roman dogs and free his chieftain, burned hot within him. He could almost taste the blood, hear the satisfying crunch of bones beneath his blade. It would be glorious, a tale to rival the great deeds of old.

But caution stayed his hand. He forced himself to take a deep, steadying breath, remembering hard-learned lessons. "You win the battle before it's fought," his father had often said. Rushing in now would be suicide, a pointless gesture that would leave Gar with no hope of rescue.

No, patience was the key. Bricius had to bide his time, gather intelligence, and strike when the moment was right. It galled him to watch Gar suffer the indignities of captivity, but he consoled himself with visions of future vengeance. The Romans would pay for this insult to the Iceni.

As night fell, Albinus's group made camp. Bricius observed their routines from the safety of a dense thicket, noting the guard posts and the layout of the encampment. He paid particular attention to where they held Gar and the pale woman, mapping out potential approaches in his mind.

The strangest sight came during meal time. The pale woman – Apple, he heard her called — received different treatment than the other prisoners. There was wariness in how the Romans approached her, as if they feared some hidden power. Bricius filed this information away.

Throughout the night, Bricius wrestled with his conflicting instincts. Every fibre of his being screamed for action, for the heat of battle and the feel of blade meeting flesh. But the cooler, tactical part of his mind — the part that had kept him alive through countless battles — counselled patience.

He thought of Jane's warnings, of the hints of greater forces at work. As much as he distrusted the witch and her strange magics, he couldn't dismiss the gravity of her words.

There was more at stake here than just Gar's freedom, though he couldn't understand the full scope of it.

As dawn's first light painted the eastern sky, Bricius continued shadowing the Romans, gathering what information he could.

AS THE ROMAN CONVOY WOUND ITS WAY THROUGH A narrow valley, Bricius's keen eyes caught a flicker of movement on the opposite ridge. At first, he dismissed it as wildlife, but something about the motion struck him as distinctly human. Narrowing his eyes, he focused on the spot.

There. Two figures, moving with deliberate stealth along the ridge line. One a Roman soldier, his armour unmistakable even at this distance. The other, a woman in strange garb that Bricius couldn't quite place. They were following Albinus's group, mirroring Bricius's own actions, but from the opposite side of the valley.

Confusion clouded Bricius's mind. Why would a Roman soldier be trailing his own people? Who was the woman with him?

Suspicion flared. Could this be an elaborate Roman trap to lure out any Iceni pursuers? But no, the pair seemed intent on avoiding detection by Albinus's group. Their movements were too careful, too precise to be playacting.

Bricius considered confronting them. The soldier was armed, but Bricius knew he could best a single Roman. The woman was an unknown quantity, but he doubted she posed a serious threat in close combat. Yet something held him back.

These two, whoever they were, had reason to hide from Albinus and his men. That alone made them potential allies, or at the very least, a source of valuable information.

Bricius settled into a new rhythm. He kept his primary focus on Albinus and the prisoners, but he spared regular glances for the mysterious pair across the valley. Their progress was slower, more cautious than the primary group, but they seemed to have an uncanny knack for anticipating the Romans' path.

As the day wore on, Bricius found himself impressed by

their skill. The Roman soldier moved with a grace that spoke of extensive wilderness training, far beyond what Bricius expected from the usual urban-centric legionaries.

Bricius gripped his sword hilt, drawing comfort from its familiar weight. Whatever game the gods were playing, he would see it through. For Gar, for the Iceni, and for a future that seemed far less certain than he had ever imagined.

As the days of pursuit wore on, Bricius noticed subtle shifts in the landscape. The wild, untamed forests of the north gave way to more managed woodlands. Clearings became more frequent, often revealing neatly tended fields or the occasional Roman villa perched on a distant hillside. The air itself changed, carrying hints of smoke and the acrid tang of too many humans living in close proximity.

They were nearing Londinium.

Bricius felt the tension coil in his gut. Every step closer to the Roman stronghold increased the danger, not just for him, but for Gar and his fellow captive. The Romans' vigilance would only intensify as they approached their seat of power. Any rescue attempt would become more difficult once they passed through Londinium's gates.

As he slid through the underbrush, parallel to the Roman column's march, Bricius's mind drifted to the stories he'd heard since childhood. Tales told in reverent tones around flickering campfires, passed down through generations of Iceni. Stories of Boudica, the warrior queen who had brought Rome to its knees.

He could almost hear his grandmother's voice, rough with age but alive with pride: "Londinium burned, my little wolf. Our people, led by Boudica, swept through the city like an avenging storm. The Romans fled before us, their precious buildings turned to ash."

In his mind's eye, Bricius imagined the flames licking at the sky, and heard the screams of terrified Romans as Iceni warriors exacted their revenge. The elders said the Thames had run red with blood that day, a sacrifice to appease the gods who had been so grievously offended by Roman arrogance.

Now, as an adult, Bricius understood the complexities his childhood self could not grasp. The Iceni had won a glorious victory, yes, but at a terrible cost. And in the end, Rome had tightened its grip on their lands, determined never again to be caught so unaware.

These thoughts fuelled Bricius's growing sense of urgency. He couldn't afford to wait much longer. Each day brought them closer to Londinium, closer to the point of no return. Yet he was aware of his limitations. One man, no matter how skilled, could not hope to overcome Albinus's entire retinue.

Tomorrow would bring them to the very edges of Roman civilisation. Tomorrow, Bricius would have to act. As he drifted into a light, watchful sleep, his last thoughts were of Boudica and the flames of rebellion her name had ignited. Perhaps, just perhaps, it was time for those flames to burn once more.

Modern Mysteries

Ryan Francis drummed his fingers on the steering wheel, his mind churning with possibilities as he navigated the winding roads towards Hexham. Beside him, Emma sat in contemplative silence, her notebook open on her lap, filled with scribbled observations from their meeting with the head of the Hadrian's Heroes Metal Detecting Club.

"What do you think?" Ryan asked suddenly. "About his story?"

Emma pursed her lips, considering. "It's... odd. The way he described how they found the coins. It sounds like a more recent burial, as opposed to someone hiding the coins before escaping an advancing enemy army, despite the depth."

Ryan nodded, a wry smile tugging at his lips. "My thoughts exactly. Twenty-three gold coins, all in pristine condition, found around the site where their mayor vanished? It's like something out of a novel."

"And not a very good one at that," Emma added, her tone dry. "It's not in the same league as a Clive Cussler level plot!"

As they approached Hexham, the quaint charm of the town's historic centre came into view. Under different circumstances, Ryan might have appreciated the picturesque scenery. Today, however, his focus was on the task at hand, as well as on the woman by his side.

"Do you think they're connected to the Caernarfon

heist?" Emma asked, her voice tinged with skepticism. "It seems like quite a leap. Even with Darby's analysis." She shuddered at the mention of the decapitated archaeologist.

Ryan shrugged, his eyes fixed on the road. "It's a long shot. I'll grant you. But in my line of work, you learn to follow even the most unlikely leads. As for Darby's results... Given what happened to him, I think we take it all with a grain of salt, and I'll be asking for additional analysis by a London lab."

They both tried to put the thought of Darby and his head from their minds as they pulled into the Hexham Police Station car park, a lot overflowing with both marked and unmarked cars, as well as those from media organisations from around the country.

"Ready?" he asked Emma, who was gathering her notes.

She nodded, her expression determined. "Let's see what they have to show us."

As they entered the bustling police station, the constable directed Ryan and Emma into a small, windowless room. Sergeant Bishop sat behind the table, and two other men in sharp suits stood in the corner, their presence adding an extra layer of mystery to the atmosphere. Bishop never bothered introducing them.

Bishop nodded from his stack of files. "Let's make this quick. I've got a missing mayor and a media circus to deal with."

Ryan cleared his throat, surprised by the brusque welcome. "Of course. We appreciate your time. If we could just look at the coins—"

Bishop slid a small evidence box across the table. "Here. But I don't see how this helps find Jane Badrick."

As Ryan examined the coins, he could feel the weight of multiple gazes on him. Emma leaned in close, her breath warm on his neck as she whispered, "They're incredible. The detail, the preservation..."

Ryan nodded, a frown creasing his brow. "Too incredible," he murmured. Then, louder, "Sergeant Bishop, we're here because I have reason to suspect that these coins might be from the Caernarfon Castle heist."

The effect was immediate. Bishop's face flushed red. "That's ridiculous! Those coins went missing when I was still in school uniform. I remember that. They're long gone. Melted down and sold for scrap."

"I appreciate it sounds far-fetched," Ryan began, but Bishop cut him off.

"Far-fetched? It's bloody impossible! These coins are our key piece of evidence in a high-profile missing persons case. Why are you trying to connect it to some decades-old theft in Wales?"

The two suited men in the corner exchanged a glance, their interest clearly piqued.

Emma stepped in, her voice calm. "Sergeant, we're not making any accusations. We're following a lead—"

"A lead that's wasting my time," Bishop snapped. "I just don't have time for this. Our contractors found these coins deep underground. Buried by some poor Roman running for their lives. And now you're here, ruining mine. If you want any further information, come to the next media briefing. This interview is over. Out."

After Ryan and Emma left, and in a room far from prying ears, the two silent observers finally spoke.

"I think we need to look into this new angle. There might be something to it," one said.

The second man nodded, his expression grim. "Agreed. A burglary gone wrong? And possibly involving the mayor... It fits. But how? Had she uncovered it? Or worse, was she involved?"

"Either way," Bishop replied, wiping the sweat from his face, "I think our missing persons case just got a lot more complicated."

Once outside, Emma turned to Ryan. "Well, that could have gone better."

Ryan nodded. "But did you see those two goons in the corner? They weren't local. Something's going on here, Emma. Something big."

Emma reached for Ryan's hand, giving it a brief,

professional squeeze before quickly letting go. "Hey, don't let Bishop get to you. I think we're on the right track here."

Ryan glanced at her, a mix of gratitude and lingering tension in his eyes. Although their past relationship added a little complexity to their current professional collaboration, he wouldn't want to be here with anyone else. "Thanks, Em. It's just... I know there's something else here. I can feel it."

"Trust me, I believe you!" Emma said, her voice firm but with a hint of the familiarity. "And remember, we're not bound by the same rules as the police. We can follow our instincts on this one."

Ryan nodded, a determined glint returning to his eyes. "You're right. So, where do we start?"

They began walking towards Ryan's car, the bustle of the police station fading behind them. Emma pulled out her phone, scrolling through her contacts.

"I think our next move should be to visit that pawnbroker in town," Emma suggested. "The one Clifton mentioned when he was talking about local coin enthusiasts."

Ryan raised an eyebrow. "Good thinking. If anyone in town knows about gold coins turning up, it would be a pawnbroker."

As they settled into their seats, an awkward silence fell between them. Ryan cleared his throat. "So, how's life at the Royal Mint? Must be quite a change from the Art Loss Register."

Emma smiled. "It's... different. Less exciting in some ways, more stable in others. But I miss the thrill of the chase sometimes."

As they drove through Hexham's winding streets, both were aware of the delicate balance they were trying to maintain — professional colleagues with a complicated past.

"You know," Ryan said, glancing at Emma, "I'm glad you're here. Your expertise is invaluable."

Emma nodded, a faint blush colouring her cheeks. "Thanks. I have to admit it's nice being back in the field."

They lapsed into silence again.

After parking outside the pawnshop, Ryan turned to Emma. "Ready to channel your inner Poirot?" he asked with a wry smile, referencing an inside joke from their Art Loss Register days.

Emma laughed. "Let's just hope we are just as successful as the detective in solving this one!"

Together, they stepped out of the car and headed towards the pawnshop. The faded sign above the door read Hexham Antiquities & Pawn. Through the grimy window, they could see shelves lined with an eclectic mix of items — old watches, tarnished silverware, and display cases of coins.

Ryan reached for the door handle, then paused, looking at Emma. "Whatever we find in here, whatever these coins mean — we're going to figure it out. Just like old times?"

Emma nodded. "Just like old times."

The bell above the door jangled as they entered, announcing their presence. The shop's interior was a cluttered maze of history — old-fashioned wooden cabinets displayed an array of gentlemanly trinkets, pocket watches, and gold-rimmed glasses. Royal Doulton vases that hadn't held their value, regardless of what the antique price guides had predicted in the 1980s, and a plethora of spindly walking sticks that would be more at home on the set of Bridgeton than they were on the streets of Hexham. The air was thick with leather and tobacco, and a faded green carpet muffled their footsteps.

Behind the counter stood a battle-scarred man with ears that had a life of their own. His eyes narrowed as they approached.

"Can I help you?" he asked, his voice wary.

Ryan stepped forward, offering a polite smile. "We hope so. We're looking for information about some coins that were found in the area, which may have turned up here."

"Coins, you say? Are you lot coppers?"

Ryan shook his head. "No, we're not police. I'm from the Art Loss Register, and my colleague here is from the Royal Mint. We're just following up on a lead related to some potentially significant historical artefacts."

The pawnbroker's posture relaxed, but a hint of suspicion remained in his eyes. "The Art Loss Register, eh? That's a new one. What's your interest in these coins, then?"

Emma chimed in, her expertise evident in her tone. "Has anyone brought in a gold Roman coin specifically? Or have they asked you to value one?"

The pawnbroker's eyes darted between them. "You're not the first to come asking about Roman coins," he said cryptically.

Ryan and Emma exchanged a quick glance. "Oh?" Ryan prompted.

The pawnbroker leaned on the counter, his voice lowering. "Had a fellow in here not too long ago, asking about a very specific coin. He wanted one from the reign of Decimus Clodius Albinus, if I recall correctly. Odd request really."

"Why odd?" Ryan asked.

The pawnbroker raised an eyebrow. "Well, coins from Albinus's reign are rare. He was only emperor for about three years, from 195 to 197 AD, and he had his coins minted in Gaul, not Rome. Apart from the gold ones, that is." He paused, stroking his chin. "After Septimius Severus defeated Albinus, there was a damnatio memoriae — a condemnation of memory. They destroyed or melted down most of Albinus's coins. So for someone to come in asking for one... well, that's not your everyday request. And for more than one person... that's nigh on impossible."

Emma's eyebrows shot up. "So it's quite a coincidence, then?" she asked.

The pawnbroker shrugged. "Lot of interest in Roman artefacts these days, especially with that big shindig for Saturnalia that they had up at the Bellingham."

Ryan pressed further. "The Bellingham? Isn't that linked to where the mayor went missing? Did I read that in the paper? And there's a missing girl as well?"

The pawnbroker's expression shut down. "I know nothing about any missing people," he said, shutting down that line of questioning. "But if you're serious about those coins, there's a man staying at the Twice Brewed who might answer some of your questions. You won't need me to point him out. He looks like he stepped straight out of a Dickens novel. Now, if you don't mind, I've got some work to do."

They thanked him and left the shop, the bell jangling behind them. Once outside, Emma turned to Ryan, her eyes wide.

"Why was someone else was here asking about a coin from the same period as the ones found near where Jane Badrick disappeared? This should have been the first place the police came to?"

"It makes sense to you and me, but this isn't London. The police here are probably only used to dealing with lost hikers, petty crime and domestic disturbances, with a side helping of drug and alcohol abuse," Ryan said, checking his watch. "Time for a late lunch at the pub, then?"

"Just like old times, indeed," Emma agreed, a small smile playing on her lips.

On Atlas's Shoulders

Jane leaned against the wooden balustrade of the praetorium's upper gallery, watching the early morning mist roll off the river. The Roman fortress of Londinium spread before her, a sprawling collection of timber buildings and stone foundations nestled within its protective walls. From her vantage point in the governor's headquarters, she could see the busy port where ships brought supplies from across the empire, their sails catching the first light of dawn.

The sound of clashing metal drew her attention to the courtyard below. Clodius Albinus, the soon-to-be self-proclaimed Caesar of Britain, was training with his personal guard. His pale skin gleamed with sweat, making him appear almost luminescent in the early morning light. Even from this distance, Jane could see the wild tangle of his white-blond curls bouncing as he parried and thrust.

"Still playing at being a soldier," she muttered under her breath, though she had to admit there was something compelling about his martial display. Despite his high-pitched voice that carried across the yard and his mercurial temper, he commanded respect. The men responded to his presence with an eagerness that spoke of genuine loyalty rather than mere obligation.

Jane shifted uncomfortably in her woollen stola. She missed the simplicity of jeans and a sweater. The thought brought a bitter smile to her lips. Such mundane concerns, when she was standing at a pivotal moment in history.

Below, Clodius executed a perfect disarming manoeuvre, sending his opponent's gladius spinning across the packed dirt. His victory cry carried up to her position, shrill yet triumphant. The soldiers cheered, and Jane could see his chest puff with pride. Such a fragile ego for a man who claimed he would rule an empire.

She knew what was coming. Every child learned about the Battle of Lugdunum, where Septimius Severus would defeat his rival claimant to the imperial throne. Clodius Albinus would die there, his head sent to Rome as a trophy. But knowing history and trying to change it were two very different things.

"My lady," a slave girl appeared at her elbow, head bowed. "The Governor requests your presence at the morning meal."

Jane nodded, straightening her posture. "Tell him I'll attend shortly." As the girl scurried away, Jane cast one last look at the misty skyline of Roman London. Somewhere out there, Severus was gathering his forces. Every day they delayed their departure for Rome was another day for him to consolidate his power.

But how do you tell a man he's making a fatal mistake when you're not supposed to know the future? How do you change history? Jane had spent countless nights wrestling with these questions, the weight of foreknowledge pressing down on her like a physical burden.

In the courtyard, Clodius was helping his opponent up, showing that peculiar mix of graciousness and condescension that characterised his leadership style. His pale skin had flushed pink with exertion, reminding Jane of Apple, still imprisoned in the cells below. Another impossible situation requiring impossible choices.

Jane straightened her stola and touched the copper mirror hanging at her belt — an insignificant gesture that had become a habit, a reminder of who she was and where she came from. Then she turned away from the view and headed inside. There was work to be done, and history wouldn't wait forever.

. . .

THE GUARD'S TORCH CAST DANCING SHADOWS ON THE DAMP stone walls as Jane descended into the holding cells. The smell hit her first — a mixture of human misery, blood, defecation, vomit and mouldy straw that made her stomach clench. She steeled herself, keeping her face impassive. Weakness wasn't an option, not here, not now.

Apple sat cross-legged on the cell's wooden platform, her white-blonde hair glowing in the torchlight. She didn't look up as Jane approached, but the set of her shoulders betrayed her awareness.

"Has the Governor been to see you?" Jane asked the girl through the iron bars.

Apple's head snapped up. "Why do you care?"

"Because the Governor's fascination with you is unhelpful." Jane kept her voice level, remembering how frustrating this girl was.

"Unhelpful for whom?" Apple's voice dripped with contempt.

Jane remembered the look on Clodius's face when he'd first seen Apple – that moment of recognition, of seeing his own distinctive colouring mirrored in another. She hadn't anticipated his reaction, hadn't considered how a man who'd spent his life standing out might respond to finding someone who looked like him.

"Yesterday," Jane said, "he spent an hour questioning the guards about you and your prayers." She paused, letting the implications sink in. "Why?"

"I told the guards we're related," Apple replied.

Jane moved closer to the bars, lowering her voice. "Listen carefully. Whilst you think you're playing a brilliant game, it will end badly for you. Related? You think that because you're both missing the same level of melanin in your skin, that you can claim a kinship, and reverse his decision to put you to death? You're dreaming. But I can help you live, as much as that pains me to say. "

"You never wanted me alive back in Hexham. Why's that any different now? What do you want? That's what it boils down to, like always. What's in it for the great Jane Badrick, Mayor of Hexham?" Apple's words cut sharp.

Jane's face flushed. The girl was right. Jane had seen an opportunity. She could turn the governor's fascination with the girl to her advantage.

If she could engineer Apple's distinctive appearance to validate Albinus's claim to greatness, then that could only be a good thing.

"Perhaps," Jane agreed, "we can help each other."

Apple's laugh was bitter. "Help you manipulate him, you mean?"

"Help keep us both alive." Jane met the girl's pale eyes. "There are worse things than being useful."

She turned to leave, her mind already working through the possibilities. Behind her, Apple's voice drifted through the bars, soft but clear: "I know what you're doing. Playing with people like they're pieces on a chess board. But remember, the pawn is just as powerful as the king."

Jane smiled as she climbed the stairs back to the upper levels. The girl was right, of course. But sometimes, playing the game was the only way to survive it.

THE WAR COUNCIL GATHERED IN THE PRAETORIUM'S MAIN hall, where maps covered the long oak table and the afternoon sun filtered through oiled parchment windows. Jane took her place behind Clodius's right shoulder, a position that let her observe while maintaining a feminine deference these Romans expected.

"Severus gathers strength in Pannonia," the messenger reported, his voice steady despite his obvious exhaustion. "His legions move west. The Danube garrisons have declared for him."

Jane watched Clodius's pale fingers drum against the table's surface. She'd seen this behaviour before in countless council meetings back in Hexham – the telltale signs of a leader who didn't want to hear uncomfortable truths.

"The Danube garrisons are irrelevant," Clodius declared, his voice carrying across the hall. "Our strength lies here, in

Britain. In the loyalty of these legions." He swept his arm across the map, knocking over the wine cup at his elbow.

The generals exchanged glances. Jane had learned to read these men over the past few weeks. She saw the doubt in their eyes, the same doubt she'd seen in her own council members when budgets didn't align or promises weren't kept.

"My lord," she breathed, letting her voice carry just far enough, "perhaps we might consider how to best use that loyalty?"

Clodius's head snapped toward her, his pale eyes narrowing. "You have a prophecy for us? Speak, then."

"The legions' loyalty is indeed precious," she continued, choosing her words. "Too precious to waste defending Britain when Rome itself lies vulnerable. Severus moves west, yes, but Rome looks north, to you."

She saw the shift in his expression — the way her words stroked his ego while planting the seed of action. This was no different from persuading the council to back the new shopping centre. Just with higher stakes.

"Rome," Clodius murmured, and for a moment his face showed the shrewd intelligence that had made him governor. Then his expression darkened. "But these reports of Severus – they're lies! Provocations! He wouldn't dare move against me!"

The nearest general flinched at the sudden shift in tone. Jane had seen this before too – the mercurial swing from rationality to rage. But where others saw unpredictability, she saw opportunity.

"Of course they're provocations," she soothed. "He fears you enough to keep you here, defending Britain, while he consolidates his power in Rome." She paused, letting the idea take root. "Unless that's exactly what you want him to do?"

Clodius stood, his chair scraping against the stone floor. "You suggest I'm hiding like a coward?" His voice rose to an almost feminine pitch.

"I suggest," Jane said calmly, "that you're exactly where Severus hopes you'll stay. Safe. Contained. Away from Rome's gates."

The silence that followed was broken only by Clodius's

rapid breathing. Jane could almost see the thoughts churning behind his pale eyes. She'd seen that look too, in countless meetings – the moment when a politician realises they're being backed into a corner of their own making.

"Perhaps," he said finally, his voice settling back into its lower register, "we shouldn't wait for better weather."

Jane allowed herself a smile.

Sometimes, the best way to move someone forward was to make them think retreat was the only other option.

Later that night, in Clodius's private chambers, Jane accepted the cup of wine he offered. The room spoke of power – Persian carpets, Greek bronzes, the trappings of a man who saw himself destined for greater things. She watched him pace, his pale skin ghostly in the flickering light.

"You spoke well today," he said, his voice softer here, away from his men. "The gods have blessed me with your counsel."

Jane took a careful sip of wine. "The gods have blessed you with much, my lord. Your military prowess, your loyal legions…" She paused deliberately. "Your beautiful wife Cornelia, your strong son."

His expression flickered. "You needn't remind me of my family obligations."

"Never, my lord." Jane set down her cup. "I speak only of your blessings. Your advantages over Severus. Although he has powerful allies in Rome."

Clodius waved his hand dismissively. "Allies can be bought, or married."

"True," Jane said. "And what better way to secure such alliances than through family ties?" She watched his face. "A daughter of marriageable age, for instance, could secure loyalty faster than any amount of gold."

"I have no daughter," he snapped.

"Are you sure?" Jane queried. "Could it be conceivable that you have a daughter Rome was unaware of? A daughter you kept hidden from view until now? A girl who so overtly shares your blood that there can be no question of her parentage? One of marriageable age that you now offer to Rome?

Clodius stopped pacing. "The prisoner? That Iceni spy?"

"Is she?" Jane asked softly. "The same pale skin, the same

hair, the same noble bearing. Can it be coincidence?" She stepped closer, lowering her voice. "The gods themselves have sent you a sign. A girl who could be your daughter in every way that matters."

"You yourself said she was a spy," he said, but uncertainty had crept into his tone.

"I was wrong," Jane admitted. "When I spoke with her today, I watched how she carried herself. She believes, fervently, that she is off your blood. Whether she is or isn't matters not. What does matter is that she's of perfect age to cement an alliance with one of those powerful families in Rome who might otherwise support Severus."

Clodius stared out the window at the darkened city. "Cornelia would never accept it."

"As your wife, shouldn't Cornelia accept your word? You are, after all, her husband, head of the household. Wouldn't it be wise to accept this gift from the gods? And bring her to Rome, where her presence might... open doors?"

She watched the idea taking root as Albinus's pale features glowed with the possibility of cementing his claim to the throne.

"A daughter," he murmured. "My daughter."

"We must seize such opportunities before Severus can act," Jane pressed.

Clodius turned back to her, his eyes bright. "We sail with the morning tide," he declared. "Have my daughter prepared. She'll need... suitable attire. For a governor's daughter."

Jane bowed her head to hide her smile. "Of course. I'll see to everything."

As she left his chambers, Jane felt the weight of her manipulation settle around her shoulders like a familiar cloak. She had given Clodius his army, and now she had given him a daughter. All the pieces were in place.

History said Clodius Albinus would die in Gaul. But history hadn't counted on Jane Badrick – or on a pale-skinned girl from the future who might just change everything.

Don't Kill The Messenger

Neumegen squinted at the newspaper spread across Pramod's desk, his finger tracing the grainy photograph for the hundredth time. The lead box looked innocuous enough in the black and white print of the Hexham Herald, but the markings along its edge made his heart race. They weren't random scratches. They couldn't be.

"You're going to wear a hole in that paper," Loretta said from behind him. She set a cup of tea at his elbow, her hand trembling. She'd been jumpy, checking her watch every few minutes, as if expecting to disappear at any moment. Six weeks in one timeline was a record for her, and they both knew it.

"Look at this section," Neumegen said, tapping the photo. "The way these lines intersect — it's just like the diagrams Pramod showed me last year. The ones about temporal markers."

Loretta leaned closer, her breath warm on his neck. "You think Pramod is sending a message?"

Neumegen pushed back from the desk, his chair scraping against the bare wooden floor. "Remember what he told us about communication across timelines? About leaving markers that only other travellers would recognise?"

"I remember you both getting very excited about Roman lead curses," Loretta said, perching on the edge of the desk. She glanced at her watch again. "But that doesn't mean—"

"That's exactly what this is!" Neumegen stood, pacing between the towering bookshelves. "Pramod theorised that lead was the perfect medium for cross-temporal communication. Something about its atomic structure making it more stable across timeline shifts." He paused, running his hands through his dishevelled hair. "And now this box shows up, with these specific markings, just when Pramo—"

He couldn't finish the sentence. They both knew Pramod had risked everything to travel back in time.

"When did he first tell you about this?" Loretta asked.

Neumegen closed his eyes, remembering. "Last autumn. We were talking about curses, of all things. He'd been reading about Roman curses, and back then, instead of posting on the internet, disgruntled Romans would etch their curses into pieces of lead, and fold it over and over, thus disguising the ill words, but, the intricate folds sent the curse out across temporal planes." He smiled at the memory. "I thought he was just being poetic. You know how he gets. But then he showed me his research..."

Loretta picked up the newspaper, studying the photo. "And you think these markings match?"

"Not just match. They're identical to one specific diagram." Neumegen took the paper from her hands, pointing to a series of intersecting lines along the box's edge. "See how these form a double helix pattern? That's not Roman. That's pure Pramod."

Loretta's watch beeped, making them both jump. She checked it, then let out a slow breath. "I worry about Lillian," she mumbled. "We should be with her. Guiding her. Pramod will be okay."

"Did you have any help the first time you travelled?" Neumegen asked.

Loretta shook her head. "You know I didn't. And you didn't either. But that doesn't mean that we have to leave those girls out there on their own. We should be trying to get to them."

"Which is why we need to know where in the 'when' they are."

"Just don't get too fixated on this. Sometimes a box is just a box. Those scratchings might mean nothing."

"I know, but trust me on this," he said, reaching for Loretta's mobile phone. "I need you to make a phone call for me."

"Mr Fletcher? This is Henry Neumegen. I'm calling about your article on the lead box found near Hexham."

Jasper balanced his phone while shuffling through papers on his desk. "The box with the tablets in it? What about it?"

"There's something significant about the box itself. I'm not interested in the writing tablets, although I'm sure that they will be fascinating once they've been deciphered, but I need to see your photos of the box."

"They're all on the website. Thanks for calling—"

"Hold on," Neumegen begged, "what I'm trying to convey is that based on the photos I've already seen, I believe the box is a form of a Roman curse."

Jasper put the phone on speaker, catching Charley's eye across the newsroom. She wheeled her chair over, curiosity piqued. "You're saying the box is an ancient curse?"

"Indeed. I realise how mad this makes me sound, but you are familiar with curse tablets? The markings I can see on your photos, whilst indistinct in the photos I've seen, appear to be very similar to other Roman curse tablets. I just need to see the original photos, or the box itself. Your article mentioned Matthew Badrick has possession of the box?"

Charley leaned toward the phone. "He's already held one media conference about it, so I doubt that they'll be another one. You realise his wife is missing? He has better things to do than to answer every crack pot's crazy theories. You don't think he's already thought of this angle?"

"Yes, yes," Neumegen's impatience crackled through the speaker. "But would he allow another examination of the box? This could be crucial to understanding—"

"Unlikely," Charley interrupted. "The police forensics team is on it now. We only have the pictures that we took."

Neumegen could hear Jasper and Charley whispering away from the phone, "What are curse tablets?"

Loretta's voice drifted into the conversation. "What about if someone from another paper wanted to cover the story? Say, from Wales?"

"Wales?" Jasper asked.

"I have press credentials," Loretta said. "From the Western Mail. Does Mr Badrick subscribe to the saying that all publicity is good publicity?"

"I would say so. He takes after his wife in that department," Jasper agreed. "Our intern took hundreds of photos at the initial press conference," Jasper added. "We could set up a meeting, go through those first. Maybe build enough interest for a follow-up viewing of the box itself."

"Perfect." Neumegen's excitement was palpable through the phone. "When can we meet?"

Rhema spread the photos across the conference table in the Herald's back office. The fluorescent lights cast harsh shadows across the images, making the box's markings stand out in stark relief.

"I took these from every angle," she explained, arranging them in sequence. "The light wasn't great during the press conference, but—"

"These are perfect," Neumegen interrupted, already hunched over the table. His fingers traced the patterns visible in the photos, his eyes intense behind his glasses. "Look at this sequence here. It's not random damage."

Loretta leaned in, playing her part as the interested Welsh journalist. "It looks like scratches to me."

"No, no," Neumegen pulled out a pen, sketching on a notepad. "See how these lines intersect? There's a pattern. Here, and here." He drew rapid lines, connecting points across multiple photos. "It's a sequence."

Charley frowned, studying the images. "Like a code?"

"More like..." Neumegen hesitated, glancing at Loretta. "Like coordinates. Temporal coordinates."

Jasper looked up from his notebook. "Temporal? You mean time?"

"Remember those coins they found?" Neumegen's voice took on a lecturer's tone. "They're not just valuable because they're Roman. They're valuable because they're perfect. Untouched. As if someone buried them yesterday."

"And?" Charley prompted.

"And look at this box. The lead is oxidised, yes, but these markings..." He shuffled through the photos, finding one that showed the box's base. "Here! This pattern is identical to one I've seen before. In a theoretical paper about quantum entanglement across temporal planes."

Rhema snorted. "You're saying someone used time travel to bury Roman coins?"

"I'm saying," Neumegen replied, "that this box and those coins might be connected in ways we don't yet understand." He paused at one particular photo. "Do you have any more shots on this side?"

Rhema dug through her laptop bag, producing a memory card. "There are some alternates. The lighting was better when they first brought it out."

They huddled around her laptop as she pulled up the images. Neumegen's excitement grew with each new photo.

"There!" He jabbed at the screen. "That's what I was looking for. The sequential progression. It's exactly like in Pramod's notes."

"Who's Pramod?" Jasper asked, scribbling notes.

"A colleague. A brilliant man who..." Neumegen swallowed hard. "Who theorised about methods of communication across different times. He's very ill now, but his work..." He turned to Loretta. "We need to see that box. The actual box."

"Hold on," Charley interjected. "You still haven't explained what these markings mean."

Neumegen gathered the photos, arranging them in a specific order. "They're instructions," he said. "Or maybe warnings. But they're definitely a message for someone specific."

"Who?" Jasper asked.

Neumegen's eyes met Loretta's. "Someone who would

know how to read them. There's one more thing," Neumegen said as he pulled out a printout of the coin analysis. "The coins date to the reign of Clodius Albinus. Early 195 AD."

"CE," Loretta responded.

Neumegen shook his head at her. "Yes, CE. Common Era. At my age, it's hard to wrap my head around the change."

"Moving on," Charley asked, interested despite her skepticism. "Are you saying that the coins are the same period as the box?"

"At first glance, you'd think so," Neumegen spread the photos out again. "But look at the oxidation patterns. This box should be roughly the same age as those coins, but these markings..." He traced the sequence. "These are different. They're newer."

Loretta checked her watch again. "We should focus on getting access to the box itself. I'll make those calls this afternoon, work the Welsh media angle."

"About that," Jasper interrupted. "Why Wales? What's the connection?"

"The Caernarfon theft," Rhema interrupted. Everyone turned to look at her. "What? I did my research. That's why the Art Loss Register is here, isn't it? Some connection between these coins and a decades-old heist in Wales?"

The blood drained from Loretta's face, and her hand went to her pocket, where a single gold coin pressed against her thigh through the fabric. How on earth was there any connection to Caernarfon? Her coin had been stolen during the chaos of preparing for a royal investiture, but that didn't explain why the same Roman coins might surface decades later. But regardless of that, she'd expected no one to draw a line between then and now. Her daughter was grown now, and her husband... She pushed the thought away, forcing herself to focus on the present.

Neumegen's eyes lit up, oblivious to her distress. "Of course! That gives us another angle. If we can convince Matthew Badrick that there might be a connection between the box, the coins, and his wife's disappearance..."

"Through the coins?" Charley sounded doubtful.

"Through the message carved into that box," Neumegen

insisted. "These aren't random scratches. They're too intentional."

"We need to go," Loretta cut in. "Things are... happening. With Pramod. If these markings really are what Neumegen thinks they are..."

"What does he think they are?" Charley asked.

But Neumegen was already gathering his notes. "Get us in to see that box," he said to the journalists. "Whatever it takes. Whatever story you have to spin. I need to see it before—" He stopped himself.

"Before what?" Jasper pressed.

"Before it's too late," Neumegen finished.

As their unusual guests left the office, Charley caught Jasper's arm. "You're not buying any of this, are you?"

Jasper watched Neumegen and Loretta walking away, deep in conversation. "I don't know," he admitted. "But something's not right."

"So, what's our next move?"

"We follow up on Rhema's research. See what else we can find about that Caernarfon connection? We check with Bishop to see if he's holding out on us." He paused. "And maybe do some digging into our mysterious Welsh journalist. Something tells me there's more to her story than she's letting on. And as for you Rhema, why the hell didn't you tell us about the guy from the Art Loss Register? The first rule of being a journalist is that you share all your info."

"Don't listen to him, Rhema. He's got no idea what a proper journalist does, which is why he's still here, instead of in Newcastle, with me," Charley smiled at the man next to her.

Disturbing the Past

Badger's phone buzzed again. Another message from Holly:

He tossed the phone onto his bed, the memory of Holly's behaviour right before Lillian's disappearance still raw in his mind.

His father's shout from downstairs made him jump.

"My God! Are you absolutely certain? How many? No, no, don't touch anything. I'll be right there!" A pause, then: "ANDY! ANDY, COME DOWN HERE!"

Badger found his father in the kitchen, phone still in hand, face flushed with excitement. Matthew Badrick looked younger. The weight of Jane's disappearance temporarily lifted from his shoulders.

"You'll never believe what they've found in the barn at Ithaca Farm," his father said, hands trembling as he poured coffee everywhere except into his mug. "Altars. Roman altars. Not one, not two, but a whole bloody collection of them. Bishop's just called — they were hidden behind some hay bales. There was a woman tied up in there. No, not your mother..." He trailed off at the sight of Badger's face.

"Anyway," he continued, his excitement too huge to contain. "That woman escaped, or was rescued, or something, and she told the police about the altars. Bishop's up there now with her, the woman that was tied up. And he's just rung me. I mean, it can't be real. They have to be replicas, but Bish knows his stuff, and he thinks they're real. And the woman with him, she's an antique dealer. Can you just imagine if she'd just loaded them all up and had driven them away? Can you imagine?" Here his father took a breath. "We nearly lost them, Andy. But they're ours now. I can see the headlines."

"Altars?" Badger's stomach clenched. In Lillian's barn? What if she needed them to come back to him?

"This is unprecedented," his father continued, oblivious to Badger's distress. "A cache of this size, all in one place? This isn't just significant, son — this is career-defining. History-making!" He grabbed Badger's shoulders. "I need your help. We have to document everything, prepare them for transport. Christ, I'm going to need umpteen pairs of hands, but hands I can trust. Do not breath a word of this to anyone."

"Transport?" Badger's voice cracked. "You're moving them?"

"Of course we're moving them! To the university's storage facility. This is too important a find to leave in a barn. We need proper facilities, proper security." His father was already pulling on his coat. "The press will be all over this. It'll overshadow even the coin find. Finally, something good coming out of this whole mess."

Badger watched his father's transformation with a mix of wonder and dread. For weeks, Matthew had been a shadow of himself, going through the motions at work while obsessing over Jane's disappearance. Now he was animated, bouncing around with academic enthusiasm. The find of the century had accomplished what no amount of rum or support had managed — it had given his father purpose.

But all Badger could think about was Lillian. The altars were her way back — she'd explained it to him that last night, about the objects acting as anchors across time. If they moved them, scattered them...

"Andy? Are you listening? Get your boots on. Bishop's already rung Newcastle, but I want us to get there first. This is history, son. Our history."

Badger nodded, knowing he had no choice. He guessed that it was better to be involved and to protect Lillian's secret from the inside. But potentially they could also be about to destroy any chance of Lillian finding her way home.

ITHACA FARM HAD BECOME AN IMPROMPTU CAR PARK. University vans with Newcastle logos jostled for space with police vehicles and news crews. Badger watched from the barn doorway as his father consulted with a group of archaeologists, their excited gestures visible even from this distance.

"Ladies and gentlemen," Sergeant Bishop's voice carried across the yard. "If you'll gather round, I going to make a statement."

The press surged forward, microphones extended. Badger recognised Jasper from the Herald, and the young intern Rhema, who was already snapping photos.

"During our ongoing investigation into Jane Badrick's disappearance," Bishop continued, "forensic teams discovered what appears to be a significant cache of Roman artefacts in this barn. Initial assessment suggests these are ritual altars, dating from the second century CE. Dr Matthew Badrick from Newcastle University, will now explain the historical significance of this find."

Badger watched his father step forward, noticing how he seemed to grow taller under the attention. "What we have here is unprecedented in British archaeology. These altars appear to be genuine Roman artefacts, and their preservation is remarkable. The sheer number of them in one location raises fascinating questions about ritual practices in Roman Britain."

"Dr Badrick!" A voice called out. "Given that these were found on the property where your wife's car was discovered, do you think there's a connection?"

Matthew's expression shifted. "The police are exploring all possibilities. What is particularly interesting is that these altars were discovered on a property recently purchased by a newcomer to Hexham. Someone who appeared in town just weeks before my wife's disappearance."

Badger's hands clenched into fists. He knew what his father was doing — redirecting suspicion away from Jane and toward Lillian.

"The Treasure Act states—" a member of the press began.

"This isn't treasure, it's archaeological heritage," another interrupted. "Different regulations entirely."

How so many members of the press had arrived already was a modern miracle.

"What about the woman held captive here?" shouted someone else.

"That's an ongoing investigation," Bishop continued. "We can confirm that a woman was held against her will in this barn, and that she was the one who alerted us to the presence of these artefacts. We're following several leads regarding both this incident and Mrs Badrick's disappearance."

"Dr Badrick," called out a reporter from the Chronicle, "do you have any comment about the timing of this discovery?"

Badger watched his father step forward again, his academic demeanour shifting to something harder.

"The timing is interesting," Matthew said into the forest of microphones. "This collection was hidden away in a barn belonging to someone who just moved to Hexham. And now both the property owner and my wife are missing." He paused, letting the implication sink in. "What if my wife uncovered something she wasn't supposed to? What if she found out about these artefacts? And now someone has killed her for that knowledge?"

The reporters erupted with questions, but Badger couldn't hear them over the roaring in his ears. He turned away. At least no one had started loading the altars yet. The arguments about proper procedure and legal requirements would buy them some time. But how much? And what would happen when they moved them?

After the press conference, Badger lingered near the barn, watching his father and Bishop in deep conversation.

"Think about it," Matthew was saying, his voice carrying

in the quiet yard. "Jane disappears after visiting this farm. We find her car here. Then we discover the property owner has been hiding priceless Roman artefacts in her barn. And now she's conveniently disappeared too?"

Bishop nodded. "And there's the matter of the woman tied up in the barn."

"Exactly. What kind of person keeps Roman altars hidden in their barn? And takes hostages?" Matthew ran a hand through his hair. "You need to search the entire property. Properly this time."

"I'll get a warrant," Bishop agreed. "The archaeological significance alone would justify it, but with the potential connection to Jane..."

Badger's phone felt heavy in his pocket. He pulled it out, fingers hovering over Neumegen's number. He understood about the time travel. Was there something he could he do to stop any further damage being done to Lillian's way home? Or his mother's?

"The university team can document everything while we search," Bishop was saying. "Two birds, one stone."

"Good. The sooner we get these altars somewhere secure, the better." Matthew glanced toward the barn. "Who knows what other evidence we might find once we move them? Or what else we might find?"

Badger's thumb pressed the call button before he could stop himself. It went straight to voicemail. "Henry," he whispered urgently, "they're going to move the altars at Ithaca Farm. And they think Lillian... Please, I need your help."

He watched as police cars began arriving, followed by a van marked 'Forensics.' The warrant hadn't taken long, but then again, even he knew that officers from London were already in town, probing into his mother's activities.

Inside the barn, the archaeologists were setting up their equipment. Someone was talking about bringing in a crane. They were going to do it — they were going to move the altars.

Badger's mind raced. He knew things no one else here did. He knew why the altars were really here and what they were for. Lillian wasn't a criminal hiding stolen artefacts, she was trying to protect something far more important.

As he watched as another group of archaeologists and police officers entered the barn, Badger felt something shift inside him. He couldn't let this happen. He couldn't just stand by and watch them destroy Lillian's only way back.

His phone buzzed. It wasn't Neumegen calling back, but another text from Holly:

> I know what really happened to Lillian.

> We need to talk.

Badger stared at the message, an idea forming. A really terrible, desperate idea. But maybe the only way to save the altars — and Lillian's chance of return.

Choosing History

The *Twice Brewed* was quiet for a Tuesday afternoon. Holly sat at a corner table, her perfect blonde hair catching the light from the window. Badger noticed she'd positioned herself to be visible from the street — on display.

"I knew you'd come around," she said as he slid into the seat opposite her. Her overfilled lips curved into what she probably thought was a winning smile. "Those texts I sent must have made you think."

Badger forced himself to smile back, hating himself for what he was about to do. "You said you knew what happened to Lillian?"

Holly's expression hardened slightly. "Oh yes. I saw her, you know. At the *Bellingham*. Right before she disappeared." She leaned forward, lowering her voice conspiratorially. "One minute she was there, the next..." Holly snapped her fingers, the sound sharp in the quiet pub. "It's funny what people do to avoid the police, isn't it?"

Badger's heart raced. Holly had actually seen it happen. "Did you tell anyone what you'd seen?"

"Not yet." Her emphasis on yet was deliberate. "I mean, the police are looking for her, aren't they? In connection with your mother's disappearance? I should probably tell them that Lillian's actively avoiding them. What she's capable..."

"Holly," Badger said carefully, reaching across the table to touch her hand. He saw the triumph in her eyes at the contact. "Before you do anything, let me explain what's really going on."

"I'm listening." She turned her hand over, catching his fingers with hers. Her nails were perfectly manicured, painted a pale pink that probably had some ridiculous name like 'whispered promises.'

"Not here," he said. "There's something I need to show you first. At Ithaca Farm."

Her eyes narrowed. "Her farm? Where they found that old stone? I don't think so. I'm hardly wearing the right footwear to start with," she said, wiggling a foot to show off the shiny white of her fashion trainers. Some Gucci style knockoff. "I thought you asked me here for a drink?"

"I did, but I also need to take you up to the farm." Badger leaned closer, letting her catch a whiff of his aftershave — the one she'd bought him and he hadn't stopped using, more out of habit than anything else. "I need your help, Holly. You're good at getting attention when you want it. And right now, I need everyone's attention somewhere else."

"You want me to create a distraction?" A slow smile spread across her face. "Like old times?"

"Like old times," he agreed, hating the way she lit up at his words. "Remember that summer festival when you got everyone to look the other way so we could..."

"Up in the bell tower?" She giggled, and for a moment he saw the girl she'd been before ambition and jealousy had hardened her. "I told them I'd seen Ant and Dec getting ready to film something in the market square. They all went running."

"I need that Holly," he said softly. "The one who could make anything happen."

She withdrew her hand. "And what do I get out of it?"

"The truth," he said. "About everything. About Lillian, about my mother, and about the farm." He paused, then added the bait he knew she couldn't resist. "And maybe... a chance to show me that I've been making a mistake?"

Holly's smile widened, predatory and pleased.

"Give me fifteen minutes. I need to change my shoes first, and then I'll have them eating out of my hand."

As she stood to leave, Badger felt sick at how easily he'd played her. But he didn't have a choice. The altars were Lillian's only way back — and maybe his mother's too. He'd make it up to Holly somehow.

Probably.

BADGER SLIPPED INTO THE BARN, HIS HEART POUNDING. Outside, he could hear Holly's voice rising above the general hubbub, something about evidence and Jane Badrick, an exclusive story and being tied up herself. A complete fabrication. But she was a pretty blonde white girl, and as much as it was fucked up, those were the ones that got all the attention. The archaeologists and police officers who had been arguing about jurisdictions and treasure acts were now crowding around her, drawn by her performance like moths to a flame.

He moved deeper into the barn, past the photography equipment and the measuring tools. The altars stood in a rough semicircle, some already carefully numbered and tagged. His father's precise handwriting marked the labels: "Possible votive altar," "Dedicatory stone," "Funerary monument."

The first altar was dedicated to Mercury. The relief showed the god's distinctive staff with its twin snakes. The Latin was too worn to make out completely, but he remembered enough from his father's lessons to recognise the word *viator*.

Next to it stood a larger altar, this one to Fortuna. The goddess's wheel was clearly visible, along with what looked like a cornucopia. The stone was noticeably less weathered than the previous one. His father's handwritten note suggested it may have been part of a temple complex. May being the operative word.

The third altar made him pause. Dedicated to Janus, the two-faced god of doorways and transitions, it bore strange stains that seemed to seep from within the stone itself. The

Latin inscription was crisp, as though it had been carved yesterday: "To Janus, who opens the way."

But it was the fourth stone that drew him in.

Not an altar at all, but a headstone.

No dedication to gods, no fancy carvings, just a simple memorial to someone who had died far from home. The stone was rough, as if it had been carved by a novice stonemason, or by a layman.

Lillian's words came back to him suddenly: "The oldest things have the strongest pull. Time leaves marks, like rings in a tree. The more rings, the stronger the anchor."

He studied the headstone more closely, trying to decipher the remnants of the inscription.

A shout from outside made him jump. Holly was really putting on a show, her voice carrying clearly: "I have proof that Jane Badrick was investigating corruption at the highest levels of our government! Our government and its whole woke rewilding rubbish, like what was happening here, at Ithaca Farm."

Badger knew his time was running out. He had to choose. The Mercury altar made sense — the god of travellers, helping people on their way. The Janus altar too, with its connection to doorways and transitions. But his gut kept pulling him back to the headstone. It wasn't fancy or powerful or dedicated to any god. It was just... old. Ancient. Did he need to know who the headstone was for?

Sometimes the simplest answer was the right one.

He glanced at his father's notes one last time. The headstone was also the smallest of the stones — still devastatingly heavy, but just possibly manageable. If he was going to do this, it had to be now.

Outside, Holly's performance was reaching its crescendo. He could hear his father's voice among those questioning her. It was time to make his choice.

Badger took a deep breath and moved toward the headstone, praying he was right.

Holly's voice rose to new heights of indignation outside. "And I have screenshots! Text messages! Proof of a conspiracy reaching right to the top of the council!"

The headstone was heavier than Badger had anticipated. He wrapped his arms around it, trying to find purchase on the rough surface. His muscles strained as he attempted to lift it, managing only to shift it slightly on its base.

"We're going to need those screenshots," Bishop's voice carried from outside.

"Oh, they're in my car," Holly replied smoothly. "Let me just go and—"

"Nobody's going anywhere," Matthew interrupted. "Sergeant, this is critical evidence about my wife."

A scraping sound from behind made Badger freeze. He turned slowly, still gripping the headstone, to find Nicole Pilcher watching him from the barn's side entrance. She looked different from when he'd last seen her — smaller somehow in an oversized police jacket, her usually composed demeanour shaken. The angry red marks on her wrists made his stomach clench.

"I'm pleased it was you coming back for the altars," she said quietly, rubbing at her wrists. "And not anyone else."

"Nicole," Badger started, remembering their conversations at the farm, how he'd always sensed she knew more than she was saying. "What happened to you? Were you really tied up in here?"

"Yes," she said simply. "By Darby, but he's dead now. I just can't wrap my head around it. Nothing makes sense." She moved closer, examining the headstone. "You're trying to what? Keep the way open for Lillian's return?"

Badger studied her face, remembering how she'd coloured when he'd asked about the dig site that day. "You knew these were here all along, didn't you? The altars?"

"Not at the beginning. But I know... no, I suspect what they do. There's no other rational explanation, and given what I've experienced in the past... it's not as much of a stretch for me to believe it as you think it is." She positioned herself on the other side of the headstone. "Now, we need to move quickly."

Outside, the commotion was growing as Holly led everyone on a wild goose chase to her car. Nicole nodded toward the stone.

"On three," she whispered. "One... two..."

Together, they lifted. The stone was still impossibly heavy, but manageable between them. They shuffled toward the back of the barn, where bales of hay were stacked against the wall.

"Someone's coming!" Nicole warned.

They froze as footsteps approached. A shadow fell across the barn door.

"Quick," Nicole said, "behind the hay."

They barely managed to manoeuvre the headstone behind the bales when one of the archaeologists stuck his head in. "Hello? Anyone in here?"

Nicole stepped out casually, adjusting her police jacket. "Just me. Sergeant Bishop asked me to check if anything else had been disturbed while I was..." She gestured at her wrists, letting the implication hang.

The archaeologist nodded sympathetically and withdrew. Nicole waited until his footsteps faded before turning back to Badger.

"The old farm cart," she whispered. "The one Lillian was planning to restore. It's still behind the barn. We can use that."

Badger felt a surge of gratitude, remembering how Nicole had helped him look for Lillian that first day. "Why are you really helping me?"

"Because Lillian trusted you," she replied, already helping him lift again. "And because after what I've seen — both here and in London — I think some artefacts need to stay exactly where they are. There's far too much hidden away in museum storage and private collections, and not just in this country."

Together they manoeuvred the stone toward the back door, every scrape and shuffle sounding impossibly loud to Badger's ears. But outside, Holly was still holding court, her voice carrying across the yard: "And that's not even the biggest scandal! Wait until you hear about the planning permission..."

· · ·

THE OLD CART CREAKED UNDER THE HEADSTONE'S WEIGHT as they pushed it through the orchard. Holly's voice had faded behind them, replaced by the sound of sirens in the distance — probably more police responding to her claims.

"Where are we taking it?" Nicole whispered.

"The old pig shed," Badger replied. "No one goes in there anymore. The floor's too unstable." He remembered Lillian mentioning plans to renovate it before everything had gone wrong.

His phone buzzed in his pocket as they manoeuvred the cart around a fallen apple tree. Neumegen's name flashed on the screen:

Don't move the stone any more than necessary. Loretta and I are twenty minutes away.

"Bit late for that," Nicole muttered, reading over his shoulder.

The pig shed's door protested as they pushed it open, decades of rust flaking from its hinges. Inside, the air was thick with dust and decay. Badger's torch beam caught cobwebs and old farming equipment, casting strange shadows on the walls.

"Here," Nicole said, pointing to a corner hidden by a collapsed workbench. "We can—"

"Wait." Badger's torch had caught something on the headstone's surface — a glint of metal. He leaned closer, brushing away decades of grime. There, fused to the stone's face, was a coin. The metal had bonded to the stone, green-black corrosion cementing it in place.

"Look at this," he said, pointing to where the coin met the stone. The metal seemed to flow into the rock, as if the two materials had melded together. "I think... I think this is why this stone feels different. Why it was marked."

Another text from Neumegen:

> Whatever you do, don't separate any attached objects. They're part of the anchoring mechanism.

"Anchoring mechanism," Badger repeated softly. "Is that what that coin is do you think?"

"We'll know soon enough," Nicole replied, already helping him position the headstone in its hiding place. "Your friend seems to understand more than he's letting on."

"What now?" Nicole asked.

Badger checked his phone one last time:

> Stay with the stone. Don't let anyone else
> near it. L says this might be our only chance
> to find Lillian and Pramod.

He looked at Nicole, seeing the same mix of fear and determination he felt. "Hopes and prayers?"

Behind them, hidden under its shroud of ancient sacking, the headstone sat silent and heavy with possibility. Somewhere in the distance, Holly was still spinning her tales, buying them precious time. And somewhere he hoped Lillian was trying to find her way home.

The Price of Knowledge

Pramod's hand still shook as he lifted the cup to his lips. Aper, watching from across the villa's atrium, made no move to help. The Praetorian Prefect's cold eyes noted every tremor, every sign of weakness. He was improving, Pramod knew that. But progress was still too slow.

"The Senate grows restless," Aper said, pacing between the columns. "Severus advances from Pannonia, Albinus postures in Britain, and Pescennius Niger builds support in Syria. Three men who would be Caesar." He paused, studying a fresco of the wolf suckling Romulus and Remus. "And you, my friend, will help me choose which one to back."

The words caught in Pramod's throat; another gift from the stroke. "The Senate fears Civil War."

"The Senate fears backing the wrong horse," Aper corrected. "Niger claims the support of Syria's legions, but he's too far east. The real power lies with Severus or Albinus." He turned back to Pramod. "Tell me — which would make a better emperor? What do you know of their futures?"

Pramod knew exactly how this would play out. Severus would ultimately triumph, but not before civil war tore the empire apart.

He'd read about it countless times in history books. But now, trapped in the past, that knowledge was both burden and weapon.

"Severus commands more legions,"

"Yes, yes," Aper waved impatiently. "But Albinus has Britain's loyalty. And now this prophet who travels with him..." He produced a scroll from his toga. "The latest reports say she makes predictions that come true with uncanny accuracy. As well as having a prophet to guide him, Albinus now has a daughter, one who shares his... distinctive features. Do you know what a daughter means?"

Pramod froze. A daughter? No such person mentioned in any historical account he'd read. Unless...

"How old is she? And does she lack colouring, like Albinus?"

"Of marriageable age. The worst sort. With a daughter, and a prophet by his side, he may have just turned the tides in his favour." Aper continued reading from the scroll. "The prophet has convinced Albinus that his destiny lies in Rome. They've written her name as Jane, but surely they must mean Julia? I have never heard the name Jane before. Is it from Gaul? Or Britannia?"

The name struck Pramod like a physical blow. Jane Badrick. It had to be. He remembered her from the council meetings in Hexham. If she was using her modern knowledge to influence Albinus...

"That she speaks of omens and portents. That she knows things she couldn't possibly know." Aper's eyes narrowed. "Your hands shake more than usual. Does this news disturb you?"

Pramod forced himself to remain calm. If Jane was with Albinus, everything he thought he knew about history could change. And this mention of a daughter — that wasn't in any account he'd read either.

"Prophets can be... unreliable," he said.

"Perhaps." Aper rolled up the scroll. "Or perhaps the gods truly speak through her. Either way, the Senate will look to me for guidance, and I must be ready to back the right candidate. It doesn't have to be one of those three."

And profit from it, Pramod wanted to say, but didn't. He watched Aper move toward the door, his mind racing. Jane Badrick in ancient Rome, playing prophet to Clodius Albinus. The implications for the future were staggering.

"Rest well," Aper said from the doorway. "I'll return tomorrow. We have much to discuss about these... prophecies."

After Aper left, Pramod slumped in his chair, exhausted. He had to figure out exactly why Jane Badrick was playing with history itself.

As Aper's footsteps faded, Pramod pulled the lead tablet from beneath his cushions. His fingers trembled as he traced the symbols he'd already carved into its surface — temporal coordinates that might guide someone in the future to understand what was happening.

If only his hands would stop shaking.

A slave boy appeared at his elbow with fresh wine. "Dominus, a messenger arrived while the Prefect was here. News from Britannia."

Pramod gestured for the message, then waited until the boy retreated before breaking the seal. His eyes struggled to focus on the text – another legacy of the stroke – but what he could make out made his blood run cold. Albinus was delayed in Londinium due to the bad weather. But they would be travelling soon, together with Albinus's secret daughter, and a captive Iceni chieftain.

There could be only one person who could have been Albinus's secret daughter — Apple. It had to be. Jane was using the girl's albinism to convince Albinus she was his daughter, while simultaneously creating a convenient asset to marry off.

He turned back to his lead tablet, his stylus leaving uneven marks as he tried to record what he knew about the anchors. 'The oldest points are strongest', he scratched into the surface. 'Time leaves marks that echo. Look for the patterns in...'

His hand spasmed, sending the stylus skittering across the floor. Cursing his weakness, Pramod closed his eyes, trying to focus. Somewhere in the future, Neumegen would find this tablet. Would he understand what it meant?

He retrieved the stylus and continued writing: 'The anchors must remain in place or the doors will close', he wrote, his letters becoming increasingly erratic.

His vision blurred. He was pushing too hard, he knew. But what choice did he have? History was being rewritten around him, and somewhere in Londinium, Jane Badrick was orchestrating changes that would reshape everything about the future.

With trembling fingers, he added one final line. It wasn't enough. There was so much more to explain, about the anchors, about Jane's interference, about the danger to the timeline. But his body was betraying him again, darkness creeping at the edges of his vision.

The last thing he saw before consciousness slipped away was the lead tablet, its surface covered in his desperate warnings to the future.

METELLA HEARD THE STYLUS FALL BEFORE SHE REACHED THE atrium. She had been waiting for her father to leave, knowing how these visits exhausted Pramod. When she found him collapsed beside his chair, the lead tablet still clutched in one hand, her heart nearly stopped.

"Pramod!" She knelt beside him, checking his breathing. His chest rose and fell steadily, but his face was drawn with exhaustion. "Someone fetch the physician!"

The slave boy who had brought the wine earlier darted away. Metella gently pried the lead tablet from Pramod's fingers.

"Me... tella." His voice barely a whisper.

"Don't try to speak," she said, cradling his head in her lap. "The physician is coming."

But his good hand gripped her wrist with surprising strength. "Must... leave. Find Julius."

"Julius is safe," she soothed, thinking of their son, safe in Britannia. "He's well-protected."

Pramod's eyes opened, filled with an urgency that frightened her. "No. Not... safe. None of us. Changes coming."

The physician arrived then, his slaves helping to lift Pramod onto a couch. Metella watched as they checked his responses, administered the medicines that had helped after his first collapse. This wasn't like the initial stroke — he was more aware, more determined to speak despite his weakness.

"The brain needs rest to heal," the physician said quietly, "These setbacks can happen if—"

"Metella!" Pramod's voice was stronger now, though slurred. "Listen. Must get Julius. Before... before Albinus sails for Rome."

She moved to his side, taking his hand.

"What are you talking about?" she whispered, checking to see if the physician had overheard. Of course he had. Rome operated on whispers and secrets and pacts and alliances. Like shifting sands, you could never be sure where you stood.

"Jane is coming... changing everything."

"Who is Jane?" Metella asked, but Pramod's eyes were already closing again.

"The anchors," he mumbled. "Must keep the anchors. Only way back..."

The physician pressed a cup to Pramod's lips, some concoction of herbs that would help him sleep. Metella watched Pramod's face relax as the medicine took effect, but his words echoed in her mind. Changes coming. Must get Julius. The urgency in his voice had been real, even if his words made no sense.

She felt the physician staring at her. "He needs complete quiet," the doctor said.

"That will be impossible here," Metella replied, more to herself than to her father's man.

Frozen Waters

The Thames was frozen solid. Lillian watched from the window of their rented room as people ventured onto the ice, testing its strength with tentative steps. In her time, the river would be tamed by embankments and bridges, its waters warmed by centuries of urban development. But here it was a wild thing, both beautiful and deadly.

"More news from the governor's palace," Julius said behind her. "They say Albinus won't sail until the ice breaks."

Lillian turned from the window, pulling herself away from the desire to clamber out and rescue her friend. They'd barely ventured out in days, afraid someone would notice the resemblance to Pramod.

"What else did the messenger say?"

"That Albinus parades his new daughter around like a prize."

Apple. Lillian's hands clenched at her sides. What game were they playing, presenting Apple as Albinus's daughter? To what end?

Through the thin walls, she could hear their neighbours arguing, although she couldn't determine which language they were speaking. Londinium was a city of merchants and soldiers, spies and informants. Everyone watching everyone else, especially now with civil war threatening. The press of humanity felt suffocating.

"We can't stay here forever," Julius said, pacing the small room. Six steps one way, six steps back. "Someone will recognise me eventually. Or wonder why we never attend the temple ceremonies."

"Just a little longer," Lillian soothed, though she shared his frustration. "Until we figure out what Jane's planning."

"The prophet?" Julius snorted. "She has convinced Albinus that Rome awaits him. That his destiny lies across the water." He paused. "I know what you have told me of Albinus's fate, and that Severus is destined to rule the empire. But I cannot shout that from the rooftops. They'd have my head off faster than I could shit. You must know a way to stop this woman's lies? You are, after all, the same."

Lillian squared her shoulders. "We are nothing alike. Other than both being women. She is a snake oil salesman, selling lies for her own advancement. You have to be the one to persuade Albinus, or his advisors, of this."

"I can't knock on the door," Julius argued. "I'm meant to still in guarding Ithaca Fort."

The pair lapsed into silence, their angry whispers lingering in the frigid air.

A commotion rose from the street below, sending Lillian back to the window, where she watched bundled figures hurrying through the frozen city. Her London was a sprawling octopus, a metropolis of miles of glass and steel and concrete and grime. But this version of London still breathed with promise, its skyline unburdened by towering monoliths of industry. The air smelled of damp earth and fresh mortar, of fires burning in hearths and bread baking in bustling taverns. Buildings stood crisp and new, their stones unstained by centuries of soot, their facades unweathered by time. This was a city still forging its destiny, where anything—everything—seemed possible.

"They say the ice might hold another month," Julius said quietly. "That's how long we have to decide what to do."

About Apple, he meant. About Jane. About whether to risk everything by interfering.

Lillian watched her breath fog the window, remembering the day she'd first travelled through time. She hadn't chosen this power, this responsibility. But now lives depended on how she used it.

"A month," she repeated softly. "Let's hope that's enough time."

The answer came sooner than expected. That afternoon, in the smoky warmth of the Boar's Head tavern, they watched Marcus the wine merchant hold court at his usual table. He was on his fourth cup of heated wine, his face flushed as he shared the latest gossip with his eager audience. But today, his news made Lillian's blood run cold.

"The Iceni prophet has Albinus's ear completely now," he announced. "His most trusted advisors — men who've served him for years – dismissed like common slaves. She tells him they're all Severus's spies." He spat. "She's a fine one to talk, changing sides to us from the Iceni."

"All of them?" Julius asked quietly, keeping his hood pulled low. In the tavern's dim light, he might pass for a merchant, as long as no one looked too closely.

"Anyone who questions her visions." Marcus gestured for another cup of wine. The serving girl hurried over, steam rising from the freshly heated drink. "Only those who agree with her prophecies are allowed near. The rest are branded traitors."

Lillian shifted uneasily on her wooden bench, all too aware of the other patrons around them. A group of soldiers huddled near the door, their red cloaks dark with melting snow. Merchants and artisans crowded the tables, sharing warmth and news. Any one of them could be an informant.

"And what of his daughter?" she asked.

"The White Tart?" Marcus leaned forward, wine sloshing dangerously close to the cup's rim. "The Iceni whore has been writing to all the great patrician families of Rome. The Cornelii, the Claudii, the Aemilii – any with eligible sons. A marriage alliance with Albinus's only daughter? The patricians are falling over themselves to offer terms."

A burst of laughter from the soldiers' table made Julius start. Lillian touched his arm, steadying him.

"Pale as milk, like her father. She looks like moonlight," Marcus sighed, the alcohol letting loose his poetical prowess.

"And what do the augurs say of her future marriage?" Julius asked, careful to modulate his accent.

"They stay silent. The prophet has convinced Albinus that only she can interpret the gods' will." Marcus drained his cup. "Strange times we live in. A woman with that much power?"

They waited until Marcus had stumbled out into the snowy street before leaving themselves, taking care to follow a different route back to their lodging. Only when they were safely behind closed doors did Lillian allow herself to process what they'd learned.

Jane wasn't just changing the details of history — she was fundamentally altering the power structures of Rome itself. A strategic marriage for Apple could cement alliances that never existed, shift loyalties that shaped the empire's future.

"We have to stop her," she repeated for what must have been the ten-thousandth time.

"How?" Julius demanded, shaking snow from his cloak. "We can barely show our faces in public. And if she sees you..."

He didn't need to finish. Jane knew exactly who Lillian was, what she could do. One word from her, and they'd both be arrested as spies.

"There might be a way," Lillian said slowly. "But it's dangerous. And it involves using something Jane won't expect. The truth."

Julius raised an eyebrow.

"Not the whole truth," she amended. "But enough to make Rome's noble families question whether Albinus's miraculous daughter is really who she claims to be."

"You're talking about spreading rumours against Apple? Your friend. Surely that would put her life more at risk?"

"Only if she really was his daughter." Lillian met his eyes. "And we both know she isn't."

The Viper's Shadows

Bricius nursed his watered wine in the darkest corner of the Boar's Head, watching Lillian and Julius through the tavern's smoky air. He'd tracked them from Ithaca Fort, learning their patterns, watching them watch others. They were good at staying hidden — but not good enough to spot him.

The wine merchant's drunken voice carried across the room: "The Iceni prophet has Albinus's ear completely now."

Bricius's fingers tightened around his cup. Iceni prophet. The words tasted like bile. Jane Badrick was no more Iceni than the Roman dogs who'd captured Gar. She was a serpent who'd slithered into their midst, poisoning everything she touched with her lies.

"His most trusted advisors — dismissed like common slaves. She tells him they're all Severus's spies."

The memory of Gar's capture rose unbidden. Jane using her Iron Beast to double cross them, allowing the Roman's to slaughter his brave warriors and to capture their chieftain.

Bricius spat. Iolo had been right about her. The old druid had seen through her lies, his sunken eyes blazing with hatred as he'd demanded her sacrifice. But Gar had refused, and now... now he had no idea where Iolo was, and Gar lay in Roman chains.

Perhaps if he'd sought out Iolo before coming to Londinium? No. The thought of the druid's fanaticism still made his skin crawl. The way Iolo used his beliefs as an excuse to torture others. To kill...

"The White Tart?" Marcus was saying now, wine sloshing. "The Iceni whore has been writing to all the great patrician families."

Across the room, he saw Lillian tense at the words. So, she cared what happened to the pale girl. Interesting. Bricius had wondered about their connection.

He watched Julius touch Lillian's arm. There was something more there. Bricius filed that away for later.

Bricius drained his cup and stood, leaving a coin on the table. Outside, snow was falling again, thick enough to mask his footsteps as he followed the path Julius and Lillian had taken. It was time to see what other pieces were in play before he made his move to free Gar, and to take his revenge on what the Roman's were calling the Iceni Whore. Jane Badrick. The Betrayer.

BRICIUS FOUND MARED'S POTTERY SHOP BY FOLLOWING THE smell of clay and wood smoke. To Roman eyes, it was just another workshop in the artisan quarter, producing the everyday vessels that kept the city's commerce flowing. But the spiral pattern scratched into the doorpost marked it as a gathering place for those who needed a place of safety. Even Kim Philby would be proud of the subterfuge, the way Iceni secrets were hidden in plain sight of the Romans.

Inside, the warmth of the kilns drove back the winter chill. Mared herself stood at her wheel, her grey hair tied back in the Roman style, her hands shaping clay with practiced ease. She didn't look up as he entered.

"The ice holds," she said, her fingers never stopping their work.

"But spring always comes," Bricius replied, completing the recognition phrase.

Only then did she lift her head. "We expected you sooner." Her eyes were sharp despite her age. "We heard about Gar's capture. And about the woman prophet."

"Jane Badrick," The name tasted like poison on his tongue. "She calls herself an Iceni prophet now."

"We know." Mared's voice was bitter. "Her lies echo through every street. The Romans lap up her every word, and why shouldn't they? She tells them exactly what they want to hear."

Other figures emerged from the shadows of the workshop — men and women Bricius had known in better days, before they'd chosen to live among the Romans. Cadoc the merchant, wearing a toga now instead of tribal clothes. Young Rhiannon, who'd married a Roman soldier but still kept the old ways in secret.

"They say Albinus plans to take Gar to Rome," Cadoc said. "Once the ice breaks, they're shipping him to Rome as if he were nothing more than a shipment of ale."

"That's why I'm here." Bricius's hand went to his knife.

"To die uselessly?" Mared's hands slapped clay onto the wheel with unnecessary force. "Look around you. This is how we survive now. We adapt. We blend in. We—"

"We forget who we are?" Bricius challenged. "Like you've forgotten? Trading our pride for Roman coins?"

"My pots keep our people fed," Mared snapped. "What has your pride done except fill graves?"

Rhiannon stepped between them. "Both paths have their place," she said quietly.

"What we need," said a new voice from the door, "is to deal with the Betrayer before she destroys everything."

"What we need," said a new voice from the door, "is to deal with the Betrayer before she destroys everything."

They turned to find Ennion, the metalworker, shutting the door against the snow. His face grim. "Jane visited the temple with Albinus today," he reported. "She trying to convince Albinus that Gar's execution will appease the gods. That it will guarantee his victory over Severus."

The news hit Bricius like a physical blow. Mared's wheel stopped turning.

"How long do we have?" Bricius demanded.

Ennion shook his head. "The man didn't seem persuaded,

yet. The priests made noises against it. He's not fully under her spell."

The crackle of the kilns filled the silence as Bricius looked at each of the Iceni – his people — who'd found their own ways to survive in the shadow of Rome. There were few that they could trust, and even fewer who had the skills to fight the Romans on their turf.

"We need an ally," he said. "Before it's too late. I followed a couple from Ithaca Fort to Londinium," Bricius said carefully. "Julius, and a woman."

"The centurion Julius? The deserter?" Rhiannon looked up sharply.

"Is that what they're calling him?" Bricius had fought against Julius enough times to know his worth as a soldier. "Together with the woman, they followed Albinus's retinue, but stayed clear of his scouts, and of mine."

Mared's hands stilled on her wheel. "You want to trust a Roman deserter?"

"He has deserted for a reason, and clearly it is not in support of the governor of Britannia. He may... be prepared to assist us."

"You've lost your mind, Bricius. Iolo warned us all that someone would betray us from inside. Is that you?"

"Lies. It was the woman they call the Prophet. This fighting does nothing to move us forward. In the absence of Gar, I make the decisions. And I say we trust the deserter. He will help get us inside."

"Gar is in the cells beneath the praetorium. Two guards, rotating every three hours. The cold makes them sloppy — they huddle around braziers instead of watching the shadows." Cadoc offered.

"The ice works both ways," Mared warned. "If something goes wrong, there's no escape from the city. We'd all pay the price."

"We're already paying it," Bricius countered. "Every day the Betrayer's lies increase the risk to Gar's life."

Rhiannon's voice was quiet. "There is another way. The old way."

Bricius's stomach clenched. He knew what was coming.

"Iolo still has followers in the city," she continued. "The Romans think that they have crushed the druids, but their power remains. The people still believe."

"Iolo is a madman," Bricius spat. The old beliefs ran deep, especially now, with their world crumbling around them.

"A madman who saw Jane for what she was before any of us," Mared pointed out. "And his followers have ways of moving unseen, even in winter."

Bricius remembered Iolo's sunken eyes, the way they'd blazed with fanatical certainty as he'd performed his rituals. The thought of working with him made Bricius's skin crawl. But he couldn't deny the druid's influence, or his network of devoted followers.

"The people need a sign," Rhiannon pressed. "Something to remind them of who we are. Iolo could provide that."

"Along with how many sacrifices?" Bricius demanded. "How many more hearts ripped out to feed his bloodlust?"

"Sometimes," Cadoc said softly, "blood is the only language Rome understands."

In the silence, Bricius understood that they needed every advantage they could get, every weapon they could wield. Including the druid.

"Find him," he said finally, the words tasting like ash in his mouth. "But make it clear — we do this my way. No sacrifices. No rituals. Just Gar's freedom and Jane's downfall."

"And the deserter?" Mared asked. "His woman?"

"We watch them first," Bricius decided. "See what game they're playing in all this. Julius was no friend to us before – I need to know what's changed."

The ice would hold a while longer. Time enough to gather allies, even ones he'd rather run through with his dagger.

Don't Drop A Stitch

As Ryan and Emma ate their lunch at Greggs. Loretta watched them through the window of the Bellingham Tea Rooms, her knitting needles clicking as she worked on what appeared to be a Roman legionnaire's helmet. They made an attractive couple; she thought — both sharp-featured and intent, heads bent together over their laptops.

If only they weren't so good at their jobs.

She'd looked up Ryan Francis on the internet — one of the Art Loss Register's star investigators, known for recovering stolen artefacts across Europe. And Emma, with her connections to both the Royal Mint and the Register... they were getting too close. Far too close.

Her fingers fumbled, dropping a stitch. The drilled coin in her pocket seemed to burn, a constant reminder of that day. July 1st, 1969. The day everything changed.

Dafydd had access to all the treasures at Caernarfon Castle – he was the only one with a key to the coin cabinet. That morning, he'd been preoccupied with the upcoming investiture of Prince Charles and all the security arrangements it required. But he'd still remembered their anniversary.

"I saved this one for you," he'd said, slipping the coin into her jewellery box. "A proper piece of history."

She hadn't known that her husband's minor act of sentiment would change her life forever.

The first jump had been that evening. One moment she was alone in their bedroom, holding the coin, the next she was standing in a Roman street, the smell of wood smoke and humanity overwhelming her senses. She'd barely had time to register the impossible before snapping back to 1969, the coin burning hot in her palm.

"More tea, dear?"

Loretta started. The waitress hovered beside her with a pot of Earl Grey. Through the window, she could see Ryan pointing something out in his files to Emma.

"Yes, please," her voice was steady, despite her racing heart. They couldn't know. How could they? The investigation into the missing coins had been cursory at best – the investiture was the primary focus. And she'd just expected everyone would assume that the thieves would have melted down the coins straightaway.

They were asking questions about Caernarfon Castle. About the missing coins. Ones which matched the ones she'd buried all those years ago, the ones that had started this whole mess. And somewhere in those files might be Dafydd's name, his position at the castle, his access to the coin cabinet. And next to Dafydd's name might be hers.

Her knitting showed the strain — the pattern becoming erratic, the wool twisting as timelines shifted and reformed around her. She'd learned to read these signs over the years, recognising how her handicraft reflected the delicate fabric of time itself.

Movement across the road. Ryan stood up, closing his laptop with Emma following in his wake, her hand brushing his arm in a gesture that spoke of familiarity. They were heading toward the door of Greggs, and for one heart-stopping moment, Loretta thought they were coming to the tearooms.

But they turned the other way, toward the police station. The message clear that they weren't giving up.

Sooner or later, they'd start asking the right questions.

Loretta touched the drilled coin in her pocket. This was

why she never came back to this time. She was only here because of Pramod. Because she'd heard of another time traveller. Someone who needed guidance. Lillian. A fat lot of use she'd been to her.

After that first accidental jump, learning to control it had been like learning to ride a bicycle — terrifying at first, then exhilarating. The drilled coin responded to her wildest imaginings. But the jumps were erratic. Until she discovered the knitting.

It started with a scarf she was making, the familiar rhythm of the needles somehow steadying her through the temporal shifts. Later, Pramod would explain it — something about repetitive patterns creating anchor points in space-time. He'd carved her that little Welsh dragon, another focus point, and suddenly she could navigate time like sailing a well-mapped sea.

The Beatles had been her first deliberate destination. February 1961, the Cavern Club in Liverpool. She'd sat in that dank cellar, watching four young men who didn't know they would change the world, and had thought to herself that this was better than any history book. Better than any life she'd left behind.

Then came the real adventures. London, 1888. She'd been determined to solve the Ripper mystery—what good was time travel if you couldn't crack history's greatest cases? She'd found him too or thought she had. A Polish barber in the Ten Bells pub, his broken English masking an educated mind.

Over steaming mugs of gin-laced tea, they had spoken of their time in the city, of how different it was to home. When he'd suggested fresh air, she'd followed, confident in her own abilities to protect herself. Outside, the cold bit through her thin coat as they stepped into the shadows of the street. Then the clatter of hooves on wet cobblestones, and the harsh bark of a constable's voice as he rounded the corner. The barber stiffened, his posture shifting as if he'd just thought better of something before he tipped his hat and melted into the night.

Had she been in danger? Or had she misread him, her own

suspicions twisting harmless conversation into something darker? She would never know.

And as she watched his silhouette disappear into the mist that night, she had the strangest feeling that history had been watching her.

Her knitting needles clicked faster as she remembered. Each project became a map of her journeys – Roman legionnaires, Viking longships, medieval castle keeps. The wool remembered where she'd been, what she'd seen. Sometimes the patterns would shift under her fingers, warning her of temporal disturbances, of history trying to rewrite itself.

"Joyce would be what, fifty now?" she mused, surprising herself with the thought. Her daughter's face had faded in her memory, replaced by the faces of history – Marcus Aurelius remained her white whale, the one historical figure she was determined to meet. She'd caught glimpses of his reign, but never the man himself. Not yet.

The truth was, she'd never been meant for that life in Wales. The endless routine of housework, the demands of motherhood, the suffocating smallness of it all. Dafydd was kind, but limited — unable to see beyond his little corner of Wales.

She had freed those coins. Given them purpose. Used them to witness the great sweep of time itself. This was what she was meant for. Not darning socks or attending parent-teacher meetings, but walking through history's pivotal moments, the fabric of time shifting around her.

The Roman legionnaire's helmet on her needles was taking shape, the pattern complex but familiar. She'd seen the real thing now, touched it, understood the working of the metal. Her knitting was no longer an artist's impression — it was a memory.

Pramod understood. That's why she'd agreed to help guide others like Lillian. But sometimes she wondered if she'd made a mistake getting involved. The past had a way of catching up.

The wool twisted in her hands, a warning. Something was changing. And a terse phone call from Neumegen reinforced that.

. . .

Neumegen's car smelled of old books and money. Loretta watched the historic streets of Hexham slide past, each turn bringing them closer to Ithaca Farm.

"You're quiet," he said, navigating around a pothole.

"Henry..." She touched the coin in her pocket. "What if I told you I know exactly where those coins came from? The ones the metal detectorist found?"

He glanced at her.

"I buried them." The words came easier than she'd expected. "In 1969, I took them from Caernarfon Castle and buried them here. But that's not the beginning of their story, or their end."

Neumegen's eyes stayed on the road, his silence almost more that she could bear.

"I only know what happened to them in the middle, after they were missing from the castle." She laughed, but there was no humour in it. "The same coins, spinning through time like tops. Making the same journey over and over."

"How were you were part of that journey?"

"Dafydd – my husband, worked at the castle. Gave me one coin as an anniversary gift. He didn't know what it was, what it could do. I guess it only works for the right people." She stared out the window at the passing fields. "Once I discovered its power, I had to have the rest. The investiture was the perfect cover. Everyone was too busy watching the prince to check on a display of old coins."

"And your husband?"

The question hit harder than she'd expected. "Dafydd... he loved his quiet life. I wanted more than just being a wife or a mother."

"You're a mother?" Neumegen's voice was quiet, but she heard the judgment underneath.

"You don't understand—"

"I understand the selfishness of wanting more," he interrupted. "And I understand ambition, curiosity, the pull of the past. But I also understand cruelty, and abandonment, and regret. And the weight of choices that can't be unmade."

They stopped on the side of the road abutting the bottom of the lower fields of Ithaca Farm.

"It doesn't take long for children to reach an age when they don't need you. When your mere existence is just annoying to them. Same with husbands," she debated.

"I'm not sure that's true," Neumegen said, avoiding her gaze.

The silence stretched between them, full of unspoken things. Loretta fidgeted with her knitting bag, thinking of another woman lost in time. "Will the headstone work?" she asked. "To bring Lillian back?"

"If we've chosen the right one. If we understand the markings correctly." He turned off the engine. "Your coins created paths through time. However, one can redirect paths.

"By people who know what they're doing?" She managed a weak smile.

"By people who understand the cost of their choices." He met her eyes. "And who chooses to make things right, anyway?"

THEY HAD TO CIRCLE AROUND THROUGH THE REMAINING hedgerows to avoid being seen, keeping to the shadows of the ancient oaks which had escaped the woodcutter's blade. The pig shed loomed ahead, its weathered boards barely visible in the grey afternoon light. From the barn came the sound of voices — archaeologists still arguing among themselves and with the police.

Nicole met them at the door. "Quickly," she whispered, ushering them inside, where they could see Badger kneeling next to the headstone.

"Don't touch it," Neumegen said, moving closer. "Let me have a closer look."

Neumegen crouched next to Badger, his eyes scanning the Latin inscription. "Sacred to the shades of the dead. Gaius Cossutius Saturninus of Hippo Regius, soldier of the Sixth Legion Victrix Pia Fidelis..."

"You can read that?" Badger sounded impressed. "Half of it has worn away."

"The Sixth Legion was stationed in Britain during Albinus's time," Loretta said. "But Hippo Regius – that's in North Africa."

"Severus's territory," Neumegen murmured. He looked up at Loretta. "Your coins created paths through time. But this... this is something different. A marker, perhaps. Or a message."

"Should we move it somewhere safer?" Badger whispered. "They'll tire of Holly's histrionics soon, and they'll end up here, eventually."

"No," Neumegen's voice was firm. "This location is part of the equation. The coin, the inscription, the place — it's all connected." He studied the stone again. "Gaius Cossutius Saturninus... I wonder who you were? And what your connection is?"

Blood on Snow

"Be careful," Lillian said, adjusting the worn cloak around Julius's shoulders. Her fingers lingered longer than necessary, smoothing nonexistent wrinkles from the fabric. "The streets are treacherous, and not just with ice."

Julius caught the scent that was uniquely hers, something he couldn't name. They'd been dancing around this for weeks now, this growing awareness of each other that had nothing to do with their shared predicament.

"I know these streets," he said, his voice rougher than intended. "I won't be long."

She was close enough that he could see the faint freckles across her nose, the way her eyes changed colour in different lights. Sometimes green, sometimes grey, like the sea before a storm.

"If it's not safe out there, we can wait."

"We need to eat." He smiled to lighten the moment. "Unless you've developed a taste for rats and cockroaches?"

"Gods, no!" Her nose wrinkled in that way that made his chest tight. "It was bad enough eating squirrels."

"I thought you loved my roast squirrel?"

She laughed.

The moment stretched between them, filled with all the things they hadn't said, until she reached up to adjust his cloak again, but this time he caught her hand. Her fingers were warm despite the room's chill.

The kiss, when it came, was light as a snowflake. Just the brush of her lips against his, and had melted before he could register it. But it left him stunned, rooted to the spot, his heart hammering against his ribs.

Lillian stepped back, colour rising in her cheeks. "I... I'm sorry, I shouldn't have—"

"No," he said quickly. Too quickly. "I mean... don't be sorry."

Another moment stretched between them. Then she smiled, and it was like watching the sun break through winter clouds.

"Go," she said. "Before I have to catch the rats hiding in the corner."

He nodded, not trusting himself to speak.

The cold hit him like a slap as he stepped into the street, but he barely felt it. His lips still tingled where hers had touched them, and the world seemed brighter than it ever had before.

As he made his way through the frozen city, Julius touched his fingers to his lips, checking if the sensation was still there. It was madness, of course, and yet he couldn't stop smiling, couldn't stop his heart from lifting every time he thought of that moment.

The market stalls huddled together against the cold, their awnings heavy with snow as Julius moved between them, nodding to merchants he'd met over the past few weeks. The old woman who sold salt fish, and the Greek with his exotic spices. The boy who always seemed to have fresh bread, no matter the hour.

Their funds were running low. He'd learned to haggle like a local, but prices rose with the ice. Everyone knew the supply boats wouldn't return until the thaw.

"Two denarii for this?" He held up a small wheel of cheese. "Last week it was one."

The merchant shrugged. "Last week, snow didn't block the roads. Take it or leave it."

Julius dug in his purse, aware of how light it had become. They'd need to find more money soon, or—

"By all the gods! Julius? Is that you?"

The booming voice hit Julius like a blow to the chest.

Julius turned, hoping he was wrong. But there was no mistaking that massive frame. Gaius Cossutius Saturninus. A man he'd last seen at Ithaca Fort. A fellow soldier whom he thought was still at Ithaca Fort.

"What in Hades are you doing here?" Gaius's voice carried across the market square, drawing looks from nearby shoppers. "Why aren't you at Ithaca Fort?"

"Gaius," Julius managed, his mind racing. "You're... with the governor's retinue?"

"Of course! Someone has to keep the big man safe while he plays politics." Gaius clapped a meaty hand on Julius's shoulder, nearly driving him to his knees. "But you! Why are you here? Marcus said—"

"Gaius, please?" Julius tried to step back, but the larger man's grip was like iron. "Let us talk about this somewhere else, not here. There are too many ears."

"Not here? Where then? The palace? Perfect! The prefect will want to see you. He'll be pleased to know you're alive. Though perhaps not for long, eh?" Gaius laughed at his own joke, the sound bouncing off the frozen buildings. "Come on, old friend. Let's get you somewhere warm. And get some food into you. You're nothing more than a shadow."

"I can't," Julius said, trying to keep his voice steady. "Gaius, please. Just let me go."

But Gaius was already steering him toward the main street, his friendly grip becoming something else entirely. "Nonsense! What kind of friend would I be if I let you freeze out here? Or worse, get arrested as a deserter? No, no, we'll sort this out properly. Together."

"Let's not make a scene," Julius said.

Gaius's laughter drowned him out.

"A scene? My friend, it's an unexpected delight to see you here in Londinium! Shocking, though. You wouldn't be a deserter, would you? Not the great Julius Stertinius Carpus?" Gaius's voice boomed.

Shoppers stopped to stare, and Julius saw several back away, not wanting to be involved in what was clearly soldier's business.

"I'm not what you think," Julius tried again, but Gaius's grip on his shoulder only tightened.

"No? Then explain it to the prefect. He'll understand, I'm sure." Gaius's friendly smile didn't reach his eyes anymore. "Come now, don't make me drag you. You know I could."

He could, too. Julius had seen Gaius lift grown men during training exercises and toss them aside like sacks of grain. The difference in their sizes was almost comical. Julius might as well have tried resisting a bear.

A woman muttered a prayer of protection as she scurried past. More eyes watched from doorways and windows. In the growing crowd, Julius caught glimpses of familiar faces — merchants he'd been trading with minutes ago, now looking away.

"Gaius, listen to me." Julius planted his feet, forcing them to stop. "There are things happening you don't understand. Bigger things than—"

"Bigger than desertion? Than betraying your post?" Gaius's voice had lost its jovial edge. "You were my friend, Julius. And now I find you here, skulking like a thief?"

"Please," he whispered. "It doesn't have to be like this. A drink? Let's have a drink. And talk as old friends."

Gaius's face darkened. "Friends do not desert their brothers." His massive hand moved to the hilt of his sword. "You really have forgotten everything we—"

A blade appeared at Gaius's throat. Thin and sharp, it caught the winter light like ice. The holder's voice was soft in the sudden silence. "Let him go."

Julius froze. The sight of the Iceni warrior here in Londinium was enough to make him believe that the gods had finally forsaken him.

No one moved. Even the crowd seemed to hold its breath. Julius noted the muscles in Gaius's neck tense, could read the calculations in his old friend's eyes.

"Don't," Julius said, his fear of the Iceni warrior palpable, but he was too late.

. . .

GAIUS MOVED QUICKLY FOR SUCH A BIG MAN, SPINNING away from the blade, reaching for his own sword. But his attacker was faster. Bricius's knife disappeared and reappeared, finding the gap beneath Gaius's ribs that every soldier knew was there.

Gaius sounded almost surprised as he looked down at the spreading red stain, then back at Julius, confusion replacing the anger in his eyes.

"Why?" he managed, before his legs gave way.

Julius caught him as he fell, the weight of him driving them both to their knees in the snow. Behind them, someone screamed. The crowd scattered like startled birds.

"It wasn't me," Julius cried. The last thing he wanted was for Gaius to believe it was him who'd sent him to Hades. "It wasn't me."

"Time to go," Bricius said, his hand closing on Julius's collar. "Now."

In the distance, metal boots rang on frozen cobbles. The garrison was coming. But all Julius could see was the red snow, and the look in his friend's eyes as the life left them.

Everything happened at once. The crowd surged away from them like a receding tide, screams mixing with the sound of running feet on frozen ground. Doors slammed shut. Merchants abandoned their stalls. A cart overturned in the chaos, spilling cabbages across the snow.

"Move!" Bricius yanked Julius to his feet, but Julius couldn't tear his eyes from Gaius's face. The big man's expression still looked confused, as if he'd died still trying to understand what had happened.

"Why?" Julius managed as Bricius dragged him down an alley. "We were going to have a drink, to talk."

"He was taking you to the governor." Bricius's grip was iron-strong, inexorable. "To execution."

"No, he wouldn't—" But even as he said it, Julius knew it was true. Gaius had always been loyal to a fault. It was what had made him such a good soldier. Such a good friend.

They ducked through a baker's courtyard, steam from the ovens providing momentary cover. Julius's mind was spinning.

Bricius.

Here.

The Iceni warrior who'd fought against them at the fort, who'd nearly killed him twice before, had just saved his life.

"Why are you following me?"

Bricius didn't answer or slow his pace.

Behind them, horns were sounding. The garrison mobilising. They'd find Gaius soon, if they hadn't already. Slumped in the snow, his blood spreading like a crimson flower blooming in winter.

"Why?" Julius asked again as they ducked into a narrow passage between buildings. "Why help me?"

Bricius finally stopped, turning to face him. "Because I need you to save Gar. And to kill the woman who calls herself a prophet."

Julius sagged against the cold stone wall.

"The garrison will be searching every street," Bricius said. "We need to move."

Julius nodded, but as they slipped away through the warren of Londinium's back alleys, he couldn't shake the last image of Gaius lying in the snow. It would stay with him forever, he knew. Just like the memory of Lillian's kiss — his first moment of pure joy in months, now tainted by what followed.

Two moments. One perfect, one beyond terrible. Both had changed everything.

Somewhere in the city, bells tolled. The sound echoed off the frozen buildings, calling soldiers to arms. Calling time on Julius's dreams of a second kiss. Of a new life.

Snow began falling, covering their tracks, covering Gaius's blood. Covering everything in a blanket of white that would soon be stained with more red.

Waiting

Lillian touched her fingers to her lips for the hundredth time, still feeling the ghost of that kiss. The empty room seemed to mock her foolishness — a university-educated environmentalist falling for a Roman centurion. It sounded like the plot of a bestselling historical romance.

And yet...

She moved to the window, watching snow collect on the sill. Their rented room was growing colder as the day wore on, but she barely noticed. Her mind kept circling back to that moment, to the look in Julius's eyes, to the way time itself seemed to stop.

"You're ridiculous," she told herself, the words lacking conviction.

Where could they go? What kind of life could they build? Her mind cataloged the possibilities, mapping out safe havens in the vast expanse of the Roman Empire. Not Gaul – the civil wars would tear it apart. Not Africa – Severus's power base would make it too dangerous. Greece, perhaps? Or one of the quieter eastern provinces?

She paced the room, five steps one way, five steps back. The real question wasn't where they could go, but when. Could Julius adapt to her time? The thought of him confronting cars, phones, electricity...

The fire had burned down to embers. She added another

precious log, thinking of central heating with a pang of longing. Living in the past wasn't like visiting it. Every day brought a hundred small challenges — keeping warm, staying clean, finding safe food and water. Things she'd read about in books but never truly understood until now.

And what about Apple? Could she really abandon her friend to Jane's machinations? The memory of Apple being presented as Albinus's daughter still made her blood boil. If she and Julius left...

A cart rattled past in the street below, its wheels crunching through fresh snow. Lillian wrapped her arms around herself, suddenly aware of how cold the room had become. How long had she been standing here, lost in impossible dreams?

"Face facts," she muttered. "You don't even know if he felt what you felt."

But she did know because she'd seen it in his eyes, and felt it in the way his hand had caught hers. Whatever this was between them, it was real. Real enough to make her consider giving up everything — her time, her work, her whole world.

Or he could come forward with her. But would it be cruel to ask him to leave everything he knew? At least she'd chosen this jump through time. She'd had a modicum of understanding of what she was walking into.

The room grew darker. Buying food shouldn't take this long, even with the inclement weather.

Lillian touched her lips again, remembering that perfect moment. Such a small thing, a brush of lips, the meeting of hearts. But it had changed everything, opened doors she hadn't even known existed.

If only she knew which door to walk through.

THE SHADOWS LENGTHENED FURTHER UNTIL THE ROOM WAS almost black. Lillian spread her time travel items on the bed: the gold Roman coin that had started everything, Pramod's exquisitely carved wooden tiger, the fibula brooch shaped like a dolphin. Each piece felt warm to her touch, as if holding memories of their journeys through time.

But how did it really work?

She'd jumped through time twice now — once during Saturnalia at the Bellingham, when the very fabric of time had seemed malleable, and once... she pushed away the memory of that forced journey, of being dragged through time against her will. Neither experience had given her any real understanding of the mechanics.

She fingered the woollen cape wrapped tightly around her that still somehow smelled of Julius. Would these items be enough to take him with her? The gold coin had been her first key, found in the field behind her house. But she knew now it wasn't just any coin. It was one stolen from the soldier's pay chest at Ithaca Fort. Did that matter? Did objects need their own history to work as temporal anchors?

The sound of running feet in the street below made her heart jump. But it was just children, chasing each other through the snow. Still no Julius.

The altar at Ithaca Farm had been crucial — a door between times, Pramod had called it. But here in Londinium? She had no idea which temples or shrines might hold that kind of power.

She touched each item in turn, like worry beads: coin, tiger, brooch. Could she even take someone else through time with her? The question had been haunting her since the kiss. No. Before the kiss. Weeks ago. The exchange of gifts had been important during Saturnalia – did that mean something? Was there another date of significance she could leverage?

She should light a lamp, but her hands shook as she reached for the flint. Where was he? The market would be closing soon, if it hadn't already. A commotion erupted somewhere in the distance — shouting voices, the sound of metal on metal. Military boots on cobblestones.

Lillian pressed her forehead against the cold window, straining to see through the gathering gloom. She should have asked more questions while she had the chance. About how it all worked, about whether two people could travel together, about how to choose your destination in time rather than just jumping blindly.

Another sound of running feet, this time accompanied by

the blast of a horn. Something was happening out there in the darkening city. Something that made her stomach clench with fear.

The stairs creaked as she crept down to street level.

The landlord's dog growled softly from somewhere in the darkness, but didn't bark. Outside, torchlight flickered against the walls as people hurried past, their voices hushed but urgent.

A crowd had gathered at the end of the street. Lillian pulled her cape tighter and edged closer, trying to blend in with the other onlookers. Roman soldiers formed a barrier, their red cloaks dark in the torchlight.

"What's happened?" she whispered to the woman next to her, the baker's wife she recognised from the market.

"Murder," the woman replied, her voice thick with excitement. "One of the governor's own men, killed in broad daylight. They say it was a deserter from the army who did it."

Lillian's heart stuttered. "A deserter?"

"That's what they're saying. In the middle of the market, if you can believe it."

Before Lillian could ask more, a disturbance at the edge of the crowd made her turn back toward her lodgings. Better to wait for Julius there.

The knock came just as she'd bolted the door. Three sharp raps that made her jump.

"Rent," her landlord's voice came through the wood. When she opened the door, his lamp cast harsh shadows across his face. "With the governor in residence, prices have doubled. Pay now or find other lodgings."

"But we paid for the week—"

"That was before. This is now." His eyes were hard in the lamplight. "The city is busy. Housing is scarce. Those who can pay, stay. Those who cannot..."

Lillian felt the weight of the gold coin against her chest where she kept it on a leather thong. Her only guarantee of getting home, of having any control over when and where she might land in time.

"Please," she said softly. "One night. Julius will be back soon with—"

"One night," Marcus Flavius agreed. "But only because I like the look of you." At this, his eyes travelled up and down her body before he spat on the ground.

"There are always alternative ways to pay," he smiled, his rotting teeth highlighted in the lamplight, before he shuffled away, his oil lamp bobbing down the corridor. Lillian closed the door silently, not wanting to attract any further attention from the landlord.

Night crept by in agonising increments. Lillian hugged herself in the darkness, not daring to waste the last of their oil, straining to listen to every footstep in the street below, every creak of the building's timbers. Each sound could be Julius. None of them were.

The gold aureus hung heavy against her skin. A coin that could buy a month's lodging, or get her killed for carrying it. The same paranoid thoughts circled through her mind: What if Julius had been the deserter they spoke of? What if he'd been the one killed? What if he'd been arrested? Or worse, what if he'd simply decided to abandon her? She'd initiated the kiss.

Her stomach growled, reminding her she'd last eaten the night before. She'd give anything for a sandwich from Greggs right now, or even one of those dubious pasties from the local street vendors that Julius loved so much.

Dawn's weak light finally crept through the window, painting the room in a hundred shades of gloomy grey. Lillian stood, her joints stiff from sitting still for so long. She needed a plan. The governor's residence would be her best bet — if Julius had been arrested, that's where they'd take him. And if not... well, perhaps she could throw herself upon the mercy of the governor, or even reveal herself to Jane.

But first, she needed to leave this room. After the landlord's suggestion last night, staying wasn't an option.

She piled their belongings onto the straw pallet – Julius's spare tunic, her few items of Roman clothing, the precious tools for making fire, packing each object into Julius' rough sack. The fabric was coarse against her hands, nothing like the technical materials she was used to. No ergonomic shoulder straps or weight distribution here — just crude rope handles that would dig into her shoulders.

Her time travel items went into a separate pouch that she could keep close: the coin on its leather thong, Pramod's carved tiger, the fibula brooch. She wouldn't risk losing those, no matter what happened.

The sack was awkward, easily twenty-five kilos of dead weight. In her time, she'd had backpacks specially fitted for hiking, adjusted to her size and shape. Here, she had to make do with what felt like a bag of rocks strapped to her back.

"Come on," she muttered, adjusting the rope handles yet again. "You've carried heavier stuff on the farm."

But she hadn't, not really. Even her heaviest modern equipment had been designed for modern farming life. This was like trying to move an elephant with a medieval sack.

A noise in the corridor made her freeze. Heavy footsteps — the landlord making his morning rounds. She needed to leave now, before he came to collect his "alternative payment."

Lillian took one last look around the room. Somewhere in the city, Julius was either dead, arrested, or... No. She couldn't think about the "or." She had to focus on survival. On finding him. Finding a way forward, or back. As long as whatever she chose didn't end with her dead in a Roman ditch.

The sack was ungainly, the straps already cutting into her increasingly bony shoulders. But she had no choice. It was time to go.

Despite the street being eerily quiet at dawn, Lillian kept to the shadows. The heavy sack made stealth impossible but at least it gave her the appearance of a local about legitimate business.

The attack came from nowhere. Rough hands grabbed her from behind, pulling her toward a doorway. Lillian swung the sack wildly, using its weight as a weapon. Her attacker grunted but didn't let go.

"Stop fighting," a woman's voice hissed.

Lillian froze. In the dim light, she could make out grey hair tied back in a practical style, pottery-stained hands.

"I'm here to save you," the woman hissed. "But you have to trust me and stay quiet," the woman breathed into her ear. "Julius sent me."

The world lurched.

Lillian felt it first in her chest, where the coin hung against her skin—a sudden heat, like touching metal left in the sun. Then came the familiar pressure behind her eyes, the dull throb. A sickening twist followed, as if the world were unspooling around her, reality fraying at the edges.

"No," she gasped, reaching for the woman. "Wait—"

But it was happening too fast. The street dissolved, the grey dawn light fracturing like broken glass. The last thing she saw was the woman's back disappearing around the corner, the woman who was taking her to Julius. Then the darkness took her as Lillian fell back through time.

Evidence Trail

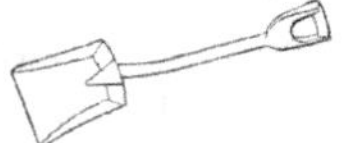

Bishop stared at the wall of his office, his uniform jacket draped over his chair, tie discarded hours ago. The water bottle at his elbow was lukewarm — he'd switched from coffee after his hands started shaking around dinner time. Not that he'd eaten dinner.

Yellow post-it notes covered the wall in neat rows, each one representing another piece of this mess. The project management course he'd taken last year had stressed the importance of visual organisation. Right now, it was the only thing keeping him sane.

First row: MISSING PERSONS
- Jane Badrick (Mayor)
- Lillian Armstrong (Farm owner)
- Apple Collings

Second row: PHYSICAL EVIDENCE
- Roman coins (perfect condition)
- Darby's head (no body found)
- Cache of weapons (Jane's car)
- Roman altars (still being documented)

His phone buzzed again — probably another message from the Chief Constable about London's "growing concerns." Everyone wanted answers, but they kept focusing on the wrong things. Newcastle Uni's archaeology department was breathing down his neck about proper handling of artefacts, while he was trying to solve what might be multiple murders.

"It's a police investigation," he muttered, adding another note to the wall. "Not a bloody *Time Team* episode."

Jane Badrick's face stared at him from the incident photo pinned in the centre. She'd been difficult since she'd first arrived in Hexham, but she'd gotten things done. The new shopping centre, the library renovation, the tourism initiative. She wasn't the type to just disappear.

Unless she had to.

Bishop added another note:

WEAPONS - SOURCE?

The guns in her car suggested connections he didn't want to think about. Arms dealing? Organised crime? But nothing in Jane's background suggested anything like that. Twenty years of public service, clean record, model citizen apart from a small problem with alcohol. Until she vanished.

Bishop rubbed his eyes. He needed sleep, but his mind kept circling back to the elements that didn't fit. The Roman coins that looked fresh from the mint. The weapons cache that seemed staged. The witnesses who kept disappearing before, or after, giving statements.

And now these altars. Everything seemed to connect to Ithaca Farm.

He added one final note to the wall:

CONNECTED???

They had to be. He just wasn't seeing how yet.

He tried sipping his water, but the bottle was empty. Outside his window, Hexham put itself to sleep for the night, unaware of the puzzle spread across his office wall. Tomorrow there would be more pressure, more questions, more complications. But tonight, he had his notes, his method, his training.

It was a police investigation. And he was going to treat it like one, no matter how many ancient artefacts turned up.

Despite his exhaustion, Bishop added another row of post-its:

WITNESSES
- Nicole Pilcher (kidnapped, escaped??)
- Holly Corben (unreliable??)
- Metal detector club

NICOLE PILCHER'S STATEMENT SAT OPEN ON HIS DESK. Found tied up in the barn at Ithaca Farm, she'd given a clear account of her captivity — right up until she started talking about her escape. Then the details got fuzzy. "I don't remember exactly" appeared five times in her statement. Bishop had interviewed enough witnesses to know when someone was holding back.

He moved to the window, stretching his back. The Art Loss Register's involvement had added a migraine to his list of complaints. His call to their London office had confirmed Ryan Francis was legitimately investigating the Caernarfon Castle theft—Roman coins stolen during Prince Charles's investiture in '69. He didn't remember that ever making the news. But then, he guessed that the last thing the Royal Family needed was another scandal. And if he remembered that time correctly, in 1969, they were already dealing with the fallout from that ill-advised *Royal Family* documentary— the one they quietly buried after realizing it had made them seem a little too ordinary.

But Ryan Francis asked questions that seemed to lead nowhere. Bishop surmised that Francis clearly knew something he wasn't sharing.

Bishop returned to his wall, adding another note:

CAERNARFON CONNECTION?

He wished he'd thought to ask the Welsh journalist for her ID. There was no record of her credentials at any Cardiff paper.

Even Holly Corben's performance at Ithaca Farm seemed suspiciously well-timed, and over the top. And now she wasn't answering her phone.

"They can't all be involved," he muttered, but the evidence suggested otherwise. Every person connected to this case either vanished, changed their story, or suddenly developed memory problems.

The Art Loss Register should have simplified things. Instead, Francis's involvement had only created more problems for him.

A new post-it went up:

FRANCIS - REAL OBJECTIVE?

Bishop stepped back, studying his wall of notes. Three missing women. One kidnapping victim who couldn't remember who had rescued her. A headless archaeologist. An investigator from London who seemed to be working a completely different case than the one his boss described.

"What aren't you telling me?" Bishop asked the wall.

The answer, he suspected, was somewhere at Ithaca Farm.

The Game of Thrones

Publius Septimius Aper, Consul of Rome, unrolled another scroll on his marble desk, adding its intelligence to the web forming in his mind. Three men who would be Caesar. Three paths to power. And he had chosen his path months ago, before Pertinax's convenient removal from the game.

Severus was the obvious threat. His Pannonian legions were battle-hardened, loyal, and crucially close to Rome. The scroll in Aper's hands confirmed what he'd feared — that more garrisons along the Danube were declaring for him daily. The man had a gift for inspiring loyalty, Aper had to admit. Or at least for inspiring fear.

From the east came reports of Pescennius Niger building support in Syria. Niger was popular with the people. The man had the gall to style himself as a new Marcus Aurelius. But popularity was fleeting, and Syria was far from Rome. Distance had killed more imperial ambitions than any assassin's blade, or mushroom soup.

Which left Albinus in Britain. Aper's chosen piece in this game of empire. The decision had seemed perfect at the time — a commander with the loyalty of three legions, a noble background, and most importantly, a malleable nature. The sort of man who could be guided, shaped, controlled.

"Like Pertinax," Aper murmured, remembering how easily that particular obstacle had been removed.

Aper's fingers tightened on the scroll. He'd chosen Albinus because the man appeared open to his guidance. Indeed, Albinus appeared amenable to the whispers in his ear, leading him down the path to power. But Aper had never anticipated someone else's whispers. And this woman, this Iceni spy, was whispering her own words, painting her own pictures of destiny. And Albinus was listening.

The reports from Britain were troubling. Talk of omens and portents. Of a miraculous daughter appearing from nowhere. Of a governor who seemed increasingly convinced of his divine right to rule. Aper had heard the stories of omens before, the kind that turned men into legends. But this was different.

The tales from Britain spoke of a girl who had emerged from the wilderness, a child born of mist and prophecy, whose very presence had sent the governor's household into hushed reverence. A daughter of the gods, they said. A sign. A claim to destiny as undeniable as the seven eagles that had once circled Albinus' cradle.

Aper's mouth pressed into a thin line. Superstition had always been a tool he'd wielded with precision when it served his purpose. But he had no use for omens beyond his own making. If Albinus began to believe that fate had a better hand guiding him, then Aper's influence would slip through his fingers like sand.

And this woman, this Iceni spy—she was dangerous. Not for her knives or poisons, but for the insidious power of belief. She was weaving a myth around the governor, a story that no doubt curled through his mind like smoke, taking shape with every telling.

Aper exhaled slowly, steadying himself. Aper had wanted a puppet, not a true believer. Someone who could be controlled through ambition and fear, not divine conviction. Stories could be countered with other stories. Prophecies could be rewritten. And if this girl was an omen, then perhaps she could disappear just as suddenly as she had arrived. But first, he had to see her for himself.

He returned to his desk, pushing aside reports of troop

movements to focus on the latest intelligence about the Iceni prophet.

His informants wrote of how she spoke knowingly of troop movements and of events in distant provinces. Things she couldn't possibly know.

"Unless..." Aper paused, a new thought forming. Unless she had help. Unless someone else was involved, feeding her information in order to influence Albinus in ways Aper hadn't anticipated.

The empire was delicately balanced between three men. But Aper was starting to wonder if he'd chosen the wrong piece to play.

ANOTHER DAY, ANOTHER DAWN, AND ANOTHER SLAVE appeared at Aper's elbow with fresh reports. More movement from Severus. The Illyrian legions had declared for him now. The man gathered strength like a ball of horse shit rolling downhill, growing larger with each turn.

"And Niger?" Aper demanded.

"Still consolidating his position in Syria, Consul. The eastern provinces remain loyal to him, but..." The slave hesitated. "There are rumours he plans to declare himself emperor within the month."

Aper dismissed him with a wave. Syria was too far to matter immediately, but Niger's declaration would force everyone's hand. Time was running out.

Another slave appeared, this one bearing worse news. "The Indian has collapsed again, Consul. Metella said to say—"

"Take me to him." Aper was moving before the words were fully spoken. Pramod's chambers were still shuttered, heavy with the smell of urine and sweat. The man lay still as death, except for the slight movement of his chest.

"Leave us," Aper commanded the slaves, but open those shutters, before I too die from this stench. When they were alone, he gripped Pramod's hand. "Wake up, man. I have no time for this now."

Pramod's eyes flickered open, unfocused. His stroke-damaged voice was barely a whisper. "Time... changes..."

"Yes, yes, time changes everything. But I need you awake and about. Albinus readies himself to sail, and I must know what happens."

"No," Pramod's grip tightened. "You must... stop him."

Aper studied the man who had become more valuable than he'd anticipated. More valuable even than Metella. His daughter was beautiful, yes, and her marriage could cement alliances. But this man knew things. Things that had helped Aper stay three steps ahead of everyone else.

Until now.

"I promised Metella I would find you the finest physicians," Aper said softly. "That I would arrange a suitable marriage for her. That I would protect her son." He leaned closer. "But you must understand, the empire itself hangs in the balance."

Pramod's eyes cleared briefly. "The woman... she knows..."

"What woman? Albinus's Iceni woman? She knows what?" But Pramod had slipped away again, back into the darkness.

Aper straightened, his decision made. The Iceni prophet would have to be eliminated. Quietly, in a way that wouldn't alienate Albinus. But she had to go. Aper wasn't prepared to risk all that he'd worked for.

"Bring me Silas," he commanded the waiting slave. Some tasks required more of a personal touch.

The Potter's Wheel

The pottery studio reeked of wet clay and wood smoke. Julius paced between rows of drying amphorae, their curved sides still damp to the touch. Gaius's death played over and over in his mind. The look of betrayal in his old friend's eyes, the spreading red stain in the snow. They could have talked their way out of it. Gaius might have listened. Might have understood. Instead, Bricius's blade had found that gap beneath the ribs that every soldier knew about.

"Keep still," Bricius growled from his position by the door. "You'll knock something over."

The Iceni warrior cleaned his nails with the same knife he'd used to kill Gaius. Casual. As if taking a life was nothing more than clearing dirt from under his fingernails.

Julius's hands clenched. He needed to get back to Lillian. She'd be worried by now, perhaps even searching for him. The thought of her venturing out into the streets, with the garrison on alert...

A potter's wheel creaked in the back of the workshop, reminding him of the siege engines at Ithaca Fort. More amphorae waited on wooden racks, their surfaces scored with the maker's mark. Made with clay dug from the banks of the Thames.

"Your friend was a soldier," Bricius said suddenly. "He would have done the same."

"Gaius was worth ten of you," Julius spat. "He didn't kill unarmed men."

"No? Ask the Iceni about Roman mercy." Bricius's knife stilled. "Your friend would have taken you to the governor. To execution. I saved your life."

"I didn't ask you to."

Another Iceni appeared at the door, whispering something to Bricius. Julius noted the way they'd disguised themselves as potters in an attempt to blend in. The workshop was just a front, a way to move through the city unnoticed, to gather intelligence while trading in clay pots.

Clever. But it wouldn't save them when the garrison found this place. And they would find it, eventually. Roman efficiency would see to that.

"If you're thinking of running," Bricius said, reading his expression, "remember why you're here. Remember who you're protecting."

Lillian's face filled Julius's mind. She'd understand about Gaius, wouldn't she? She knew what it was like to make impossible choices. To live with the consequences.

A fresh batch of pots emerged from the back room. More Iceni warriors in disguise. How many were there?

He resumed his pacing, counting steps, burning the layout of the room into his memory, to fill the time until he could return to Lillian.

MARED BURST THROUGH THE DOOR, HER FACE ASHEN. FOR A moment, Julius thought the garrison had found them. But the potter's next words struck harder than any Roman blade.

"She's gone," Mared said. "The woman... Lillian. I turned the corner and when I looked back, she just... wasn't there anymore."

Julius moved without thinking, shouldering past Bricius toward the door. Strong hands grabbed him, held him back.

"Let me go!" He fought against their grip. "I have to find her!"

"Have to what?" Bricius's voice was curt. "Search every street in Londinium? With the garrison hunting for us?"

But Julius barely heard him.

Mared stepped forward. "One moment she was following me, the next…" She shook her head. "It was like she'd never been there at all."

"Gone?" His voice sounded strange to his own ears. "Someone must have grabbed her?"

"I saw no one else on the street," Mared said.

"People vanish all the time in Londinium," Bricius said matter-of-factly. "The city swallows them whole."

But Bricius's blithe explanation did nothing to dull the pain. First Gaius's death, now this. In the space of a morning, he'd lost his oldest friend and the woman he… the woman who…

Anger rose like bile in his throat. "Was this your plan?" he accused Bricius. "To keep me here while she slipped away?"

"This wasn't us," Bricius said firmly. "We needed both of you."

Julius wrenched free of the hands holding him, but didn't run. What would be the point? Where would he go? The room suddenly felt too small, too full of eyes, watching him process this loss.

Suddenly, the temperature dropped. Julius felt it first in his bones, then he saw the Iceni warriors draw back from the doorway, their faces tightening with fear.

The druid entered like a shadow made of flesh. Draped in a cloak of black wool that seemed to drink in what little light remained. Empty pools for eyes surveyed the room, settling briefly on each face before moving on. When they reached Julius, he felt the promise of death.

"Iolo," Bricius's voice held carefully controlled disgust. "We didn't send for you."

"The old gods sent me." The druid's voice rasped like dead leaves. A knife of bone hung at his belt, its surface stained. "They want me to close the door."

Julius saw Bricius's hand twitch toward his knife, but the practicality of needing every ally clearly won out. Even the ones that made the skin crawl.

"Your woman," Iolo said suddenly, those hollow eyes fixing on Julius. "Has been returned to her people."

"What have you done to her?" Julius demanded.

The druid's bloodless lips curved in what might have been a smile. "The gods give, and the gods take away. She was never yours to keep."

"Enough riddles," Bricius snapped. "If you're here, we need to focus on rescuing Gar."

"Yes," Iolo agreed, his smile widening to reveal teeth filed to points. "The chieftain's fate hangs by a thread. But to see which way it will fall…" He reached into his robes and withdrew something that made Julius's gorge rise. A human hand, freshly severed, its fingers still curled as if grasping at life.

The Iceni backed away. Even Bricius paled at the sight.

"Is that Lillian's?" Julius asked, his heart slowing to a standstill.

"She was not Roman, and I needed a Roman hand to stop the fates," Iolo explained, as if Julius were a child and his question was of no consequence.

Lillian wasn't Roman? The words filtered through to Julius's consciousness.

"The old ways are sure ways," Iolo continued, laying out the rest of his equipment, and the raw materials… "The entrails will show us the path. The blood will speak of what is to come."

A bronze bowl appeared, its surface marked with spirals that seemed moved in the dim light. The hand went in first, followed by things that squelched and slithered.

"This is how we will save Gar," Iolo said. "This is how we will know when to strike." His eyes found Julius again. "And perhaps, Roman, we will see other things as well. Other fates."

Julius wanted to look away, but couldn't, as Iolo worked with practiced efficiency, arranging his tools in a spiral pattern on the workshop floor. The severed hand lay in the centre of the bronze bowl, fingers splayed like a pale starfish in dark water. Julius had seen men gutted in battle, had watched executions, but this was different. This was an intimacy with death that made his skin crawl.

"The stars align," Iolo muttered, adding something that

looked like dried flowers but smelled of rot. "The paths converge."

The liquid in the bowl began to bubble without heat. The hand's fingers twitched, as if still trying to grasp at life. Julius heard one of the Iceni warriors retch quietly in the corner.

"Watch," Iolo commanded, his hollow eyes reflecting the dark liquid. "Watch and see what comes."

Shapes stirred in the bowl's depths—shadows and movement shifting like oil on water. Julius imagined he could see armies moving across frozen ground, banners whipping in the wind, falling, rising, falling again. The corpses strewn like broken dolls across the trampled earth.

A horse reared, its iron-shod hooves coming down hard on a body beneath it. A body wrapped in imperial purple.

Iolo's lips barely moved. "A man once named emperor. A body ground to dust beneath the heels of victory." He stirred the liquid with a bony finger, and the image shifted. "His head will hang in triumph, a lesson in fate. And yet his bloodline lingers, twisting through the dark like roots beneath old stones."

The liquid swirled again, the battlefield dissolving into something else. A pale face surfaced, strange and luminous, eyes like twin moons.

"The chieftain must be freed. Tonight. While the moon hides her face."

"How?" Bricius demanded. "The garrison—"

"Will be distracted. The girl with moon skin will see to that."

Apple, Julius thought.

"The paths split here," Iolo continued, his fingers trailing through the dark water. "Some lead to death, others to... stranger places." His gaze fixed on Julius. "You think of searching for your woman. But she is beyond your reach now."

"You said if I helped save the moon girl—" Julius started.

"Help free her, help free the chieftain, and perhaps..." Iolo's bloodless lips curved. "Perhaps the door that closed will open again. But only if you choose right. Only if you follow the path the gods show."

The liquid in the bowl had turned to smoke, rising in patterns that obscured Julius's vision. The severed hand was gone, dissolved into whatever dark magic Iolo had conjured.

"Tonight then," Bricius said, eager to end the ritual. "We free them both."

"Choose quickly, Roman," Iolo hissed. "Time flows like blood, and some doors only open once."

Julius squared his shoulders. He was a soldier. He understood duty. And maybe, just maybe, duty would lead him back to her.

"Tell me what you need me to do."

The Doorways of Carmenta

"The Romans believed today belonged to Carmenta," Neumegen said, adjusting the lamp Nicole held over the headstone. "The goddess who looked both forward and back. Rather fitting, don't you think?"

"Postverta and Antevorta," Loretta murmured. "Future and past."

Badger ignored them. Instead, he studied the coin fused to the stone's surface, his fingers tracing the metal's edge where it seemed to flow into the rock. "Will this bring her back?"

"Why do you think I drove like the devil to get here?" Neumegen settled back on his ankles. "We should never have allowed Lillian to travel at all. So today we must do all that we can to bring her back." Neumegen closed his eyes, his mind drifting into knowledge that had seemed redundant when he'd first been at university. "Carmenta was the goddess of technological innovation, of 'opening what was closed.' If there was ever a day to bring her back..."

"Henry," Loretta's voice warned. The wool twisted in her hands, the pattern distorting as if viewed through water.

Neumegen stepped back, letting Badger take his position by the stone. "Carefully now. We don't want to damage either surface."

Badger's hands were steady as he selected his tool.

The coin gleamed dully in the lamplight — an aureus of

Clodius Albinus, identical to the ones found in the field. But this one had somehow merged with Gaius's headstone. Creating... what? A door? An anchor point?

"It's warming up," Badger reported, his tool barely touching the metal's golden edge.

The coin resisted Badger's efforts, clinging to the stone as if it had grown there. The chisel slipped once, twice, finding no purchase between metal and rock. Sweat beaded on his forehead despite the January cold.

"Steady," Neumegen whispered.

Loretta's knitting needles stilled completely. The wool hung limp between them, as if waiting. Even Nicole's breathing seemed too loud in the sudden quiet.

Then something changed. The air in the pig shed grew thick, heavy with possibility. Badger's tool found an edge, the barest separation between coin and stone. He pressed harder, feeling resistance, then—

The coin came free with a sound like a sigh. Or a door opening.

"Henry?" Loretta's voice shook.

Wind filled the shed, though all the doors were closed. Nicole's lamp flickered wildly, throwing strange shadows on the walls. The coin in Badger's hand grew hot, then cold, then hot again.

A crack like summer lightning split the air and in that impossible moment, Lillian fell through.

She hit the ground hard, gasping like someone who'd been underwater too long. Her clothes were wrong — a Roman stola instead of her modern dress. Her hands clutched at nothing, trying to find purchase in a world that had suddenly changed around her.

"Easy," Loretta said, reaching for her. "You're safe. You're back."

But Lillian's eyes were wild, unfocused. "Julius," she managed. "I have to... Gaius... the blood..."

"Lillian," Badger's voice cut through her panic. "You're home."

She stared at him, recognition slowly dawning. Then at the others. Nicole was holding the lamp, her face as shocked as Lillian's. Loretta with her frozen knitting. Neumegen looking like all his theories had been proven at once.

"Why?" she whispered. "Why now?"

The headstone stood as silent as they crowded around it. Outside, thunder rolled across Hexham, though no storm had been forecast.

Lillian tried to stand, her legs unsteady. "Send me back!" Lillian's voice was on the edge of hysteria.

"We should go," Neumegen said finally. "Before the search reaches us."

But Lillian wasn't ready to move. Her eyes had found the headstone, reading the name carved there. Her fingers traced the space where the coin had been.

"Gaius," she whispered. "Oh God, Gaius."

"We need to move," Neumegen insisted, one eye on the farm's distant lights where searchers moved with torches. "The police will work their way here, eventually."

"You don't understand." Lillian struggled against Loretta's supporting arm. "Julius is in danger. Apple is in danger. I have to go back—"

"The coin's fusion with Gaius's headstone created a temporal anchor," Neumegen continued as if she hadn't spoken, already shepherding them toward his car at the bottom of the field. "The combination of the festival of Carmenta and the personal connection—"

"I don't care about that!" Lillian's voice cracked. "Send me back!"

"The doorway's closed now," Loretta said gently.

They hurried through the darkness, Lillian still protesting, still trying to turn back. Badger followed behind, the coin heavy in his pocket, watching how she leaned away from him toward the barn. Toward the past. Toward Julius. And something cold settled in his chest. He'd saved her. He'd brought her home. But it wasn't him, she thanked.

"The festival matters," Neumegen was explaining as they piled into his car. "Carmenta's dual nature — looking forward and back — creates a possibility of transition. But it has to align with personal connections, with objects of significance—"

"Like a headstone and a coin from the same time period," Loretta added, helping Lillian into the back seat.

"Julius will think I abandoned him," Lillian whispered. "Like Jane abandoned Apple."

The name cut through Neumegen's academic excitement. "Jane? You saw her?"

"She's with Albinus. She's using Apple. Claiming that Apple his Albinus's daughter—"

"We can discuss this somewhere safer," Loretta interrupted as lights came across the field. "Henry, drive."

"I have to go back," Lillian said again, softer now. "He needs me."

"You can't," Neumegen said from the front seat. "Not yet anyway. We shouldn't have let you go in the first place."

Badger watched Lillian's reflection in the car window, saw how her hand kept rising to touch her lips. Remembering someone else's kiss. His fingers closed around the coin in his pocket. If objects of significance could open doors through time... maybe it was time to create some significance of his own.

Sometimes the cost of playing with time wasn't measured in physics or theory. Sometimes it was measured in broken hearts and bitter revelations.

And sometimes it created monsters.

A Gilded Cage

The silk felt wrong against Apple's skin. Everything felt wrong — the perfumed air, the soft bed, the constant attention of slaves. A week ago, she'd been in chains. Now she wore gold bracelets instead of iron shackles, but the weight was the same.

"More wine, daughter?" Albinus gestured to a slave. His pale features, so like her own, caught the afternoon light streaming through the villa's windows. Sometimes, watching him was like seeing her own reflection aged and masculinised.

"No, thank you... father." The word stuck in her throat.

Jane sat between them, as always, her smile fixed and watchful. "Tell Apple about Hadrumetum. About how you overcame such odds."

Apple didn't need to hear it again. She'd memorised his story over the past week — the boy born different in North Africa, mocked for his ghostly appearance until his military prowess proved stronger than prejudice. His rise through the ranks, his governorship of Britain, his dreams of Rome.

"The sun was cruel there," Albinus said, warming to his favourite topic. "Not like here. I learned to fight in full armour even in summer heat, while other boys wilted. My... our condition made us stronger."

Apple nodded, the expected response to his familiar words.

She couldn't help being drawn in by the pride in his voice,

the way he included her in his triumph. No one had ever understood what it was like to be so different.

"They called me names too," she found herself saying. "In my vil... in my home."

Jane's eyes sharpened, but Albinus leaned forward eagerly. "But you survived. You thrived. As I did. As our kind always has."

"Our kind," Apple repeated. The words felt dangerous, like admitting something she shouldn't.

"The gods marked us," Albinus continued. "Made us special. And now they've brought us together, just when I need an heir most."

Jane's hand covered Apple's. "Already there's talk of marriage alliances. The noblest families in Rome..."

Apple pulled her hand away, standing abruptly. "I need air."

But even the balcony offered no escape. Slaves followed at a discrete distance. Guards watched from below. And always, always, Jane's presence lingered like smoke.

"Don't wander far, dear," Jane called. "All manner of dangers lurk in dark corners..."

Apple gripped the balcony rail, staring out over Londinium. Somewhere below her, Gar remained in real chains. Somewhere, Lillian might still be searching for her. And here she stood, dressed in silk, playing daughter to a man long dead.

Her life was more than surreal, as was the growing fear that she was starting to believe her own performance.

THE BANQUET HALL BLAZED WITH LAMPLIGHT. APPLE SAT on Albinus's right, exactly where Jane had positioned her. The elaborate hairdo pulled at her scalp, and the weight of borrowed jewels made her neck ache.

"Smile," Jane murmured from behind her. "People are watching."

Apple felt the weight of dozens of calculating stares. Romans assessing her value, measuring her influence. A pale curiosity with a governor's backing — or perhaps an emperor's, if the whispers about Albinus's ambitions proved true.

The guards dragged Gar in during the third course. They positioned him where everyone could see the mighty Iceni chieftain in chains, proof of Roman dominance. His eyes were fixed on the floor, refusing to meet anyone's gaze.

Look at me, Apple pleaded silently. Just look at me.

"The girl has her father's bearing," someone said loudly. "See how she holds herself?"

"A touch of the barbarian about her, though," another voice countered. "That wild look in the eyes."

Albinus's hand tightened on his cup. "My daughter," he said, his voice carrying across the hall, "has the blood of kings in her veins. The gods themselves marked her as special."

Jane smiled her serpent's smile. "And such a devoted daughter she is. So eager to learn our Roman ways."

Apple forced herself to nod, to smile, to play her part. But her eyes kept straying to Gar. Once, just once, his gaze flickered up, met hers – and the disappointment she saw there cut deeper than any blade.

"The Julii have expressed interest," a senator was saying. "Their youngest son—"

"The Claudii have better connections," someone else interrupted.

Apple felt the walls closing in. The marriage proposals, the political machinations, the web Jane was weaving. Even Albinus, with his dreams of empire, was caught in it.

"Eat, daughter," Albinus commanded.

She lifted a piece of meat to her lips, tasting nothing. Gar was being led away again, shackled in his real chains, while she sat here in her pretend ones. The irony of it burned like acid in her throat.

"Such a lovely family gathering," Jane announced to the room. "A father restored to his daughter, Rome's power displayed, and new alliances forming. Truly the gods smile upon you, Albinus."

Apple watched as slaves cleared away another course — roasted dormice drowned in honey, their tiny bodies arranged in elaborate patterns. Food that should have been stored for winter, wasted on display. The ice-locked Thames meant no fresh fish, but Albinus's kitchens served preserved mullet from clay amphorae, shipped from the Mediterranean months ago.

While people starved in the streets of Londinium, they feasted on imported olives, dried figs, and wine that had crossed an empire. Even the bread was different — fine white loaves that used precious stored grain, nothing like the rough winter bread of the common people.

A slave appeared at her elbow to replace her barely touched plate of salted pork with something swimming in garum sauce. As he cleared the dishes, she felt something press into her palm. A scrap of papyrus, folded tiny.

Her heart stopped. The slave was already moving away, anonymous among dozens of others. She let her napkin fall, using the movement to conceal the note as she unfolded it.

Two words, written in a precise hand: "Trust Mared."

Who was it from? And who was Mared?

"Something wrong, dear?" Jane's voice cut through her thoughts.

Apple crumpled the note in her fist. "The sauce disagrees with me."

"Perhaps some preserved quince?" Jane gestured to a slave. "The governor had it brought specially from his estates in Africa."

More waste. More showing off wealth while winter tightened its grip on the city. Apple forced herself to accept the fruit, her mind racing. Trust could be dangerous. She'd learned that lesson well enough from Jane. Even now, watching the woman orchestrate the banquet like a general commanding their troops, Apple could see how trust could be turned into a weapon.

The note burnt her palm. Hope was dangerous too. But like the preserved quince she pretended to eat, she would hold it close, keep it safe, wait for the right moment.

Somewhere in this city, someone was moving pieces into place to rescue her. And she needed to be ready.

$\cdot \quad \cdot \quad \cdot$

THE RICH FOOD SAT LIKE STONES IN APPLE'S STOMACH AS she made her way back to her chamber. Three watches of the night had passed — the soldiers changed guard as she walked down the corridor, their torches casting long shadows on the walls.

"River's breaking up," one guard muttered to another. "Three days till the next Kalends, and we'll be on our way to Rome."

Three days. The knowledge settled as heavily as the dormice and quince in her gut. She'd heard the servants talk about the Kalends – the first day of each Roman month, when debts came due and new ventures began. A fitting time for Albinus to begin his venture toward empire.

From her window, she could see fires dotting the darkness of Londinium. Not all of them were for warmth. The sound of breaking pottery echoed up from the streets — someone's precious winter stores being looted. Hunger made people desperate.

"They're at it again in the eastern quarter," a guard called from below.

"Let them fight over scraps," another answered. "Better than another Boudica."

Boudica's name whispered like a curse in Roman circles, and like a prayer in British ones. Apple had heard the stories, even in her time. How the warrior queen had burned Londinium to the ground, how she'd slaughtered thousands. The ruins still lay beneath their feet, a layer of black ash in the foundations that every new building had to acknowledge.

Roman mothers told their children to behave, or Boudica's ghost would come for them. British mothers told their daughters to be strong, like the queen who'd dared to challenge Rome. And tacticians studied the maps, determined never to let such an uprising happen again.

More sounds of unrest drifted up from the city. This wasn't a rebellion, though, just hunger and desperation. The winter had been too long, the river's ice too thick. Even now, with thaw coming, food would be scarce until spring.

Apple moved away from the window, still feeling the

papyrus note crushed in her palm. Who was Mared? And why should she trust them?

The sounds of the palace settling for the night filtered through her door and she thought of Gar in his cell. Of the disappointed look he'd given her at the banquet. What would Boudica think of her — dressed in Roman silks, playing Roman games, while her people suffered?

But maybe that's what was needed. Maybe sometimes you had to play their game to beat them at it.

Three days until the Kalends and they left for Rome.

Whatever was going to happen, it would have to happen soon.

The clatter of cart wheels on cobbles woke Apple from her uneasy sleep. Voices filtered up from the courtyard — complaints about the hour, about the cold, about deliveries that couldn't wait until morning.

"The governor sails with the thaw," a woman's voice insisted. "These storage vessels must be loaded now, before the crowds return."

Apple crept to her window. Below, massive amphorae were being unloaded from a cart. Each one stood taller than a man, their necks sealed with pitch, their sides marked with the potter's spiral. A grey-haired woman supervised the unloading, her hands stained with clay.

"And what's so precious it can't wait for dawn, Mared?" the guard demanded. "Have you no man in your bed to help you sleep?"

"Keep your insults inside you mouth. This is garum sauce from the coast. The governor's personal supply for his journey to Rome. You want to explain to him why his favourite fish sauce was left behind?"

Apple's breath caught. The note had said to trust Mared. And here was a potter, delivering impossible amphorae in the dead of night.

The guard laughed and waved them through, but not before tapping each vessel with his spear shaft. The hollow sounds seemed to satisfy him, but Apple noticed how carefully the slaves handled the amphorae, how they didn't tip or roll them as they usually would.

"Store them in the cool room," the potter instructed. "The sauce spoils easily."

Apple counted six massive vessels disappearing into the storage rooms beneath the palace kitchens. Six amphorae, each large enough to hold... what? Or who?

She remembered stories from her own time about smugglers hiding people in wine casks, about resistance fighters concealed in cargo. But surely the Romans would have heard similar tales too? Helen of Troy and the Trojan Horse came to mind.

Unless the Romans were too proud to imagine anyone would dare such a thing. Unless they were too certain of their own power to look closely at a woman's pottery.

More voices from below: "The governor's seal? These vessels don't have—"

"Here." The potter produced something from her cloak. "Will this satisfy you?"

Whatever she showed him must have worked. The guards stepped back, letting the last amphora pass.

Apple's heart raced. This had to be the rescue the note hinted at. But how many warriors could fit in those vessels? How long could they survive sealed inside? And how would they get out again?

The potter glanced up, straight at Apple's window. Their eyes met for just a moment before Apple stepped back into the shadows.

Three days until the Kalends. But maybe she wouldn't have to wait that long after all.

Sealed Hopes

The darkness was absolute. Bricius was pressed so tightly against the walls of the amphora it was as if he'd melted into the clay himself. How strange it was to be sealed in darkness next to a man who should have been his enemy. But Julius had proven himself more an ally than an oppressor.

Outside, Bricius knew his people were creating chaos. The sounds of breaking pottery, of fire taking hold, of shouts and conflict that would draw the soldiers away from the palace. Their distraction had to be precise — enough to pull attention, but not enough to trigger a full military response that would crush their people.

"How much longer?" he heard Julius whisper.

"Quiet," Bricius murmured back. "Not yet."

He felt the amphora rock slightly, and Bricius thought of the others — warriors who had volunteered for this impossible mission. They were six, crammed into a space that would make a wolf whimper. Six warriors, six blades, one purpose: to rescue Gar.

Gar would be furious. Bricius knew that the Iceni chieftain would see this as a foolish mission. That if the gods had meant for Gar to die in Rome, then so be it. But Gar hadn't counted on the arrival of Bricius, the Roman, or Iolo.

Bricius thought of his mother's words. "Sometimes, to save the tree, you must cut away the diseased branch." At one point, he'd imagined cutting Gar down, when Jane had first appeared and had started spreading her poison, before she'd turned into a viper. But even he knew that would have angered the gods, regardless of whether he believed in them or not.

Julius shifted in the amphora next to him. Bricius imagined he could smell his fear. One wrong breath, one misplaced sound, and they would be discovered.

Mared had been specific. Six amphorae of garum sauce, each large enough to hide a warrior. Each sealed with pitch, each marked with the correct seal, each handled with the casual indifference of a routine delivery. The Romans loved their systems, their bureaucracy. They would see what they expected to see.

His hand touched the small blade hidden against his thigh. His only weapon.

Through the walls of the amphora, he heard footsteps approaching. He held his breath.

A scrape and a muttered curse broke the silence. Someone was moving the storage vessels. Bricius tensed, his hand gripping his blade.

The amphora rocked. A shift. A scrape. Then a crack.

Bricius heard the distinctive sound of pottery breaking. Not the violent smash of combat, but the careful split of something under precise pressure. Someone was deliberately opening one of the vessels.

A whispered curse, then light filtered in. A sliver at first, before widening to reveal the outline of a calloused hand, then an arm, then a shoulder of the slave working to open the amphora.

In one fluid motion, Bricius exploded from the clay prison.

The slave scuttled from the storage room, his job done.

Bricius worked quickly, using his knife to continue cracking open the other amphora. Julius emerged first, then Iolo, then the others. Each man moving with the precision of hunters, silent as shadows.

The stench of death clung to Iolo like a second skin as he emerged from his clay coffin. Bricius couldn't bring himself to trust Iolo. The man moved like something only partially alive, with empty eyes.

But Iolo was on their side, and thus Bricius could use him. Until he didn't need to anymore...

"We don't have much time," Bricius whispered, scanning the cool room for anything weapon like. Clay vessels and amphorae lined the walls, with preserved meats hanging from hooks. The space smelled of salt and decay and damp. There was nothing there they could use.

Bricius looked at his companions. Julius, the Roman. Iolo, walking death. The other warriors, silent and deadly.

"We move now," he said.

The rescue of Gar had begun.

Bricius led the way, Julius close behind. Iolo moved like a phantom, his unnatural stillness more terrifying than any warrior's charge. The other three Iceni warriors — Rowan, Brennan, and Cynric — spread out in a loose formation behind them.

The cool room opened into a narrow corridor. Torches flickered in wall sconces, casting long shadows that danced and shifted. Bricius knew every shadow could conceal a guard, every corner could hide a trap.

Julius touched his arm, pointing. A set of stairs leading down, down to the cells, most likely.

Bricius motioned to the others, and silently they inched their way down the stairs. Each step was carefully placed. Each breath controlled. Ice seeped up through the stone under their feet. How many prisoners had walked these same steps? How many had never returned?

The first guard they encountered didn't even see them coming. Iolo moved first — a blur of motion that was more spirit than man. His blade found the guard's throat before the man could draw breath to cry out. The body dropped, silent as a fallen leaf.

Bricius didn't flinch. He'd seen worse.

Julius grabbed his arm. "We don't need to kill them," he hissed.

"The Romans killed my family. All of my family," Bricius replied, his eyes black in the shadowy light.

Julius released his grip and stepped back, nodding.

The cellblock was a warren of narrow corridors and iron-barred doors. The smell of human misery hung in the air. Bricius produced a ring of keys taken from the fallen guard.

"Spread out," he whispered.

"Gar will be in the most secure cell. Closest to the centre," Julius advised.

As they moved deeper into the cellblock. There was a shift of movement in one of the cells.

Bricius raised a hand. Stop.

Iolo pressed forward, his face a mask of something not quite human. A scavenger tracking an animal close to death. He listened at the cell door, his head cocked at an impossible angle.

"Here," he said. The word was more breath than sound.

Julius worked the keys. One. Two. None fit.

Cynric stepped forward, a skinny blade in his hand. He began to work at the lock, fingers moving with the precision of a craftsman.

Minutes passed like hours.

A click.

The cell door swung open.

Gar sat in the corner, chains around his wrists, his ankles. He looked up, eyes hard as flint. No surprise. No relief. Just the cold calculation of a chieftain whose expectations had been met. No more, no less.

"You should have been here earlier," he said.

Bricius nodded. He hadn't expected thanks, nor did he require them. Only half the job had been done. They still needed to get Gar, and themselves, out of the place alive. And then he would kill the prophet. He would kill Jane Badrick.

The manacles had left deep marks on the chieftain's wrists, but Gar said nothing as Cynric twisted and turned and tugged at the manacles whilst wielding his blade with practiced efficiency.

Julius kept watch at the cell door, ears straining for any

sound of approaching guards. The chaos outside had begun to fade. Their window was closing.

"A Roman?" Gar's only words.

"We need to move," Rowan whispered from further along the corridor.

Iolo's presence was a dark weight in the cell. He vibrated with an energy that was neither alive nor dead.

"Something's wrong," Iolo muttered.

Brennan tensed. "More guards?"

"No," Iolo replied, his voice a rasping whisper. "Something else."

Gar struggled to his feet. He scanned the cell, then the corridor beyond.

"The prophet?" he said. The words were a statement, not a question.

Bricius froze. "Jane?"

Gar nodded. "We take her with us."

The temperature in the cell dropped even lower as Bricius chose his words carefully. "She needs to die."

"She will," Gar said. "But by my hand."

"We need to move," Julius insisted, his Roman pragmatism cutting through the tension.

Cynric produced a set of rough clothes — merchant's clothes and a worn cloak. "For you," he said to Gar. "To blend in."

Gar dressed quickly, sloughing off his filthy prison outfit.

The energy of the group changed.

"She's coming," Iolo said.

No one questioned him.

Bricius readied his blade. "We go now," he said.

They moved as one. Gar in the centre, with Julius and Bricius on either side. Rowan and Brennan watching the flanks. And Iolo – Iolo moving like a shadow given form, his presence more threat than protection.

The stairs wound upward where the predawn silence was broken only by the occasional creak of settling wood and the distant sound of a guard changing watch.

Bricius's eyes scanned every shadow. Jane. He could think

of nothing else. The woman who had poisoned everything she touched.

"We need to save Apple," Julius whispered, pulling Bricius from his thoughts.

"Quiet," Bricius hissed.

Iolo began to mutter, his voice a low, raspy sound that seemed to come from somewhere between the walls. "A false emperor. A pretender on the throne. Blood of kings spilled on Roman stone."

Rowan placed a hand on Iolo's shoulder. The touch seemed to calm him momentarily, but the mumbled mutterings continued, each breath making less and less sense.

They reached a corridor lined with doors. Servants' quarters, perhaps. Or guest rooms. The governor's residence was a maze of potential dangers.

"Jane," Bricius whispered. "We find her first."

Julius stepped forward. "Apple," he countered. "Is the priority."

Gar's voice cut through their argument. "Neither."

They both turned to him.

"We find a way out," Gar said. "First. Everything else is secondary."

Iolo laughed. The sound was like dry leaves scraping stone. "No. Something worse is coming. Can't you feel it?"

Brennan shifted uncomfortably. "What do you mean?"

Bricius raised a hand.

Stop.

They pressed themselves against the wall. A slave, barely more than a boy, emerged from a room, rubbing sleep from his eyes. He carried a stack of linens, moving with the unconscious routine of early morning service.

The boy froze when he saw them.

Julius moved first. Not to attack. Not to silence. But to speak.

"The governor's chambers," he said quietly. A command disguised as a question.

The boy's eyes darted between them. Slaves knew everything. Saw everything. And feared everything.

He pointed down the corridor to the left.

Bricius wanted to kill him. To ensure their silence. But Julius's hand on his arm stopped him.

"He's just a boy. We don't need to spill more blood," Julius whispered.

Gar said nothing. But his eyes told a different story.

Iolo had stopped muttering. Now he was perfectly still, listening. "She's here," he said suddenly. "The viper's silken nest is close."

Bricius tried the first door. Locked. The second. Locked.

Cynric worked at the locks with the same precision he'd used in the cell below. His fingers moving like water, finding the weaknesses in metal and wood.

A click and the door swung open to reveal a study of Roman excess. Silk hangings. Intricate mosaics. A bed with linens so fine they looked like they'd been spun from moonlight. And curled on the bed was Apple herself.

Iolo moved first. Faster than an eel avoiding the spear of the hunter.

His laugh began low, a rattling sound that seemed to emerge from the underworld. It grew, rising in pitch and madness, until it became a high, keening cackle that made Julius take an involuntary step back.

"The moon child," Iolo cackled. "My trophy."

Revulsion rose in Bricius's throat. The way Iolo looked at Apple was worse than any battlefield horror he'd witnessed.

Julius recovered from the shock of Iolo's reaction and his hand went to his weapon. The druid was a madman. "Get away from her, you filthy beggar," Julius warned.

Apple stirred at the sound. Her pale eyes widening at the scene.

Iolo's laughter continued as he took a step forward, his arms outstretched like a supplicant before a god.

"My little viper," he crooned. "My beautiful weapon."

Bricius moved between Iolo and Apple. The action was instinctive. Protective. Something in Iolo's approach was fundamentally wrong.

"Grab her and let's go. We need to move," Bricius hissed. "And you," he said to Iolo. "You shut up, unless you want your tongue removed. You'll get us all killed."

But Iolo wasn't listening. His attention was completely and utterly fixed on Apple.

"You're perfect," Iolo whispered. "Just as the gods promised."

Outside, dawn began to break. The palace was already stirring. Their window of escape was closing faster than the sun was rising.

Iolo took another step forward.

Bricius's blade flicked up to Iolo's scrawny neck.

"Not another step," he said.

"He won't kill me," Apple said, sliding from the bed. "But Jane will."

Julius nodded at Apple, and took her arm, guiding her past the druid like a gallant knight in a Mills & Boon book.

Allies or Enemies

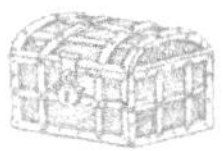

The corridors blurred into a maze of shadows and torchlight. Bricius lead with his blade ready. Julius kept Apple close, one hand guiding her, the other holding his short sword. Gar moved with the silent precision of a chieftain used to escaping impossible situations.

Iolo remained a problem with his constant muttering, and his eyes darting in directions that didn't exist, seeing things none of them could perceive.

"Quiet," Bricius hissed for the hundredth time.

They reached the servants' corridor. Dawn's first light crept through narrow windows. Soon, the palace would fully wake.

The sound of footsteps on flagstone floors. The group froze.

Marcus appeared around the corner. Shock flooded his face.

For a moment, nobody moved.

"Well," Marcus said. "This is unexpected."

"You will help us escape," Gar announced. "As payment for what we did for you."

"What? What did you do for him?" Julius asked.

"It was nothing," Marcus said, straightening his shoulders.

"What. Did. You. Do."

"He paid us to kill Romans," Gar said, as if he were

reciting nothing more exciting than the time of the next train.

Julius still looked confused, before a sick understanding flooded his face.

"The pay chest," Julius started. "You used the Iceni to be a distraction so you could empty the pay chest from the strong room."

Marcus shrugged. "As I said, it was nothing."

"Nothing? Nothing? My men died. Your friends. Men, we had both known for years. Our friends. For what? For money?"

"You really shouldn't hang about here," Marcus said. "It's inevitable that you'll be caught if you do. And with the Governor's daughter. He will be doubly upset. I hear there's a very fortuitous betrothal awaiting her in Rome. Although I would have liked to have been considered. We did have a connection, didn't we?" Marcus said, leering at Apple.

"You sold your own for gold," Julius spat. "Not for survival. Not for your people. Just for yourself." Julius took a step forward, rage rolling off him. "I will kill you."

Bricius recognised this moment. The moment when war became personal.

Apple stepped between them. "He's not worth it, and we don't have time," she said, staring into Julius's eyes, her back to Marcus.

Iolo began to laugh. That terrible, scraping laugh that seemed to come from somewhere between worlds. "The gods are coming," he muttered. "Time changes with every breath."

Outside, Mared would be waiting with the cart. Their escape route was planned with the precision of a military campaign. But plans, as they all knew, were the first things to die in moments of chaos.

Marcus cocked his head. "I have my uses, even if you hate me," he said.

"Not to us," Julius said. "You'd only be useful as a fertiliser in the fields."

Gar's voice cut through the tension like a blade. "We need him."

Julius looked ready to argue, his face a storm of barely

contained rage. Marcus stood there, infuriatingly calm, a small smile playing at the corner of his mouth.

"No," Julius said. "Absolutely not."

"Yes," Gar replied. His tone brooked no argument. "He knows the palace. He knows the way out."

"The routes are changing," Iolo muttered, his voice rising in pitch. "The rivers run backward. The stones speak. Can't you hear them?"

Bricius shot him a look that would have silenced most men. Iolo continued.

"Blood and gold," Iolo proclaimed. "And the breath of gods!"

The other Iceni shifted uncomfortably. Even they had limits as to how much madness they could tolerate from the druid.

"We move now," Gar said. "With or without agreement."

Julius's eyes never left Marcus. His hatred was almost visible in the air between them.

"I will kill you," Julius whispered. It wasn't a threat, but a promise.

The corridors of the governor's residence were a maze of potential discovery. Each shadow could hide a guard or conceal a trap.

Bricius had already dismissed the animosity between the two Romans. His mind was elsewhere — on Jane. His quest to find her burned like a fever.

"Jane," he muttered. "She needs to die."

Gar shook his head. "Survival first, vengeance second."

As someone well-versed in looking after his own skin first, Marcus jumped in. He recognised an opportunity to get everything he wanted—life outside the Roman army, access to his buried gold, and the chance to settle an old score.

For years, he'd watched Julius rise through the ranks, earning the respect of their superiors while Marcus remained overlooked and under appreciated. He had convinced himself that it was Julius's fault—that the other man had schemed, whispered, and manoeuvred to block his progress. Now, with the chaos of their desertion providing the perfect cover, Marcus could seize what he was owed.

A fortune in stolen gold lay waiting for him, enough to buy the kind of idle, indulgent life he had always craved. No more marching through mud, no more following orders barked by men he despised. He would slip away from the discipline of the legions and into the embrace of wealth, where he could live as a man of status, not a footsore soldier scraping by on a legionary's pay.

But first, there was Julius. That smug, self-righteous bastard who had always seemed to be one step ahead. The chance for revenge burned as hot as his hunger for gold. He imagined the look on Julius's face when the knife slid between his ribs, when he realised too late that Marcus had bested him at last.

Yes, Marcus thought, his pulse quickening. This was the moment he had been waiting for.

"Follow me. I know the back passages," he said. "Ways out that the guards don't patrol."

Julius's rage seeped through his pores. "I don't trust a word from your mouth."

Iolo's laughter grew madder. "The stones are singing!" he proclaimed. "Can't you hear them?"

No one answered.

Apple touched Julius's arm. "Let's go," she said. "Together, and then you can take me to Lillian."

He didn't have the heart to tell her Lillian was gone. Not yet, anyway.

And so they moved together as a group of broken things — warriors, traitors, madmen. And a girl who was both everything and nothing.

A Bitter Pill to Swallow

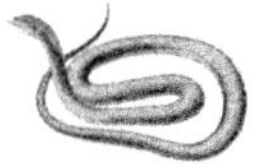

The drizzle matched Badger's mood. He kicked a loose stone along the footpath, hands shoved deep in his pockets, muttering to himself about the injustice of it all.

Lillian and her precious Julius. Always Lillian and Julius. As if nothing else in the world mattered.

And then, of all people, Holly appeared.

"Badger," she said. Not a greeting. More like an accusation.

He stopped, guilt flashing across his face as the memory of asking her a favour surfaced.

Holly had always been territorial. When they'd dated, she'd been possessive to the point of obsession. And now, after everything, she still looked at him like he was something she'd once owned and might want to reclaim.

"Hey, thanks for your help before, up at Ithaca Farm," he said.

She smiled. Not a nice smile. "Did you know Bishop threatened to charge me with wasting police time? That's such a harsh phrase, isn't it? Wasting police time. I prefer to think of it as more like deploying a secret shopper. My 'creative expression' provided an opportunity for Bishop to assess the abilities of his staff against nationally accepted police performance criteria."

Badger snorted. "And were you creative enough to avoid charges?"

"Of course," Holly said. She fell into step beside him, uninvited. "So. What's new?"

And just like that, the floodgates opened. The frustration and the shame Badger was carrying burned inside him, and Holly – well, Holly had always been a good listener when it came to other people's drama, given that gossip was one performance area she excelled in.

"Lillian," he spat the name. "After everything I've done for her, she couldn't care less. Dropping me like a hot potato to chase after some bloody Roman soldier. And all of them have got one of those coins. Those stupid gold coins that even my father thinks are more important than me, his son. Or his bloody wife. No one cares about her. But I do."

Holly's interest sharpened. "Coins?"

"Those gold coins up at Ithaca Farm. The ones they think my mother stole. She had nothing to do with any of it. They're all acting like they're some kind of precious artefacts. But you know what? They should be in a museum!" His voice rose. "Do you know how much one of those coins is worth?" Badger continued. "Just one could get me out of my parents' house. Start a new life. But no. No one is allowed to know what they've got. Well, the jokes on them, because they found all the Roman altars, right? And most of the coins. It makes me sick to think that they can get away with it. Uttering some absolute shite about time travel, and bloody fucking Roman emperors." Badger left out the part of seeing Lillian and Apple disappear the night of the Saturnalia festival at the Bellingham. He left out the part of Lillian materialising in front of his eyes in the pig shed at Ithaca Farm. He left out the part of feeling like his heart had been ripped in two when he thought he'd never see Lillian again.

Holly patted his arm, and made soothing sounds, her comforting presence opening the floodgates even further.

"Those coins," Badger muttered. "They could have given me one."

The rain continued. A steady backdrop to his anger.

"Lillian thinks she's so special," he said. "With her plans to rewild the farm, and her precious Julius, and her archaeological discoveries. You know that woman tied up in the barn?

She's an antique dealer from London. Lillian was going to sell everything. Like, what the actual hell? All that stuff would have gone into private collections, and would have ruined any chance my dad had at seeing them and studying them." Here Badger seemed to run out of steam, and he rested his head against Holly's perfumed shoulder.

Holly's smile was poison. "Tell me more."

HOLLY'S MIND WAS ALREADY SORTING THROUGH BADGER'S drunken outpouring of information like a skilled prospector sifting for gold.

Coins. Archaeological finds. Roman artefacts. And a rival not in her right mind.

Holly excelled at collecting information. Not for any noble purpose. She viewed information as a currency and knew how to trade better than any Wall Street financier.

With Badger's head still resting on her shoulder, and his breathing ragged with emotion and what seemed like exhaustion, Holly wiggled her body closer.

"Tell me everything," she murmured, stroking his hair with a practiced tenderness that was more calculation than comfort.

Holly's mind went to Sergeant Bishop at the Hexham police station, and to the narrow escape she'd just managed. Another opportunity was presenting itself, and Holly was nothing if not an opportunist. But perhaps not one involving the police... There was another young man in town who had tried on more than one occasion to catch her eye. Although there was no way on God's green earth that she would ever give Jasper Fletcher more than the time of day, he wasn't without his purposes.

Now she could envisage a reason to invite Jasper over, and imagined that he'd agree to do whatever it took to get between her sheets. She shuddered at the thought. There was no way she'd let him get that far, but she could let him imagine he had a chance...

This town had overlooked her too many times. Dismissed her as a stupid blonde. But now she held all the power.

"So," she crooned, "tell me more about these coins. Where are they?"

With his face buried into her shoulder, Badger missed the predatory glint in her eye.

Holly was going to turn his information into something valuable. And she didn't care who got hurt.

A Siren's Call

Jasper Fletcher was riding the highest wave of his life.

The Hexham Herald had transformed. Where once it had been a struggling local rag, now it was the talk of the county. John Revell, his editor, couldn't stop singing his praises. The exposé on Jane's mayoral misconduct had been more than just a story — it was a journalistic earthquake that had shaken the entire local political landscape.

"You've saved this paper," Revell had told him just last week. "Circulation's up, advertising's up. Everything's up!"

And Charley. Beautiful, brilliant Charley Scott. She was everything Jasper had ever wanted. Smart. Driven. Supportive. And right now, she was beside him, her hand resting on his leg as he drove. The morning light caught her hair, turning it into a halo of copper and gold.

The phone rang. *Holly Corben.*

He hadn't spoken to her since school. Or rather, she hadn't spoken to him. He'd said hi in massing, but she'd never reciprocated. Those years of casual cruelty seemed like a lifetime ago. Holly, the most popular girl. Him, the quiet, bookish kid who consistently outperformed her in English Literature.

"Hello?" he answered.

Her voice was honey and poison. "Jasper! It's Holly, Holly Corben. I need to talk to you. It's important."

He tried to beg off. "I'm kind of busy—"

"Roman coins," she said. The words stopped him cold.

Charley looked over, curious.

"I have information," Holly continued. "About those coins found at Ithaca Farm. You're a journalist, right? Don't you want to know?"

Jasper hesitated. A story was a story.

"What do you know?" he asked.

"It's safer if I tell you in person. After all, I don't want to lose my head like poor Darby. I mean, they haven't even found the rest of his body yet, have they?"

"Okay, where do you want to meet?"

"My place," Holly replied, with an implied expectation that Jasper knew exactly where that was. Which he did. Everyone knew where Holly Corben lived, even if you had never been invited to one of her parties. Which he hadn't.

Charley's eyebrow rose, as if to say, "Are you sure about this?" They'd been at school together, and Jasper knew that Charley was no fan of Holly, either.

"I'll be right over," Jasper said.

They pulled up to Holly's house — a detached monstrosity that screamed new money and bad taste. The kind of house that tried too hard to impress, and failed at every turn.

"Do you want me to come with you?" Charley said. "I'd rather face whomever murdered Darby than face Holly Corben alone."

"No," Jasper replied. "I'll be fine." *Famous last words.*

Jasper kissed the ends of Charley's fingers, before clambering out of the car.

As he walked up to the imposing front door, he couldn't help but wonder if this was what Daniel had felt like walking into the lion's den.

Holly opened the door before he'd even finished knocking. Her foreign smile was something else entirely. He'd never had the full wattage of one of Holly's smiles directed at him before. And although the journalist inside him recognised it for what it was, a lie. The bullied teenage boy he'd once been lapped it up.

· · ·

THE SITTING ROOM WAS A STUDY IN CAREFULLY CURATED perfection. Everything designed to impress.

Jasper sat on the edge of an expensive leather sofa, notebook in hand, with Holly perched opposite him, her posture open and overly inviting. She took a sip of tea – Earl Grey, served in bone china, and let her eyes dart around the room as if checking they were truly alone.

"It's about Lillian Arlosh," she began, her voice a conspiratorial whisper. "She's back."

Jasper's pen hovered over the page. Holly was playing a game, and he knew it. But a story was a story.

"Since when? The police haven't said anything?" he prompted.

"Badger found her in the pig shed at Ithaca Farm. Fitting really for someone so underhanded." She leaned forward. "Can you believe that Lillian was going to sell everything to that antique dealer from London – all these precious artefacts they found in her barn? Do you know what that would have done?"

"Tell me."

Her finger traced the rim of her teacup. "That would have destroyed any chance of proper historical research. And as for the coins — oh, the coins, she's basically been handing them out like party favours. Like Oprah giving away cars. You get a coin, and you get a coin. I'm amazed she hasn't tried to bribe you with one, to make sure you show her in a positive light..."

"Who has she been giving coins to?" he asked.

Holly's smile was a weapon. "They're worth a fortune, you know. I'm not surprised someone has already died. Lillian is completely unstable. She's not right in the mind. Badger said she kept talking about travelling through time. Can you imagine? Now we know what sort of defence she's going to use if she's ever caught."

Holly placed her cup on the table and moved next to him. She leaned in, her voice low. "You remember those metal detectorists, the ones who looted that Anglo-Saxon hoard and got sent down for years? They stole history, Jasper. And that's exactly what Lillian's done, only on a far grander scale," Holly paused for a dramatic breath.

"She didn't just pocket a few coins. She has manipulated everyone, lied, and ripped something priceless out of its rightful place. The courts didn't hesitate to lock those men up, and with your skills, and with the right angle, we can make sure Lillian faces the same fate. Longer, even. She thinks she's untouchable, but she's not. Not if we expose her for what she really is."

He knew she was feeding him a carefully selected version of the truth. She was playing him like a fiddle. And he was buying it, hook, line, and sinker.

CHARLEY WATCHED HOLLY'S HOUSE, HER BREATH FOGGING the window. Minutes ticked by. Ten. Fifteen. Twenty. The car was freezing, and she'd had enough.

"Sod this," she muttered.

The front door was unlocked. Of course it was. Who in this small town ever locked their doors?

She stepped into the hallway, her footsteps silent on the plush carpet. Voices drifted from the sitting room, so it wasn't hard to follow them.

And there she was. The beautiful Holly Corben. The darling of Hexham. Northumberland's very own Barbie lookalike. And she was sitting far too close to Jasper, her lips nearly brushing his ear. Any normal girl would have slapped some sense into the guy, but nothing about the scene felt genuine. Charley knew she'd walked straight onto a stage, where Holly was the lead actress, and Jasper was playing the fool.

Charley cleared her throat.

Jasper jumped up, guilt written all over his face. His notebook went flying, his ink pen smearing the pristine white of the expensive leather sofa.

Holly's smile froze as anger flickered in her eyes. Anger she quickly masked, but not before Charley clocked it first.

"Oh," Holly said. "I didn't realise you were here. Did you knock?"

Jasper collected himself. "We should go," he told Charley,

preparing to bundle her out of the house with an urgency that spoke volumes.

"You came together?" Holly asked, confusion replacing the anger in her eyes.

"Yes, we're a couple. Didn't you know?" Charley purred, sliding her hand into Jasper's, and enjoying the shock on Holly's face far more than she thought she would.

"Thanks for the information," Jasper stuttered, as he pulled Charley out of the sitting room, along the hall, and through the front door, and back into his car.

Charley laughed as she tried to imagine what was colder. The air outside? Or Holly's reaction to the news that Jasper couldn't be bought with faux affection.

The car roared to life, and gravel sprayed as they pulled away from Holly's perfectly manicured drive.

"Well, that was fun. Where are we going?" Charley asked.

"The police station," Jasper replied, his eyes fully on the road, and not on her.

It was funny how guilt worked in the mind of a man. Charley smiled again, pleased that she'd come in when she had, before anything happened. She placed her hand on Jasper's knee.

"Why? What did she tell you?"

"I'm not sure which of her statements were lies. But there was definitely a kernel of truth in there. And in the interests of public safety, I'm taking this to Bishop, before I take it to the paper."

Everything Unravels

Dawn had only just broken when the messenger arrived. Jane was already awake — she rarely slept more than a few hours at a time, her mind too active, too full of plans.

The slave who brought the messenger was trembling almost as much as the man himself. Something was very wrong.

"Speak," Jane commanded.

The messenger's hands shook so violently that the scroll he carried danced in the lamplight carried by the slave.

"I'm to tell you that the prisoner," he stammered. "Gar. Has gone."

Jane's eyebrow raised, and it was a struggle to stop any emotion from crossing her face. This was a setback, but not a derailment. "Explain."

The words tumbled out. Iceni warriors, hidden inside the giant amphora. An impossible escape from the governor's residence. And they'd taken the moon girl too.

"Who?" Jane asked. Her blood was like ice as realisation hit.

"The governor's daughter."

Jane sat perfectly still.

"Repeat everything," she said. "Every detail you know."

The messenger's voice cracked as he repeated the story.

Jane's mind was already moving. This was an unexpected

complication, but not the end. As long as it didn't stop their journey to Rome, she could get through this. She had to get to Rome.

"When did it happen?" she asked.

"Just before dawn," the messenger whispered. "The governor hasn't been told yet."

A small smile played at the corner of her mouth. Information was power and now she had something Albinus did not.

"Leave me," Jane said.

The messenger and the slave fled.

She rose, moving to the window. Londinium was only just waking, oblivious to the catastrophe that had just unfolded within the governor's residence.

She couldn't let Gar's escape stop what was meant to happen. And Apple's abduction, if that was it was, could be overcome. But first, she needed to contain the damage and decide on the narrative before anyone shared the news with Albinus. He could not know. Not yet.

ALBINUS WAS STILL HALF-ASLEEP WHEN JANE ENTERED HIS bedchamber. The morning light caught the white of his hair, making the lines of his face more pronounced. He looked older, more vulnerable, and nothing at all what a man claiming to be emperor should look like.

"What?" he demanded, sitting up. The silk coverlet fell away.

Jane stood at the foot of the bed. Her posture was rigid. Controlled. "Gar has escaped."

For a moment, nothing moved.

"Gar?" Albinus's voice was dangerously quiet.

"The Iceni chieftain," Jane repeated. "Escaped. With help from inside the palace. And your... daughter was involved."

"Apple? she would never—"

"She betrayed you," Jane cut him off. "One of your guards died trying to stop her." There was no harm in embellishing the truth.

Albinus rose from his bed.

Even in his nakedness, the pain of deceit was clear to see. "I want every painted Iceni dead. And I want Gar's head!"

Jane remained perfectly still. "No," she said simply.

"You defy my orders?"

"We cannot delay our journey to Rome," she explained. "You have to go to Rome. To stay here is certain death. Severus will destroy you. I have seen it."

"They have taken my daughter!" Albinus roared with real pain in his voice.

Jane knew he saw Apple as more than a political tool. As a family member. So her voice was cold when she answered. "She was never truly your daughter. She was a means to an end."

Albinus's hand caught her chin, and for a moment, Jane thought he might strike her. But he stopped.

"She is my daughter, sent by the gods. We will send the legions," he said finally. "Not to capture. To slaughter." A dangerous smile spread across Albinus's face. "Every Iceni will know the price of defiance."

Threads of Fate

Pramod's fingers trembled slightly as he took Aper's seal. The weight of history pressed down on him — one wrong move could unravel everything.

The letters would be crafted with surgical precision. Each word chosen to nudge events toward the path he knew must happen. Severus must defeat Albinus. The empire's future depended on it.

Using Aper's seal was a risk. But Aper was perfectly positioned — a cripple with just enough access and just enough credibility to be ignored.

The first letter. To a legion commander in Gaul.

Subtle hints about Albinus's weakness. The recent escape of Gar from Londinium. The loss of the governor's daughter. Implications of instability. Enough to plant seeds of doubt.

The second letter. To a senator in Syria.

Whispers about Albinus's ambition. Carefully worded suggestions that he might be preparing to challenge Severus more directly. Creating the narrative of inevitable conflict.

The third letter. To the Praetorian Prefect.

Pramod's hand was steady now. He knew how to balance suggestion against fact.

Each letter sealed with Aper's mark. Each a thread in a tapestry that must remain unchanged if the future wasn't to change.

Pramod understood the delicate nature of time. One

wrong move could shatter everything. The battle of Lugdunum must happen. Severus must defeat Albinus. The empire's future hung in the balance.

He thought of the histories he'd studied. Of the precise moment when Severus would emerge victorious. When 75,000 men — mostly from the Pannonian, Moesian, and Dacian legions, he would crush Albinus's forces.

The letters were more than messages. They were anchors keeping history's ship on its predetermined course.

Pramod looked at the sealed documents. Each one a potential turning point. Each one a whisper that might change everything.

The fate of an empire balanced on these small pieces of parchment.

Aper could not know.

Pramod's hands, once steady enough to craft the most delicate silver filigree, now trembled with each scratch of the stylus against the wax tablet. The stroke had stolen more than just his ability to create. It had stolen his precision.

But not his mind.

A librarian understood misdirection better than most. Information was a weapon. And weapons were most effective when they seemed to strike by accident. So he would not send the letters directly. That would be suicide.

Instead, he would create a trail. A carefully constructed illusion of intercepted correspondence. Letters that looked like they had fallen into the wrong hands. Missives that appeared to be stolen, read, passed between the wrong people.

First, he would use a messenger known for his loose tongue. A young man who couldn't keep a secret if his life depended on it. The type who would "accidentally" discuss the contents of a sealed message in a tavern.

Then, he would ensure the letters took a circuitous route. A Syrian merchant heading to Gaul. A trader passing through multiple hands. Each transfer increasing the appearance of chance.

The seals would be perfect. Close enough to Aper's to raise suspicion. Different enough to suggest interception.

Pramod remembered his days as a silversmith. The precision required to create something that looked accidental was an art form. His hands might shake now, but his mind was as sharp as ever.

Libraries were full of stories about how empires rose and fell. How a single piece of information, placed just so, could change everything. And he thought of the histories. Of Severus. Of the precise moment when everything must happen exactly as it was meant to.

These letters were more than messages. They were lifelines. Threads that would pull history back to its intended path.

Let Aper suspect. Let others wonder.

Pramod would ensure the message reached its destination. By what appeared to be the most unlikely of routes.

A librarian understood. Information was never just information. It was a weapon. A shield. A destiny waiting to be fulfilled.

THE FORUM FELT DIFFERENT. APER SENSED IT BEFORE HE could define it. Conversations hushed when he approached. Colleagues who had only yesterday sought his counsel now avoided his gaze. Something was shifting beneath the surface of Roman society, and he was at the centre of a storm he couldn't understand.

"Silas," he called, his voice tight with rage.

His most trusted assistant appeared silently at his side.

"Find out what's happening," Aper demanded. "Why are people avoiding me?"

Silas bowed, but Aper saw a flicker of uncertainty in his eyes. Could it be that even his most loyal servant had been afflicted by the same ailment as every other man in the forum?

Metella's cancelled betrothal was the final straw.

The family Aper had carefully selected for Metella's marriage—a connection he'd spent months cultivating—had suddenly withdrawn. The Augures had declared another match more suitable. More politically advantageous.

"Months!" Aper screamed into the empty corridor. "Months of consultations with the soothsayers! Months of careful planning!"

He had paid good money. Significant money. The soothsayers had been specific—the date, the family, the alignment of the stars. And now? Nothing.

It was supposed to have been a perfect match, sealed with all the proper rites. The auspices had been read meticulously, the flight patterns of birds studied at dawn, the livers of sacrificed lambs examined for the slightest imperfection. The confarreatio ceremony had been planned down to the last detail—Metella would have donned the traditional tunica recta, woven in a single piece, and the saffron-coloured veil that would mark her transition from girl to wife. A procession of expensive torchbearers and flute players would have led her to the groom's house, where she would speak the sacred words. Musicians he had already paid for.

But none of it would happen now. The carefully selected omens, the sacrifices made at the Temple of Juno Pronuba, the painstaking negotiations with the family—rendered meaningless by a single decree from the Augures.

Aper clenched his fists, his nails biting into his palms. He had done everything by the book. Had the gods turned against him? Or had a rival, some scheming senator, offered a larger bribe to tilt fate in their favour?

His daughter's future had been rewritten in the space of a breath. And Aper was left with nothing but broken arrangements and empty promises.

By the time he returned to his villa, rage consumed him and his study became a battlefield of his own making. Delicate pottery shattered against the marble walls. A Greek vase — already centuries old — crashed to the floor. The delicate fragments would one day confound museum curators. Some pieces missing. Some mysteriously mended.

A bronze statuette of Mercury – a piece that would one day be studied by archaeologists — flew across the room, leaving a deep gouge in the wall.

"What is happening?" he screamed.

But no answer came. Only silence.

THE MESSENGERS ARRIVED IN QUICK SUCCESSION, EACH bearing news that struck Aper like physical blows. His secretary's face grew increasingly pale as he delivered the reports.

"My lord, Albinus has departed Londinium." The first messenger's words hung in the air. "He moves with haste toward Gaul, leaving behind the Sixth Legion to continue operations against the Iceni remnants."

Aper's fingers dug into his desk. "Continue."

"There are... rumours, my lord. They say his daughter was taken. Some whisper of Iceni raiders, others of internal betrayal. The details are unclear, but—"

"Enough," Aper waved him away, but another messenger stepped forward before the first could retreat.

"News from Britannia, from Ithaca Fort." The second messenger's voice quavered. "The centurion Julius... he's gone. Deserted."

The room seemed to tilt. Julius – the one game piece he thought he had secured, his leverage over Metella, gone like smoke in the wind. His carefully constructed web of control was unravelling thread by thread.

"Deserted, or killed in battle?" Aper's voice was barely a whisper. No grandson of his would dare. Even if he'd never publicly claimed him as his flesh and blood.

"Deserted. With all his personal effects. After the governor's departure from the fort. There was a delay in notification as there was initially some confusion whether he had joined the governor's party."

"But he hasn't?"

"No. They have no record of him ever arriving in Londinium with the governor..."

"There's more?"

"Rumours—"

"Rumours? Is that all you have?"

"They report that he was in Londinium though, and killed

a Roman soldier he was acquainted with."

Aper felt a tightness in his chest, and an obscene pressure building behind his eyes. His physician had warned him about strong emotions, about the dangers of allowing his blood to run too hot. But how could he remain calm when everything was falling apart?

"Find Pramod," he commanded, his voice hoarse. "Bring him to me immediately. And do not share any of this with my daughter. She mustn't know of this news. None of it."

If anyone could make sense of this chaos, it would be Pramod. The man saw patterns where others saw only confusion. He had a way of knowing how events would unfold, as if he'd already read the ending of history's scroll.

Aper paced his study, each step sending fresh waves of pain through his temples. Albinus on the move. Julius gone, leaving him without any leverage over Metella. And now his carefully arranged marriage plans lay in ruins.

When Pramod shuffled into the study, leaning heavily against the side of a slave, Aper barely waited for the door to close before speaking.

"Tell me what is happening," he demanded. "Albinus abandoning Britain half-pacified, rushing to Gaul. My daughter's betrothal in shambles. I am being avoided in the forum. Who is plotting against me?"

Pramod's fingers trembled slightly against the arm of the slave. "Sometimes, my lord, when events align in such a way, it means we are approaching a crucial moment in time. A point where all paths converge, and the true path must be chosen."

"Speak plainly. I have no time, nor the head, for riddles." The pressure in Aper's head mounted, a dull pounding behind his temples. "What convergence? What moment?"

"The empire stands at a crossroads," Pramod said softly. "And sometimes, to reach the correct path, things must first appear to unravel."

Aper clutched his chest, the pain sharp and insistent now. "Unravel?" He struggled for breath. "Everything I've built is unravelling! And you speak in riddles instead of—"

The pain struck like a dagger beneath his ribs.

Aper staggered as the room blurred at the edges. He was

vaguely aware of Pramod standing motionless, his hand tightening on the slave's arm as if restraining him.

As darkness crept into his vision, Aper saw something in Pramod's expression. A flicker—satisfaction, or something close to it. But the thought slipped away with his consciousness, lost in the growing void, as Hades began to claim him.

Return to Ithaca

The police tape fluttered in the wind like tattered prayer flags, marking Ithaca Farm as a place of violation. Lillian sat in her car, hands still gripping the steering wheel, unable to make herself move toward the farmhouse that had always been her sanctuary. Now it felt like a stranger's home.

"We don't have to do this today," Nicole said from the passenger seat. The antiques dealer had insisted on accompanying her, but Lillian suspected she simply didn't want her facing this alone.

"Yes, I do." Lillian watched another news van pull up at the end of the drive, joining the small media encampment that had formed there. "This is my home. They can't take that from me."

But it didn't feel like home anymore. The familiar stone walls held different shadows now, darker ones. Where was Badger? The thought of her faithful companion missing tightened her chest. And Julius... every corner of the farm held some memory of him. The workshop where he'd first shown her the centurion's ring. The kitchen where they'd pored over artefacts together. The garden where—

"Ms Arlosh!" A reporter had spotted her car. "Can you comment on the historical artefacts found on your property?"

Lillian's hands tightened on the wheel. "We'll park in the

barn," she said, missing Nicole blanch at the mention of the barn.

The car bumped through the rutted driveway and straight into the barn, out of sight of the journalists. They sat for a moment, each lost in their own thoughts, before Neumegen suggested that they retire inside for a restorative cup of tea.

Lillian nodded, grateful for the suggestion. The house key felt heavier than usual in her hand. Everything felt heavier these days, weighted with uncertainty and fear for Julius. Was he safe? She had no way of knowing.

Inside, the farmhouse was eerily quiet. Police had been through every room, she knew, searching for evidence of... what? The history that had always lived here? The secrets that had protected her family for generations?

Neumegen appeared in the kitchen doorway. "I've put on some tea," he said quietly. "Loretta has arrived at the Bellingham, but she wanted me to tell you that she will probably be gone by tomorrow..."

"Tomorrow? Why? We still have to get Apple back, and Julius." But Neumegen had already retreated back to the safety of the kitchen, and his own thoughts about his friend.

Lillian moved through the house like a ghost, touching familiar objects that somehow felt different now. The antique sideboard where she'd found Julius studying the pottery shards. The old desk where they'd spread out maps of the Wall. Everything reminded her of him, of the mystery they'd begun unravelling together.

"We can leave it till later," Nicole offered. "It seems wrong to pack all this up when..." She left the last of her sentence unsaid. "We don't know if some of these things might help," she finally added, waving her arm towards the piles of antiques they'd been working on before all this happened.

"Let them wonder." Lillian paused at her study door. Yellow police tape crossed it like a warning. "Did Loretta say whether she'd received any news? Or any premonitions?"

Neumegen's silence was answer enough.

Lillian's eyes went to the window. Julius was out there. She felt it in her bones. Would he seek her out? Did he have the power?

"He'll come for me," she whispered to herself. "I know it. He'll find his way back here."

Behind her, Neumegen and Nicole exchanged concerned glances, but Lillian didn't care. They couldn't understand how the past and present were woven together here. Some things were meant to return to Ithaca, and Julius was one of them.

THE CRUNCH OF TIRES ON GRAVEL DREW THEIR ATTENTION. Through the kitchen window, they watched Sergeant Bishop's police vehicle force its way through the crowd of journalists, their cameras flashing like lightning in the grey afternoon. The reporters scattered reluctantly, like ravens disturbed from carrion.

"That's all we need," Neumegen muttered, setting down his tea. "I'd better go out and meet him."

But Bishop was already at the door, his knock more of a warning than a request. He entered without waiting for an answer, bringing with him the cold air and a tension that made the room feel smaller.

"Ms Arlosh." He nodded curtly. "Welcome home. We need to talk."

Lillian's stomach tightened.

"May I come in?"

"It seems like you already have," Lillian replied, turning around and returning to the relative warmth of the kitchen.

"There are archaeologists from Newcastle University waiting outside," Bishop continued. "Along with some representatives from the British Museum. Not to mention..." and here he began to tick off a litany of other agencies, all of whom wanted a piece of her flesh. "They're rather interested in how these particular artefacts came to be in your possession."

"Which artefacts do you mean?"

"You can't be serious? Bishop gaped. "The Roman altars in your barn. For Christ's sake, woman, it is the biggest coup of the century. And you were going to sell them to her?" He pointed at Nicole.

"Ah, not me," Nicole pushed back. "I'm here for the

walking sticks, the bed pans, the Royal Doulton Flambé bulldog, and the war medals.

I'm not the Getty Foundation. I certainly don't have the funds to buy Roman altars."

"This really isn't the best time," Neumegen interjected, but Bishop held up a hand.

"Actually, it's exactly the best time. The only time." His eyes fixed on Lillian. "Please explain how these altars ended up in your shed?"

"I didn't know that they were there. Not initially. I inherited this property, and my grandfather's things are exactly that — my grandfather's things," Lillian said, fighting to keep her voice steady. "You'll have to ask him where they came from."

"That would be quite difficult since he's dead," Bishop replied.

"Exactly."

"That's a coincidental, and convenient, answer, wouldn't you say?"

Bishop's implication hung in the air like smoke.

"I can't stop you from bringing in experts," Lillian said finally. "But I won't have them on my land. If they want to examine the altars, they can do it where you're storing them."

"That's not how this works, Ms Arlosh. They need to examine the site, document the context—"

"The context?" Lillian's laugh was bitter. "You mean what's left of it after your officers tore everything apart?"

"Lillian," Neumegen warned softly, but she was beyond caring.

"You want context? How about the context of my missing friend? Or the fact that someone broke into my home and tied up my friend—" She stopped herself, seeing the sharp interest in Bishop's eyes. She'd nearly said too much.

"And what, Ms Arlosh?" Bishop leaned forward slightly. "What exactly happened here that night?"

The silence stretched taut as a bowstring. Outside, camera flashes continued to strobe against the windows. Lillian thought of Julius, and of everything she couldn't tell Bishop without sounding mad.

Bishop cleared his throat. "I also need to ask you to have over all and any of the remaining Roman coins you found on your property."

"I think," Nicole spoke suddenly, her voice firm, "that Ms Arlosh needs her solicitor present before answering any more questions."

Bishop's eyes flicked to the antiques dealer, narrowed slightly, then returned to Lillian. "Fine. But Ms Arlosh?" He paused at the door. "Don't go far. We're just getting started."

As soon as Bishop's car disappeared down the drive, Lillian sagged against the kitchen counter. "The coins," she whispered.

Neumegen was already pacing, running his hands through his hair. "This is bad. This is very bad. I can not lose my coins. I will never be able to return home."

"What coins?" Nicole looked at them, her face pale. "Are you telling me you have more coins than what the police found? You have to declare them."

Lillian met Neumegen's eyes across the kitchen. How much could they tell her? How much would she believe?

Nicole stopped. "I think I should head back to London. I don't want to know anymore. I want to go home to my shop, and to Mel. He probably thinks I've moved on. I can't get caught up in this. I'll lose my licence. I've already been tied up and left to die by a madman who had his head chopped off. His head. I have nightmares about it every time I close my eyes. I don't think that the trauma will ever leave me."

"Please don't go." Lillian reached out, catching Nicole's arm. "I know how this looks, but I need someone here who isn't..." she trailed off, unsure how to explain what she meant. Someone who wasn't caught up in the strangeness. Someone normal.

"Isn't what?" Nicole's voice had an edge to it now. "Isn't involved in whatever this is? Because I have to tell you, finding out I've been cataloguing items in a house full of potentially illegal artefacts is not exactly what I signed up for." She took a deep breath. "Do you have more coins? Because if you do, I need to know right now if I'm party to—"

A sound cut through the gathering darkness outside. A long, mournful howl that made the hair on the back of Lillian's neck stand up. All three of them froze.

"Was that…" Nicole whispered.

"A wolf," Neumegen's voice was barely audible. "But that's impossible. There haven't been wolves in Britain since—"

"The Iceni," Lillian finished. "It's them. Preparing for war."

The howl came again, closer this time. It echoed through the night—low, guttural, ancient. From the direction of the Wall.

"What's the date?" Neumegen asked suddenly, his eyes wide.

Lillian frowned. "January 17th. Why?"

He checked his watch, his breath unsteady. "The dead of winter. The wolves would have been hungry. And the Iceni…" He swallowed. "They would have called to them."

Nicole looked at them like they'd lost their minds. "What are you talking about? What does an ancient tribe have to do with—"

Another howl, even closer. This time, it was answered. A chorus rising, layering upon itself, until the night was thick with the voices of wolves that shouldn't exist.

"The altars," Lillian whispered. "They shouldn't have moved them."

Neumegen turned sharply toward her.

"They weren't just for offerings. They were for war." Her voice trembled. "The Romans sacrificed at Lupercalia to call on the spirit of the wolf—but the Iceni did something else. They called on the wolves themselves. They called on their gods to tear Rome apart. And if the altars have been disturbed…"

Nicole's knuckles whitened on the door handle. "Are you saying we've triggered—what? Some kind of ancient battle rite?"

Outside, something shifted in the darkness beyond the kitchen windows. Something large. Too large. And behind it, shapes moved—shapes that walked like men, but not men. Warriors, wrapped in furs, their eyes catching the torchlight like hungry beasts.

Neumegen exhaled. "Something has woken up."

Lillian turned to him, her pulse hammering. "Then we

need to stop it. Before whatever's out there finds its way in here."

The Flight of the Vanquished

The night air bit cold against Julius's face as they moved through Londinium's shadows. Apple walked silently beside him, her white hair luminescent in the darkness. He kept her close, aware of Iolo's gaze following her every movement.

"We should go back," Bricius growled for the third time. "The woman betrayed us. She betrayed the Iceni. Such treachery cannot go unpunished."

"Jane Badrick isn't worth dying for," Julius countered, though he shared Bricius's disgust. The archaeologist's betrayal had cut deep, but revenge would have to wait. "Albinus's men will be looking for us. We need to move."

Gar materialised beside them, his face painted with shadows. "The roads north are watched. Romans everywhere."

"The gods demand blood," Iolo's voice came from behind, thick with hunger. "The white one would make a perfect sacrifice. Pure. Untouched. From beyond time itself." His fingers twitched at his sides, tracing patterns in the air that seemed to leave ghostly trails of power.

Julius felt Apple press closer to his leg. The last druid's madness was becoming harder to control with each passing hour. The ancient power that crackled around him made the air taste of metal and ash.

"Touch her and die," Julius said, his hand moving to his

weapon. He'd killed one person in this time already. He'd kill again if it meant protecting Apple.

Iolo's laugh was like breaking glass. "You think your Roman blade can harm me? I am the last. The only one who remembers the old ways. The true ways." His eyes gleamed with an unnatural light. "The white one's blood would open doors you cannot imagine."

"No one's opening any doors," Julius said. "We're getting out of Londinium. All of us." But he positioned himself between Apple and the druid, noting how even Bricius and Gar kept their distance from Iolo's increasingly erratic movements.

They moved through the city like water, keeping to the shadows of ancient buildings that somehow still stood in the modern world. Julius saw them both ways now — the gleaming steel and glass of present-day London overlaid with the rough stone and wooden structures of Roman Londinium. Both real, both now. And everywhere, he felt Iolo's power rippling through the air, distorting the boundaries between times even further.

"There," Gar pointed to a gap between buildings. "Way clear."

But Bricius had stopped, his head tilted like a wolf scenting prey. "She is close. I can feel it."

"The betrayer's blood would serve as well," Iolo whispered, his voice carrying despite its softness. "But not as well as the white ones. Not as pure. Not as powerful." His hands were constantly moving now, weaving spells that made reality shimmer around them.

Julius watched in horror as flowers sprouted and died beneath Iolo's feet, centuries passing in seconds. The druid's power was bleeding through, unchecked, uncontrolled. Mad.

"We need to move," Julius insisted, feeling Apple trembling against him. She could sense it too — the wrongness that surrounded Iolo, the chaos he threatened to unleash. "Now."

"The old ways demand sacrifice," Iolo continued as if he hadn't heard, his eyes fixed on Apple. "The white one comes from a time yet to be. Think of the power in that blood.

Think of the doors we could open. The barriers we could break." He took a step forward, and reality rippled around him like heat waves.

"Bricius," Julius appealed to the warrior chief. "Control your druid."

Bricius's face was grim. Even he, it seemed, feared what Iolo might do. "Iolo, enough."

The druid's laugh echoed, as if coming from multiple times at once. "Enough? It will never be enough. Not until the white one's blood feeds the earth. Not until time itself bends to the old ways."

Apple growled, the sound somehow both present and ancient, and Iolo's eyes widened with terrible delight.

"See? She understands. She knows what she is. What she could be."

"She's under my protection," Julius said, his voice hard. "Touch her, and I'll show you exactly what a Roman blade can do to a druid."

The tension crackled between them like lightning, past and present twisting together in the space between heartbeats. Then Gar's voice cut through: "Romans. Coming."

They could all hear it now — the sound of boots on stone, orders being called. Whether they were modern police or Roman soldiers hardly mattered anymore. The hunt was on.

"We run," Gar said simply.

They ran, leaving Londinium and its ghosts behind. But Julius kept Apple close, and his hand on his weapon. The druid's mad eyes followed them through the darkness, and Julius knew this wasn't over.

It was only the beginning.

Iolo stopped, raising his arms to the night sky. His voice rose in a chant that seemed to come from the earth itself, ancient words that made Julius's teeth ache and Apple's fur stand on end. The air shimmered, and then the first howl split the darkness. It was answered by another, then another, until the night was alive with the voices of wolves – more wolves than any of them had ever heard at once, their howls building to a terrible chorus.

Through the streets of Londinium, citizens hurried inside their homes, pulling their children close. In the governor's villa, Jane shivered despite the warmth of the brazier. She had grown used to the occasional wolf cry, but this was different. This was power.

Albinus stood at his window, watching the darkened streets. As a Roman, he had always respected wolves. Celebrated them even. For had not the she-wolf nursed Romulus and Remus?

But these howls carried something alien in them, something that belonged not to Rome's ordered world but to the wilds beyond the wall of Hadrian.

"I have never heard them call like this," his advisor murmured, one hand clasped around the amulet at his neck. "So many, and so close to the city walls..."

"The gods are restless tonight," Albinus replied, his voice tight. "Do not let it worry you. They are but beasts. We leave on the high tide for Gaul tomorrow."

Beyond the walls, the wolves' chorus grew stronger. In the torchlight, shadows seemed to move with new purpose, and the night air itself felt charged with ancient power. The wolves of Britain had answered the druid's call, and their hunt was just beginning.

The Price of Peace

Pramod watched Aper's chest rise and fall, each breath more shallow than the last. He held onto the slave, preventing him from running for help. There was no point. He had seen enough death in his long life to recognise its approach.

"Wait," he said softly, his grip firm on the slave's arm. "First, help me to his desk."

The slave's eyes widened in protest, but he dared not refuse him. Together they shuffled to Aper's desk, Pramod's own infirmity making each step a careful negotiation. The correspondence lay scattered where Aper had left it. The latest messages from Britannia spilled across the surface like fallen leaves.

"Wait outside," Pramod commanded. "No one enters until I call."

As soon as the slave withdrew, Pramod's trembling fingers began sorting through the papers. He had to work quickly—there would be questions about why he delayed calling for help. But some things were more important than the appearance of proper behaviour. The future itself depended on what happened in these next few moments.

A letter from the governor of Syria caught his eye. Warning about Severus's growing power in the east.

Aper had marked it with his own annotations, calculating political advantages that would never come to fruition now.

Behind him, Aper made a sound—not quite a gasp, not quite a groan. Pramod didn't turn. The gods would claim their due, with or without an audience.

His fingers moved faster now, shuffling through correspondence. He needed something—anything—that would give them a way out. Then, beneath a pile of reports, his hand hesitated. The broken wax seal. The weight of the parchment. A spy's report.

'Centurion Julius absent from post following the governor's departure. Initially presumed part of the travelling party, but no record of arrival in Londinium. Witness reports place him in Londinium after his disappearance. Engaged in an altercation resulting in the death of a Roman soldier. Circumstances are unclear. Ongoing investigation.'

Pramod's vision blurred for a moment. Julius. Their son. The words pressed against his chest, each syllable tightening like a fist. Worry flooded through him—where was he? Was he safe? Had he fled, or was he being hunted? The thought of his son, alone, pursued, made him feel physically ill.

But beneath the worry, another emotion stirred. A quiet, unexpected joy. Aper had no leverage anymore. He couldn't use Julius to keep Metella bound to Rome, couldn't dangle the boy's safety like a chain around her neck. That hold was broken.

Aper exhaled behind him, his breath shallow, wet. Dying or dead, it made no difference. His power was slipping through his fingers.

Pramod folded the report and tucked it inside his tunic. It would not be found.

They could leave.

The sound of Aper's breathing changed, with long gaps between each breath. Pramod had known that Aper's death was necessary for what must follow. The history books were clear about when certain players left the stage.

But knowing didn't make it easier to listen as a man died behind him.

At last, satisfied he had found everything of importance, Pramod turned back to Aper. The Roman's face was grey now, his lips tinged with blue. Their eyes met for a moment, and Pramod saw the question there – the confusion, the betrayal.

"I'm sorry," Pramod said softly. "But some paths cannot be changed."

Then he shuffled to the door and called for the slave. Help would come quickly now, but too late to matter. Aper's thread in the great tapestry of history had reached its end.

As servants rushed past him, as shouts for physicians echoed through the villa, Pramod made his way slowly back to his quarters. The letters burnt against his chest.

He thought of Metella, who would soon learn of her father's death. Of Julius, somewhere in Britannia, playing his own part in the great dance of history. Of Severus and Albinus, moving their pieces on a board they thought they controlled.

None of them understood. None of them could see the pattern as he did.

In his quarters, Pramod carefully secured the stolen correspondence. Then he took out his own letters — ones written in his hand but under Aper's seal — and prepared to send them on their way. The battle of Lugdunum must happen. Severus must defeat Albinus. The empire's future seemed more certain now that there was one less hand trying to unravel them.

Freedom

Metella stood in her father's study, where the physicians had finally pronounced him dead. The room still held his presence — scrolls left scattered on his desk, the lingering scent of the oils he used to ease his joints. But Aper himself was gone. His body had already been carried away, in preparation for his funeral.

Freedom and terror warred in her chest. She was legally independent after her father's death. No more arranged marriages, no more carefully orchestrated alliances. No more threats about Julius... but no protection, either. An unmarried woman of her age, even one from a good family, walked a precarious path in Rome.

Carmella, her most trusted servant, spoke softly from the doorway. "The house awaits your instructions."

The household. Gods, yes — dozens of lives now depended on her decisions. Slaves, freedmen, clients who had looked to her father for patronage. The villa itself, with its extensive gardens and workshops. All of it now teetered on the edge of chaos.

"Tell them..." Metella's voice caught. She cleared her throat and started again. "Tell them nothing changes for now. All positions remain as they were. We prepare for the funeral rites as befits a man of my father's standing."

Carmella nodded and withdrew, leaving Metella alone with her thoughts. She crossed to the household shrine, where the masks of her ancestors watched with empty eyes. Which god should she petition for help? Vesta, protector of the hearth? Juno, guardian of women? Or perhaps Fortuna, who might yet smile on her uncertain future?

Her hand found the small statue of Diana instead — the huntress, the independent one. The goddess who needed no man's protection. Her father had always frowned at her devotion to Diana, seeing it as unseemly for a woman of her status. But Diana had been her mother's favourite too, before the fever took her.

"Guide me," she whispered, placing a pinch of incense on the burner. "Show me the path through this darkness."

The smoke curled upward, carrying her prayer to whatever gods might listen. Metella watched it drift, remembering all the times she had stood in this very spot, praying for escape from under her father's thumb. She had escaped, and then she had been returned. And now her release from her father's control was final, but at what cost?

Fierce, unexpected grief hit her. For all his manipulation, all his schemes, Aper had been her father. He had taught her to read both Greek and Latin, and had encouraged her love of philosophy. He had protected her, even while using her as a game piece in his political matches.

"Mistress?" Another slave at the door. "The funeral clothiers have arrived. They require your approval for the arrangements."

Metella sighed. This was her life now — decisions, responsibilities, the weight of the household on her shoulders. Freedom, yes, but freedom was never free in Rome.

"I'll see them in the atrium," she said, her voice steady now. One last glance at Diana's stern face, one last prayer for strength, and then she turned to face her new reality. She would need to secure her position quickly. Make alliances of her own. Perhaps some of her father's political friends would transfer their patronage to her, but she couldn't count on it.

And somewhere out there was Julius. She hadn't expected to see her son again, not while her father lived.

But could she return to Britannia now? Would it make any difference to whatever path he had chosen?

After the funeral clothiers left, Metella remained alone in the atrium. Above her, the compluvium opened to the sky, where the first stars were beginning to appear. She thought of all the nights she had stood here with her father, learning about the constellations, and their power to guide travellers home.

"I am free," she whispered to those distant stars. The words tasted of both honey and ash.

Echoes of the Past

The *Bellingham's* dining room gleamed with its recent renovation, all clean lines and modern lighting that made the dated décor of their upstairs room feel even more like a time capsule. Ryan and Emma had secured a table near the window, where January's darkness pressed against the glass like black velvet.

"At least they've sorted this bit out," Emma said, gesturing at the fresh paint and new upholstery. "Though I'm getting attached to our 1970s paradise upstairs. The orange curtains are growing on me."

Ryan smiled, but his attention had drifted to an elderly woman sitting alone at a corner table, her knitting needles moving with practiced precision. Something about her...

The first howl cut through the quiet murmur of dinner conversation like a knife. Every head in the dining room turned toward the windows. The sound came again, closer this time, joined by others until the night seemed full of wolves.

"Dogs?" Emma asked, her hand frozen halfway to her wineglass. "But they don't sound like dogs. They sound like wolves?"

The woman's knitting needles stopped. In her lap, Ryan saw what looked like the half-formed shape of a wolf emerging from grey wool. She caught the attention of the waitress. "What is that sound?"

The waitress shook her head, her face pale. "I... I don't know. Dogs, maybe? From one of the farms?"

"Those aren't dogs," someone else muttered, and a ripple of uneasy agreement passed through the room.

Emma leaned across the table toward the woman. "That's beautiful work," she said, nodding at the knitting. "The detail on the wolf's face is incredible."

"Thank you." The woman smiled, but her eyes kept darting to the windows. "I've always had a fondness for wolves. Didn't expect to hear them in Hexham, though. Not tonight."

Her words struck Ryan like a physical blow. It was the accent which tipped him over though. A Welsh accent, but softened by the years away from home. He stared at her face, stripping away the decades, until he was back in Dafydd's flat in Caernarfon, staring at the photographs that had covered every wall.

Loretta. Dafydd's wife, who had vanished during the investiture of Prince Charles, along with a horde of Roman coins from the castle museum. Her disappearance had haunted Dafydd, had turned his flat into a shrine of frozen moments – Loretta young and laughing outside the Black Boy Inn, Loretta holding their daughter.

The howling grew louder.

"It's gotta be for a film?" another diner suggested.

Several people were now pressed against the cool glass, peering into the night. For what? The sight of an animal extinct in Britain for hundreds of years?

"Ryan?" Emma's voice seemed to come from far away. "You look like you've seen a ghost."

"Not a ghost," he said quietly. "But definitely someone who I wasn't expected to see here." He couldn't tear his eyes away from Loretta. How was she here? Where had she been all this time?

The wolves howled again, and this time Loretta began to pack away her knitting with trembling hands. As she stood to leave, her eyes met Ryan's across the room. He saw the moment of recognition, saw her realise that he knew who she was. For a heartbeat, time stopped. Then Loretta turned and hurried from the dining room, leaving her half-finished wolf behind.

"Ryan?" Emma reached across the table to touch his hand. "What is it? What's wrong?"

But before he could answer, another howl split the night, and the power went out.

Ryan stumbled out of the dining room into darkness. The air in the corridor ahead seemed to resist his movement. It felt like he was wading through ice water. He fumbled for his phone, jabbing at the screen, but it remained stubbornly dark.

"Loretta!" His voice echoed strangely in the darkness, as if the surrounding space had grown larger, emptier. "Loretta Wynne!"

Somewhere ahead, a floorboard creaked. Ryan moved forward, one hand trailing along the wall for guidance. The renovations had left this part of the hotel in a strange limbo — half-finished surfaces beneath his fingers alternating between rough plaster and peeling wallpaper. The cold intensified with each step until his breath fogged in front of his face.

"I know who you are," he called out. "I've been to Caernarfon. I've spoken to Dafydd."

Another creak, closer this time. Ryan's phone suddenly flickered to life, but the light was wrong — too blue, too weak, casting more shadows than it dispelled. He caught a glimpse of movement at the end of the corridor.

The door opened silently, spilling moonlight into the darkness. Ryan ran, his footsteps muffled by the thick carpet. The door began to swing closed.

"Wait!"

He caught the door just before it latched, pushing it open into what was a far nicer guest room than his. Moonlight streamed through the open window, painting the high end furniture in shades of silver and grey. Loretta stood by the window, her outline somehow less substantial than it had been in the dining room.

"Tell Dafydd I'm sorry," she said, her voice barely a whisper. "I can't stay. Tell him I never stopped loving him."

Then she was gone. Not through the window, not through

a door, just gone. Only the cold remained, and the sound of wolves in the distance.

RYAN STOOD IN THE EMPTY ROOM FOR SEVERAL LONG moments, struggling to process what he'd just witnessed. The power flickered back on, harsh electric light replacing the ethereal moonlight, making the room look ordinary. A room which was a damn sight better than his, but still empty of life other than himself.

He made his way back to the dining room in a daze. The corridor no longer felt supernaturally cold; it was just a hotel corridor, with the usual sounds of guests behind closed doors and the hum of the heating.

"There you are!" Emma called as he returned to their table. "Did you find her?"

Ryan sank into his chair, noting that the grey wool wolf still lay abandoned on Loretta's vacant seat. Around them, the dining room had returned to its normal atmosphere, conversations flowing as if nothing unusual had occurred.

"Must be that new Viking film they're shooting up by the wall," a man at the next table was saying authoritatively. "My cousin's working on the set. They've got all sorts of special effects — sound systems hidden in the trees, that sort of thing. Bit like that Hobbiton place in New Zealand. My doctor and his wife went there last year. They said it was the best thing since sliced bread."

"Of course," his companion agreed. "Makes perfect sense. Thought I was about to pass away! Gave me a hell of a shock!"

Ryan reached for his wine glass, needing something to steady himself. How could he explain what he'd just seen? That he'd just watched a woman who'd disappeared in 1969 vanish into thin air? That she'd asked him to deliver a message to the husband she'd abandoned over fifty years ago?

"Ryan?" Emma's voice was gentle. "What happened out there?"

He opened his mouth, then closed it again. The rational part of his brain was already trying to explain it away — tricks of light and shadow in a power cut, his imagination running wild after recognising Dafydd's long-lost wife. But he couldn't shake the memory of her final words, or the impossible way she'd disappeared.

"I..." he started, then shook his head. "I think I need to make a phone call. Tomorrow. To Wales."

Emma waited, but when he didn't elaborate, she simply reached across the table and squeezed his hand. "Okay," she said. "But you're going to tell me everything eventually, aren't you?"

Ryan nodded slowly, his eyes drawn to the abandoned knitting. The half-formed wolf seemed to watch him with knowing eyes, its grey wool catching the light in ways that made it look almost alive.

"Yeah," he said. "I will. When I figure out how to explain it myself."

Around them, the dining room had moved on. Dessert menus were being distributed, coffee orders taken. The wolves — or whatever they had been — were already becoming just another strange story to tell, a bit of excitement on an otherwise ordinary evening.

But Ryan knew he would never forget the impossible cold of that corridor, or the look in Loretta's eyes as she delivered her final message to the husband she'd left behind. Some mysteries, it seemed, didn't want to be solved. They just wanted to be witnessed.

Natural Explanations

The newsroom was quiet except for the clatter of keyboards. Jasper had left Charley sleeping in his flat, hoping to get some actual work done on his article. Only Rhema remained at this hour, the intern's dedication to fact-checking sometimes bordering on obsession.

The first howl stopped Jasper's fingers mid-sentence.

"Did you hear that?" Rhema's head snapped up from her computer screen.

Another howl answered the first, closer this time. Jasper pushed back from his desk and went to the window. The street below was empty, but something moved in the shadows between buildings.

"What the actual?" Rhema joined him at the window. "Those aren't dogs."

"Wolves?" Jasper said, the word feeling strange in his mouth. "That's impossible."

"Go down and check it out!"

Jasper snorted. "Hell no. I don't have a death wish." He squinted into the darkness. "Though this might explain..."

"Darby," Rhema finished his thought.

They stared at each other.

"Think about it," Rhema continued, excitement building. "What if he wasn't murdered at all? What if he was attacked by wolves? They ate most of the body but got disturbed before they could finish the head?"

Jasper frowned, his journalist's mind already connecting dots. "Like those lynx that were released illegally last year? When the proper rewilding groups were trying to do everything by the book?"

"Exactly!" Rhema was already searching the internet. "Look – Sweden just approved a wolf cull. Bunch of idiots more worried about their precious sheep than actual conservation. Even though the statistics show barely any sheep attacks."

"Never liked the Swedes," Jasper muttered, watching her pull up articles.

"Right? And now they're going completely anti-conservation." Rhema's fingers flew across the keyboard. "What if someone smuggled some wolves out before the cull? Released them here?"

The howling had grown closer, and Jasper stepped back from the window. It made sense — way more sense than ancient Roman curses or archaeological conspiracies. Just some idiot animal rights activists taking matters into their own hands.

"But his skull being found with those ancient remains..." he mused.

"Pure coincidence," Rhema finished. "Wolves would have dragged his body into the first sheltered spot they found. And that spot by the altar was perfect. Isolated, away from any humans, abandoned..."

"Protected from the elements," Jasper added. "Which would explain why the head was so well preserved."

They looked at each other, relief clear on both their faces. A rational explanation for Darby's death. One that didn't involve human trafficking, murder or ancient mysteries.

"I'll check with the police in the morning," Jasper said, already drafting the story in his head. "See if there have been any other reports of large predators in the area."

The howling had stopped now, but Jasper couldn't shake the feeling that something was still watching from the shadows. He turned back to his computer, determined to focus on facts, on evidence, on things that made sense.

"Natural explanations," he muttered to himself. "That's what we need. Not ghost stories or time travellers."

But even as he typed, he couldn't help noticing that Rhema kept glancing out the window, as if she wasn't quite convinced by their own rational explanation. And somewhere in the back of his mind, a small voice felt that the explanation was a little too convenient to be coincidental.

The Rivers Run Red

The wolves' song filled the night, but Bricius felt no fear. They were his brothers. Children of the same wild gods that had painted his soul with vengeance. As Julius led the others north, Bricius melted into the shadows, back towards Londinium.

The blue pigment still stained his skin, marking him as something other than human. A warrior blessed by Andraste, goddess of victory, and Camulos, god of war. The night wrapped around him like a cloak as he made his way to the port, where Roman ships clustered like water beetles on the Thames.

He knew which vessel would carry Albinus and the traitor. The governor's bireme stood proud among the other ships, its hull freshly painted, its deck alive with sailors preparing for dawn's departure. Bricius slipped aboard like a shadow, finding refuge among the amphorae in the hold. The smell of wine and oil would mask his presence from Roman noses.

That night, he listened to the creaking of timber and rope, to the calls of sailors and soldiers as they loaded the governor's belongings. When dawn came, he watched through gaps in the deck planking as Jane boarded, her head high, her smile bright — as if she were Boudica herself voyaging to Rome in triumph.

The ship pulled away from the dock, joining the flotilla heading for Gaul across the Oceanus Britannicus. Bricius waited as they cleared the river mouth, and the other ships grew distant, scattered by wind and current. Waited until the morning mist wrapped them in isolation.

Then he began his work. The first guard died silently, his blood hot on Bricius's hands. The second managed half a cry before the blade found his throat. Each death was an offering to the old gods, each step bringing him closer to his prey.

He found Jane near the governor's quarters at the stern. She saw him emerge from the shadows, blue-skinned and blood-streaked, and her eyes widened with recognition.

"How are you here?" she said, backing away.

"I am reborn as vengeance," Bricius said. "In blood and earth. While you played at being Roman, I became something else."

"The Iceni," she spat, "will be nothing more than a footnote to history. Your time is over. I sail to Rome to be part of an empire that will last forever."

"Our people are immortal, their lives live on in the trees, in the brooks, in the air." He lunged, his blade flashing. She ducked, but not fast enough — steel kissed flesh, drawing first blood.

Bricius was fury incarnate, blessed by gods older than Rome. His second strike opened her arm. His third found her ribs, once, twice, three times. Faster and faster.

He never saw the guard's spear. It came from behind, the iron point erupting from his chest. The force drove him forward, pinning both him and Jane to the ship's hull like butterflies mounted for display.

Their mingled on the deck, seeping between the wooden planks to feed the hungry sea below. His last thought was of satisfaction. He had completed his mission. The traitor would die with him.

The wolves' song reached him even here, carried on the salt wind.

Welcome, brother, they seemed to say.

Welcome home.

Fractured Trust

"Bricius is gone," Gar announced, materialising from the darkness. "Doubled back toward Londinium."

Julius cursed under his breath. He should have seen it coming – Bricius's rage at Jane's betrayal had been building like a storm. Him not being there could doom both him and Apple.

"One less barbarian to worry about," Marcus said, adjusting his sword belt, the bronze fittings catching the firelight, the engraved plates glinting as he shifted.

Julius caught the slight smirk on Marcus's face and his hand tightened on his own weapon. His hatred of his fellow soldier eclipsed his loathing of the Iceni and everything they'd done.

Apple pressed closer to Julius's side, and he positioned himself between her and Iolo, who hadn't stopped watching the girl with an unsettling hunger in his eyes. Julius tightened his grip on the hilt of his sword, debating whether he'd need to use it sooner rather than later.

A branch snapped in the darkness behind them. Gar swore under his breath, scanning the tree line. "We need to keep moving. Roman patrols will be everywhere by dawn." His voice was low, urgent.

Julius nodded, but his mind was torn between too many dangers. Iolo was a threat, but so were the Romans behind them.

And then there was Apple, whose safety had become his responsibility, and who was now at the mercy of a druid he did not trust. If Iolo claimed her for whatever rites the druids still clung to, how would he stop him? How could he?

And yet, even with the weight of Apple's fate pressing down on him, another thought burned through him, one he had no time for and yet couldn't shake.

Lillian.

He could still taste that first and only kiss. A stolen moment, brief but searing, before she had vanished. Before, the world had conspired to rip them apart. He had travelled across continents in the name of Rome, but in truth, his life had always been small—measured in the steps between battles, in the names of men he had buried, in the choices he had not been allowed to make.

But Lillian had been different.

Gar didn't wait. He grabbed Julius by the shoulder, yanking him forward. "Move. Now."

"Where's Lillian?"

Apple's whispered question cut through the chaos. Julius faltered. He'd forgotten their connection.

"Did they take her?"

"The Iceni think someone took her. There wasn't time to search for her," Julius explained, but Apple shook her head, her pale eyes fixed on his face.

"No," she said. "She's gone back."

"Back?" Julius frowned. "Back where?"

"To her time. Where she belongs." Apple's words carried a certainty that shook him.

Julius felt the world tilt beneath his feet. Of course. It made terrible sense – Lillian's strange knowledge, the way she sometimes spoke of things that hadn't happened yet. He knew, and yet he didn't, because he couldn't grasp the concept that she wasn't just from another place, she was from another time.

"The White One speaks the truth," Iolo's voice carried on the wind. "She sees the threads that bind time together. As do I." His hands reached toward Apple, but Julius stepped forward.

"Touch her and die," he growled. The threat only made Iolo smile.

"The blood of a creature that walks between times..." the druid mused. "Such power..."

"We're wasting time," Marcus interrupted. "The patrols will sweep north from the river. We need to move."

Julius studied the Roman officer's face in the darkness. How long had Marcus been playing his game of betrayal? Julius thought back to the missing pay, and to the death of Darius, and the convenient chaos that let Marcus position himself as both betrayer and saviour...

"You're right," Julius said. "We move north. But you walk in front where I can see you."

Marcus's eyebrows rose. "You don't trust me, brother?"

"I'm not your brother," Julius replied. "And no, I don't trust traitors."

They moved through the night like shadows, Julius keeping Apple close, watching Marcus ahead and Iolo behind. When the druid had summoned the wolves to protect their flank, he had woken something ancient in the land itself. But Julius couldn't shake the feeling their destinies were already decided. That they were just game pieces in the hands of the gods.

Apple pressed against him. "She'll be trying to get back to you, I'm certain of it," she whispered. "You should go back to Ithaca. That's where she'll find you."

Messages In Bottles

Neumegen stood at the edge of the Cockshaw Burn, watching the water tumble over ancient stones. The stream hadn't changed much since Roman times—unlike everything else in modern Hexham. Standing here made him realise how much he missed his life in Auckland, the familiar weight of his ledger books, the smell of polished wood and aged brass, the sound of horses plying their trade up and down Auckland's Queen Street.

He missed the bustling waterfront, where merchant ships from Sydney and San Francisco unloaded crates of tea, tobacco, and fine cloth, while Māori traders arrived in waka laden with flax and kauri gum. He could almost hear the rhythmic hammering from the shipyards and the chatter of dockworkers bartering over wages. In the heart of the town, the grand wooden buildings of Shortland Street housed banks, trading firms, and gentlemen's clubs, their verandahs crowded with men in waistcoats discussing gold prices and land deals over glasses of imported whiskey. And amid it all, Pramod's steady presence—his sharp mind, his quiet wisdom—had always been there to guide him. But here, in this fractured time, Neumegen was alone.

And now Loretta had abandoned them, too. Just disappeared, like she'd apparently disappeared from Caernarfon all those years ago.

The woman treated time like a playground, while he felt every displacement like a physical wound.

"Morning! Bit fresh for standing about, isn't it?"

Neumegen turned to find a cheerful-faced man approaching with a springer spaniel. The dog's tail wagged as it strained at its lead.

"Graham Ryan," the man introduced himself, extending his free hand. "Rarely see anyone else down here this early."

"Henry Neumegen." He shook the offered hand, noting the calluses that spoke of manual work. "Just... thinking."

"Best place for it," Graham agreed.

Neumegen gestured to something strapped to the other mans back. "Off to war?"

"What, this? It's my Minelab Equinox 900, but I call her Noxie." He patted the device. "I prefer searching to thinking, myself. Founding member of the Hadrian's Heroes Metal Detecting Club, and I've found some crackers over the years. We're always looking for new members."

Neumegen's interest sparked, despite preferring to avoid anything electronic. "Oh? What sort of things?"

"Bit of everything. Roman coins mostly. This whole area's thick with them. Found a beautiful fibula brooch last month." Graham's face lit up with genuine enthusiasm. "Been helping the police lately. With that business up at Ithaca Farm. It's the only time I've been authorised to metal detect up near the Wall. You have to be careful to stick to the rules for what is and isn't allowed around here. Big fines otherwise. No one wants some nighthawker ruining the area for the rest of us."

Neumegen frowned. "A nighthawker?"

"Illegal detectorists," Graham explained, shifting Noxie on his shoulder. "Sneak out under cover of darkness, dig up whatever they can find, and sell it on the black market. No reporting, no records—just lost history, gone for good. Gives the rest of us a bad name."

Neumegen nodded slowly, absorbing the information.

"Did any of the nighthawkers get to the coin hoard first," Neumegen asked. "Could some of them have gone missing?"

Graham frowned. "Hard to say. There's always talk of people sneaking around where they shouldn't be."

He scratched his chin. "Though… now you mention it, I heard that there was one chased off Ithaca Farm a while back."

Neumegen kept his expression neutral. "But isn't that near where they found the most recent hoard?"

"Mostly," Graham nodded. "The big hoard turned up closer to the lane, near where our missing mayor's car was found. Only found a scattering of coins at Ithaca Farm, but that was right by the remains of the old Roman fort's vault — where they used to keep the soldiers' pay. Makes you wonder if some of it was hidden in a hurry." He gave a half-smile. "Or stolen."

"Speaking of finds," Graham said, his eyes lighting up, "you won't believe what I turned up the other day. Best condition I've seen in years—had the finds liaison officer practically drooling." He patted the side pocket of his jacket as if the object might still be there. "Makes you wonder what else is still out there, waiting."

He pulled out his phone, swiping through photos. "Here – see? Nasty weather that day, but worth it. Look at the detail on the lid."

Neumegen leaned closer, studying the images. The box was exactly as Rhema's newspaper photos had shown, except… there, in the corner of one shot, barely visible in the mud: a small symbol scratched into the metal. His heart nearly stopped.

It was Pramod's maker's mark — the same one he'd used on his silver work in Auckland. But beside it was something else: a series of tiny numbers that could only be a date. CE 193, and what looked like an image of a Roman column. Neumegen traced a finger over the parchment, his mind slipping back to a reckless detour he'd taken when he was still new to time travel. To the vast and chaotic Rome. He had gone for one reason only: to stand before the newly completed column of Marcus Aurelius, with its spiralling reliefs crisp and untouched by centuries of weathering. But more than that, he had wanted to read the original dedicatory inscription, the very words that had once adorned its base before vanishing from history. He remembered craning his neck, heart hammering as he took in the towering monument, the stories of conquest carved in stone.

"Remarkable preservation," he managed to say about the box. "The Romans certainly knew their metallurgy."

"Don't they just? Found all sorts around here. This whole area was prime Roman real estate. The views, you see?" Graham gestured expansively. "You should come to one of our club meetings. We're always happy to welcome new members into the club, especially since you're new in town."

"Perhaps I will," Neumegen said absently, his mind already racing. Pramod was sending him a message through time — giving him an exact location and date.

"Well, must crack on," Graham said cheerfully. "Tide and time wait for no man, eh?"

Neumegen almost laughed at that. If only Graham knew. But as he watched the metal detectorist continue his morning walk, Neumegen felt hope rising for the first time in days. He had a destination now. A when and where.

He just had to figure out how to get there.

Roman Chains

Pramod watched as Metella dealt with yet another of her father's clients. She handled them perfectly — exactly the right balance of dignity and authority – but he could see the strain in her shoulders, the way her fingers twisted the rings she wore as markers of her status.

Even with her status as an independent woman after her father's death, and even with her substantial inheritance, Rome's social strictures wrapped around her like chains. The patriarchs of the great families circled like vultures, each hoping to acquire pieces of Aper's prosperous business and his extensive land holdings.

A slave appeared at his door. "The lady requests your presence in the study, when convenient."

Convenient. As if he wouldn't drop everything at her summons. But they had to maintain appearances — she the patrician daughter, he the trusted advisor. Even the slaves couldn't know the truth about their relationship.

He found her in Aper's study — her study now — surrounded by scrolls of accounts and property deeds. Her face brightened when she saw him, though she maintained a proper distance.

"The procurator wants to review father's investments," she said. "I need your expertise with the numbers."

It was a perfectly reasonable request. Aper had relied on

Pramod's mathematical skills often enough. But they both knew this was about more than accounts.

"The Western trade routes are solid," he said, scanning the documents. "The grain shipments from Egypt, the Hispanian silver mines. They are all good investments. Your father chose well."

"But will they respect contracts made with a woman?" Metella's question cut to the heart of their predicament.

Pramod considered carefully. A wealthy widow could maintain significant control over her own property in Rome, but an unmarried woman? Even one of patrician status? The vultures would seek any weakness, any excuse to challenge her authority.

"The contracts are legally binding," he said slowly. "But..."

"But I need powerful allies to enforce them." Metella's smile was bitter. "And those allies will want marriage agreements in return."

The words hung between them, heavy with implications. They both knew she would have to marry, eventually. Roman society demanded it, especially for a woman of her standing. The best they could hope for was finding someone who would respect her independence, who would allow their relationship to continue discretely. If they stayed in Rome. If they stayed in this time...

Pramod wanted nothing more than to go to her, to take her hand, to promise that given time, they would find a way out of this chaos.

"The period of mourning gives us at least a year before any marriage arrangements must be considered. And it gives me time to heal. And after that..."

"After that, what?" Metella's voice cracked like a whip. "You'll whisk me away to your magical future? Like you've been promising for months?"

Pramod stepped back, startled by her vehemence.

"I'm sick of your stories, Pramod. Your endless tales of a world to come, of mechanical horses and buildings that touch the sky. You speak of rescue, of taking me away from all this, yet where is your proof?"

"Metella, please—"

"No!" She slammed her hand on the desk. "I've listened to your promises, your fantastic tales. But what have I seen? Nothing! Just words, Pramod. Empty words while I watch my future crumbling around me. While these vultures circle, waiting to claim what's mine."

"The timing must be perfect," he tried to explain. "The threads of time—"

"More riddles! More mysteries!" She laughed bitterly. "Perhaps you are nothing but a clever storyteller. Perhaps I'm a fool for believing any of it. You're the one who left me, remember? Left me with child, only to return years later when that child is grown, and still with nothing to offer me, but happy to enjoy the fruits of my father's wealth."

The silence that followed was deafening. Pramod's heart ached at the tears he saw gathering in her eyes.

"I need more than stories now," she said quietly. "I need reality. And now that reality is here, in Rome, with responsibilities I cannot simply abandon."

Metella nodded, her face composed once more. But as she turned back to the accounts, Pramod saw her hand drift to the small statue of Diana on her father's desk — now her desk. The goddess of independence. Of defiance against society's expectations.

Old Habits

Holly shifted against Badger on the couch, acutely aware of every point of contact between their bodies. His arm lay across the back of the sofa, not quite touching her shoulders, maintaining that maddening distance she was determined to close.

"Have you heard about Lillian?" she asked, keeping her voice casual as she traced a finger along the seam of his jeans. "They're bringing her in for questioning. About those altars she was selling."

Badger tensed beside her. "What do you mean, questioning?"

"Proper interview under caution." She watched his face carefully. "Tomorrow morning."

"How do you know that?" His voice had that edge she remembered from their days together — the one that meant he was piecing things together.

Holly shrugged, letting her head rest against his shoulder. "Oh, you know. People talk."

"Which people?"

"Does it matter?" She tilted her face up toward his, but he wasn't looking at her. His eyes had that focused intensity she both loved and hated.

"Yes, it matters." Badger shifted away slightly, creating a space between them. "That's not the kind of information that just floats around. Someone told you."

"I have my sources." She tried for mysterious, but his laugh was hollow.

"Your sources." He stood up abruptly, leaving her to catch her balance. "Would that be the same kind of sources you had when we were together? The ones who always seemed to know everything about everyone?"

Holly's face flushed. "That's not fair."

"No?" He turned to face her, and she saw the hurt she'd put there years ago. "Then tell me. Who told you about Lillian?"

"It's not important—"

"Holly," his voice was quiet now. "Which constable are you sleeping with?"

The silence stretched between them. She could lie — she was good at lying — but something in his expression told her this was a moment of truth.

"Dave Matthews," she admitted finally. "But it's not what you think. We just... talk sometimes."

"Talk." The word dripped with skepticism. "Like we used to just talk?"

"For God's sake, Badger, that's ancient history! And you're hardly in a position to judge, mooning after Lillian like some lovesick teenager."

As soon as the words left her mouth, she knew she'd made a mistake. Badger's face closed off completely.

"Right," he said. "Thanks for the information about Lillian. I should go."

"Wait." Holly stood, reaching for him. "I'm sorry. I shouldn't have said that. Stay, please? We can order a takeaway, watch a film..."

But Badger was already gathering his coat. "Some habits don't change, do they, Hol? You're still collecting information like trading cards by adding notches in your bedpost, and I'm still stupid enough to think maybe this time it's different."

He left her standing there, the phantom warmth of his body still lingering on her skin, and the bitter taste of truth in the air.

BADGER DROVE TOO FAST ALONG THE DARK LANES TO Ithaca Farm, his conversation with Holly playing on repeat in his mind. What kind of fool was he, letting himself get pulled back into her games when Lillian was facing real trouble?

The farm's lights glowed ahead, and his headlights caught the flutter of police tape in the winter wind. A couple of news vans still lurked at the end of the drive, their occupants probably huddled inside against the cold, waiting for tomorrow's drama to unfold.

The antiques dealer let him in, locking the door behind him.

"She's in the kitchen," Nicole said. "I'll leave you to it."

He found Lillian in the kitchen, surrounded by paperwork spread across the table. His heart skipped a beat when she looked up, even with the shadows under her eyes and the worry etched on her face.

"I heard about tomorrow," he said, hovering in the doorway. "About the police interview."

"News travels fast." Her smile seemed forced. "Come to offer moral support, or to lambast me as well, like your father?"

Badger flinched at the mention of his father. The article in yesterday's paper had been brutal — accusing Lillian of "selling off the county's heritage to the highest bidder" and demanding a full investigation into the farm's "suspicious activities." It had brought every conspiracy theorist and amateur historian out of the woodwork, filling social media with wild theories and barely veiled threats. Some nutter had even thrown red paint over her gate last night, claiming it was "the blood of Britain's heritage" on her hands.

"That, and to apologise." He stepped into the kitchen, noting how the room felt different now — less like the warm heart of the farm and more like a command centre under siege. "I shouldn't have run off like that. I was upset..." He trailed off, remembering his childish jealousy over Julius. How could he explain that he'd been angry about competing with a man from two thousand years ago? That every time Lillian mentioned Julius, it felt like a reminder that whatever was between them wasn't enough?

The absurdity of it hit him. Here she was facing real trouble, and he'd been sulking over a Roman soldier who'd been dust for centuries.

"So you weren't chatting up your ex?" Lillian's voice was sharp. "The nurses at A&E have quite the gossip network."

Badger winced. "It wasn't like that."

"It doesn't matter what it was like." Lillian gestured at the papers surrounding her. "Look at this. Archaeological surveys, heritage assessments, police reports, solicitors' letters. They're trying to take my farm apart piece by piece, and where were you? Getting cosy with Holly Corben?"

"I'm here now."

"Are you?" She met his eyes properly for the first time. "Because I need someone I can trust, Badger, and not just when it's convenient for them."

The words hit him like a physical blow. He thought of all the times he'd pulled back, kept his distance, told himself he was being professional.

"I'm not going anywhere," he said quietly. "Whatever happens tomorrow, whatever they throw at you, I'm here."

Lillian studied him for a long moment, then pushed a stack of papers toward him. "Then help me make sense of this. They're claiming the altars were part of a scheduled monument. That I knew about their historical significance and tried to sell them, anyway. And you, of all people, know what's actually happened. You know I can't tell the police that I travelled back in time? And that's where your mother is, and Apple. And that your mother is probably the greatest threat to the world than a collection of Roman altars that some long dead ancestor happened to hide in my barn?"

Badger flinched at the mention of his mother, shame coursing through him. He'd been so wrapped up in his petty jealousy that he'd forgotten the bigger picture — that his own mother was out there somewhere in the past, plotting God knows what. That while he'd been sulking about Julius, Lillian had been carrying this impossible burden alone. How could he have been so selfish? So blind? The weight of his behaviour pressed down on him like a physical thing.

Badger pulled up a chair and reached for her hand. "We'll figure it out. Together."

She nodded, and if her eyes were a bit bright, neither of them mentioned it.

Business Meetings

Ryan stared at the note for the hundredth time, the paper crumpled from his repeated handling. He hadn't slept, his mind replaying Loretta's impossible disappearance over and over. Now this — an anonymous message slipped under his hotel room door, requesting a midnight meeting at the Roman vault on Ithaca Farm.

He shouldn't go alone. He should tell Emma, tell the police, tell someone. But after what he'd witnessed last night, who would believe him?

The wolves started howling as he parked his car at the end of Ithaca Farm's drive. The sound sent shivers down his spine — too similar to last night's supernatural chorus. He clicked on his torch, following the worn path toward the vault, its entrance now properly excavated after its discovery during the first archaeological survey.

A figure emerged from the shadows, hands raised to show they were empty. "Mr Francis? From the Art Loss Register?"

"Who are you?"

"Just... someone who made a mistake." The man's voice was thick with shame. "I never meant for any of this to happen. Never even sold a single one of the coins I found."

Ryan's torch revealed a middle-aged man, outdoorsy type, wearing a worn Barbour jacket. The kind of person you'd pass on any country walk without a second glance.

"I don't understand," Ryan said carefully. "What coins? Are you talking about Roman coins?"

The man shifted uncomfortably. "That's right, you're not a local, are you? Have you ever heard of nighthawking?"

"Should I have?"

"It's what they call us. The illegal detectorists." The man's voice was bitter. "Though that makes it sound organised. Professional. I was just... curious. It all started when I was a kid, finding Roman sinkers on the beach. Lead weights, you know? For fishing nets. Kept every one of them in my dad's old map drawers. Then I got a cheap metal detector from Argos, and..." He shrugged helplessly. "It became an obsession. Finding pieces of history, holding them in your hand. But I never sold anything. Never wanted to profit from it."

Ryan frowned. "You're telling me you just went out and dug up some Roman coins, and didn't tell anyone?"

"Not just me. There are dozens of us. Hundreds maybe. All over Britain. Most stick to public land, but some..." He trailed off, glancing toward the farm. "Some of us went where we shouldn't."

"So you found some coins, and now what? You want to sell them to me? Or what? What's going on? Why am I standing in a field in the middle of the night?"

The sound of howling split the night air. The man glanced over his shoulder.

"Look," he said, reaching into his pocket. "I want to make it right. These shouldn't be hidden away in a drawer." The man laughed hollowly. "And believe what you want, but after what's been happening around here lately — all the deaths and the missing people — I just want rid of them."

He poured a handful of coins into Ryan's palm. In the torchlight, Ryan could make out the profiles of long-dead emperors, the metal worn smooth by centuries underground.

Another howl split the night, this one so close it made both men jump. The nighthawker's face paled.

"I have to go. And Mr Francis?" He paused in the darkness. "I'm sorry about all of it. Never thought it would lead to... well, everything that's happened."

He melted into the shadows before Ryan could respond. The coins felt impossibly heavy in Ryan's hand, each one a piece of stolen history finally finding its way home.

The wolves called again, their voices echoing off the ancient stones of the vault. Ryan hurried back to his car, the coins secure in his pocket, wondering if Emma would believe any of this when he told her. Wondering if he believed it himself.

R YAN'S HANDS SHOOK AS HE TRIED TO TRANSFER THE COINS from his palm to his jacket pocket. The metal felt unnaturally cold against his skin, as if the coins had retained the chill of centuries buried in the earth. One slipped from his fingers, falling silently into the darkness near the altar.

He didn't notice its loss. Didn't see it settle into the soft earth, finding its place among the ancient stones as if it had always been meant to rest there. His mind was already on his car, on escape, on the need to get away from whatever rabid dogs were out there, whose howls seemed to be closing in from all sides.

But history noticed.

As Ryan's footsteps faded into the night, something emerged from the shadows near the altar. A wolf, but not quite solid — its form wavered like a heat haze, caught between existence and memory. Its paws made no sound as it approached the fallen coin, and when it lowered its head to sniff the metal, its breath disturbed no dust.

The wolf's eyes gleamed with ancient intelligence. Here was a piece of its time, returned to sacred ground. It threw back its head and howled — a sound that rippled not just through space, but through time itself.

The howl echoed in Roman Britannia, where Bricius heard it as his life ebbed away.

It rang through the stones of Hadrian's Wall, where Julius and Apple paused in their flight.

It resonated in the marbled halls of Rome, where Pramod's hand faltered as he wrote his letters.

And it came back to the present, where Ryan Francis

sprinted the last few meters to his car, unaware that he had just played his own small part in a story that spanned centuries.

Behind him, the ghostly wolf settled beside the coin, a guardian of the thin places where past and present merged. Its howl faded into silence, but its echo would continue, rippling through time until all the scattered pieces of history found their way home.

Sacred Hunger

Iolo's fingers traced patterns in the air as he walked, leaving trails of power that only he could see. The white one would be his soon. Such perfect timing — with the wolf moon rising, the barriers between time grew thinner. Her blood would open doors he'd only ever heard whispered about in the halls of the ancient druids. Men long gone, slaughtered by the Romans.

The journey back to the Iceni stronghold near Ithaca Fort had been torturous — not from the physical demands of the trek, but from the maddening proximity of the moon girl.

Every night as they made camp, Iolo had tried to get close to her, to perform even the smallest ritual with a strand of her hair or a drop of her blood. But the Roman had watched him like a hawk, keeping Apple always within arm's reach. Even Gar had positioned himself between them, as if sensing Iolo's hunger for her power.

The others didn't understand — couldn't understand — the significance of a creature that walked between times. But now, now they were back in familiar territory, where the old magic ran strong through the earth. Here, beside the sacred pool that would one day be known as Tyne Green, where the Romans had never found their hidden shrines, Iolo could prepare properly.

The waters remembered the old ways. They remembered

the sacrifices that fed them. They would help him when the time came.

He had prepared the grove. Nine rowan trees in a circle, their bark stripped in precise patterns. The symbols he'd carved would channel her power, prevent it from dispersing into the night air. Each cut in the living wood had been made with a bronze knife, each stroke accompanied by words in a language that Rome had tried to destroy.

The altar stone waited at the circle's centre. He'd spent hours cleaning it, scraping away moss and lichen until the ancient carvings emerged. Spirals and knots that spoke of binding, of transformation, of doors opening between worlds. The stone remembered its purpose — he could feel its hunger matching his own.

His collection of knives lay arranged on a deerskin, each one chosen for its specific purpose. Bronze to open the veins, iron to pierce the heart, stone to separate flesh from bone. The old ways demanded precision. The white one's power had to be harvested properly, each drop of blood dedicated to a different god, each breath captured in clay vessels sealed with wax and herbs.

Iolo hummed as he prepared the bindings — strips of leather soaked in a mixture of mushroom spores and his own blood. They would keep her still while allowing her to feel everything. The gods demanded suffering with their sacrifices. Pain was the key that opened their doors.

The wolves he'd called would help. They would form the outer circle, their voices raising the power, their breath creating the mist that would hide his work from mortal eyes. He could feel them now, padding through the darkness, drawn by his will and the scent of coming death.

Iolo pulled the white hair from his pouch — a few strands plucked from Apple's sleeping blanket when the others weren't watching. He twisted them into a gossamer thin cord, whispering names that made the air itself recoil. The binding would be complete once he added her blood to it.

Such power she contained!

He could see it shimmering around her like heat waves. He could taste it on the air when she was near.

A creature that walked between times, that existed simultaneously in past and future. Her death would tear open the veil between worlds.

Iolo arranged his bowls. Clay for catching blood, silver for holding power, wood for gathering her last breaths. Each one marked with symbols that would make the uninitiated eyes bleed if they looked too long upon them.

Soon. Very soon. The Roman couldn't watch her every moment. The Roman soldier's dedication to keeping her alive would make her death even sweeter. Iolo's hands shook with anticipation as he made the final preparations.

The white one would open the way, and the old gods would walk in Britain once more.

Brothers In Arms

"That's it, I'm finally done playing soldier," Marcus announced, securing his pack. "And after I retrieve the gold Darius buried for me, I'll start my new life with a farm in the northern lands. Beyond Rome's reach."

Julius blocked his path. "The pay chest gold? That doesn't belong to you. It belongs to Rome."

"Come now, brother." Marcus's smile was cold. "The empire is too busy fighting among themselves to worry about a little missing gold. They'll just send some more. But mark my words, it won't be long before they forget about this cursed edge of their filthy empire as it is. Isn't that what I heard your little snowbird saying?"

"Leave her out of this. We're talking about the coins you stole. Coins which our men need to buy supplies and to pay debts, and to live in this country."

"An unfortunate sacrifice that they've all had to make on my behalf. The army won't let them starve." Marcus adjusted his sword belt. "Now, if you'll excuse me, I have a new life to begin. Perhaps I'll even find myself a bride. I hear British women make fine farmers' wives."

"You're not going anywhere." Julius's hand moved to his gladius. "That gold belongs to Rome. Show me where it is, and I will let you leave."

Marcus laughed. "Rome? What has Rome ever given us but scars and empty promises? I've earned this retirement."

The first clash of their swords echoed through the Iceni encampment as the two Romans circled each other, their movements a deadly dance they'd practiced together countless times.

Marcus struck first, a swift thrust that Julius barely deflected. Their blades rang against each other, a familiar sound turned brutal. These were not practice blows — each strike meant to kill.

"You were always too loyal," Marcus spat, blood running from a cut above his eye. "Too concerned with duty and honour."

Julius pressed forward, his technique perfect even in rage. "And you were always a snake."

They broke apart, then clashed again. Both men had trained together since boyhood, and knew each other's moves intimately. But Marcus fought with the desperate energy of a man reaching for freedom, while Julius's strikes carried the weight of betrayal.

Blood spattered the ground as their blades found flesh. A cut here, a slash there . Death by a thousand small wounds. Marcus's sword opened Julius's leg. Julius's blade bit into Marcus's arm.

"Think about it," Marcus parried a vicious strike. "Come with me. Leave Rome behind. We could both be rich men."

Julius's response was another attack, forcing Marcus back. "You betrayed everything we stood for."

"What we stood for?" Marcus laughed, the sound ugly. "We stood for Rome's greed. For old men's ambitions. I'm taking what I deserve."

Their swords locked, bringing them face to face. Blood and sweat mingled as they strained against each other.

"You're no better than a deserter," Julius growled.

"And you're a fool," Marcus replied, then spat in Julius's face. "You should have left with your mother."

Julius' blade wavered. "What do you know of my mother?"

"Oh, I know all the secrets, brother." Marcus's laugh was cruel. "About your grandfather, the great Publius Septimius Aper.

Did you really think a prostitute's son could rise so far up the ranks without help? Aper's been watching over you your whole life, making sure his grandson succeeded — even if he couldn't publicly claim you."

The words hit Julius like physical blows. Metella was his mother? His sword arm dropped slightly as his mind reeled with the implications.

The moment of distraction was all Marcus needed. He broke away, disappearing into the darkness of the forest. Julius started after him, but his wounded leg betrayed him, sending him stumbling to one knee.

Gar emerged from the shadows. "Let him go. The wolves will find him."

Julius's gaze lingered on the blackness where Marcus had disappeared, the weight of the situation settling over him. He swallowed hard, his throat tight with unease. "Who knows what level of mayhem he will cause beyond the wall? He has to..." he paused, his thoughts heavy on his shoulders. "Die."

WHILE JULIUS AND MARCUS HAD FOUGHT THEIR PRIVATE war, Iolo had seized his moment. The white one lay bound now upon his altar — the same stone that had held Darby's head, still stained with that sacrifice's blood. The ancient grooves in the stone, carved by druids centuries before him, would channel her power properly when the time came.

Apple's white hair gleamed in the moonlight, making her glow against the dark stone as she struggled against the leather bindings. He'd had to bind her mouth with cloth to silence her blasphemous words she'd thrown in his face when he'd first snatched her.

Iolo arranged his knives with practiced precision, each one placed exactly where the ritual demanded. Bronze to open the veins, iron to pierce the heart, stone to separate flesh from bone. The order mattered. Each cut would feed a different god, each drop of blood opening another door between the worlds.

A pack of wolves emerged, padding silently into the grove.

Iolo smiled — his summoning had worked. The beasts

formed a circle around the altar as he'd intended, their eyes fixed on Apple with an intensity he didn't quite understand. Iolo shook off his unease and sprinkled dried herbs around Apple's bound form — wolfsbane, yew, and toxic mushrooms he'd gathered under the dark moon. Their poison would keep her spirit from fleeing when he began the cutting. The gods demanded consciousness during the sacrifice.

The girl twisted against her bonds, her pale eyes wide above the gag. There was something in her gaze — not just fear, but knowledge. As if she understood something about this moment that he didn't.

He raised the first knife, its edge hungry for blood – and began to chant. The words were older than Rome, older than the stones themselves. They spoke of doors between worlds, of gods who walked in darkness, of power that could reshape reality itself.

The wolves should have joined his chant, should have added their voices to his ritual. Instead, they remained silent. He couldn't stop to worry about that now. They would join in soon. He had commanded it.

Somewhere in the darkness, a shout rang out. The Roman, no doubt, finally discovering his precious charge was missing. But he would be too late. The ritual had begun, and nothing could stop it now.

Iolo pressed the bronze blade against Apple's throat, ignoring the restless shifting of the wolves around the altar. One cut to begin. One cut to start the unravelling of time itself. He smiled, caressing his knives. "The others didn't have the old knowledge. They didn't know the proper words, or the proper cuts. So many tried, and so many failed. It's why they're all dead." He held up the bronze blade, letting it catch the moonlight. "But this knife remembers. It has tasted the blood of others who walked between worlds."

Iolo increased the volume and intensity of his chant, his words in a language that made the air itself shiver. And finally, the wolves took up the sound, their howls harmonising with his voice. Power gathered like storm clouds above the altar.

"Julius will come," Apple said, but Iolo noted the first trace of fear in her voice.

"Let him come." Iolo raised the knife. "His grief will add its own power to the ritual. Now, moon-walker, let us begin," he said as his blade descended toward Apple's throat, and the wolves' song reached a fever pitch.

The time of sacrifice had begun.

Curiosity Killed The Cat

Nicole set down another antique walking stick in the 'to be valued' pile, trying to focus on the familiar comfort of cataloguing. The sitting room at Ithaca Farm was quiet except for the scratch of her pen and the murmur of voices from the kitchen where Lillian and Badger were still talking.

Her phone buzzed — another message from Mel.

Missing you.

London's not the same without you here.

She smiled, remembering their earlier conversation. He'd been so understanding about missing Valentine's Day, suggesting they could have their own celebration when she got back. Back to normal life. Back to a world where ancient artefacts didn't get people killed and where women didn't vanish into thin air.

The next walking stick in her pile caught her attention — an elegant Victorian sword stick with a sterling silver handle crafted in the shape of a wolf's head. The craftsmanship was exquisite, the wolf's eyes set with tiny garnets that caught the lamplight. As she turned it in her hands, a howl echoed from somewhere outside, making her jump. Just some local dog, she told herself, though it sounded different from any dog she'd heard before.

That's when she saw it — a flicker of light through the window, moving between the trees at the edge of the property. Someone was out there with a torch.

She should tell Lillian and Badger. That would be the sensible thing to do, especially after everything that had happened. But something made her hesitate. They were finally having what seemed like an important conversation in the kitchen, and hadn't there been enough drama already?

It was probably one of those damnable nighthawkers. Well, she'd give them a something to find. The sharp end of her tongue. Lillian had enough to worry about without having this on her plate as well.

Nicole looked down at the sword stick in her hands. The silver wolf seemed to watch her with its semi-precious eyes, as if daring her to investigate. She tested the mechanism — it was well-maintained; the blade sliding smoothly from its wooden sheath.

"This is stupid," she muttered to herself, but she was already moving toward the door. It could just as well be one of the journalists trying to get some atmospheric photos for whichever tabloid they worked for. She could tell them to clear off herself.

Another howl split the night as she stepped outside, closer this time. The sword stick felt reassuring in her hand as she moved toward the bobbing light, her sensible London self screaming at her to go back inside. But she'd already seen too much to believe in sensible anymore.

Nicole picked her way across the field, cursing her inappropriate footwear and her own stupidity. The sword stick's blade glinted in her phone's light as she swept it back and forth across the ground, more concerned about twisting an ankle in a rabbit hole than any actual need for defence.

The vault's entrance loomed ahead, its ancient archway a deeper darkness against the sky. The torch light had vanished, but something drew her forward, anyway. Perhaps it was professional curiosity?

Another howl echoed through the darkness, seeming to

come from everywhere and nowhere at once. Nicole froze, trying to pinpoint the source. The sound was strange — muffled, as if she were hearing it through water or... through walls that didn't exist anymore. The hair on the back of her neck rose as more howls joined the first, surrounding her in their ethereal chorus.

"Right," she muttered, grip tightening on the sword stick. "Time to go back."

But as she turned, her phone's light caught something near the vault's entrance — a glint of metal in the dirt. She hesitated, then moved closer, her professional instincts taking over. If someone had been digging here, she should probably call the police.

The vault's archway swallowed her phone's light as she approached. The howls grew more distinct yet somehow further away, as if she and the wolves existed in different layers of time. Like those old photographs where the image had been double-exposed, reality seemed to be overlapping itself.

Nicole shook her head, trying to clear it of such fanciful thoughts. She was an antiques dealer from London, not some character in a gothic novel. She had a shop to run, a potential boyfriend to get back to, a life that made sense.

But as she stood in the vault's entrance, sword stick in one hand and phone in the other, that sensible London life felt very far away. The darkness ahead of her felt very alive.

The wolves called again, their voices now seeming to come from behind ancient walls that had crumbled centuries ago. Nicole debated backing away from the vault, suddenly certain that whatever she'd seen, whatever had been here, might be better left uninvestigated.

Curiosity overwhelmed her, and she crouched down, directing her phone's light at the metallic glint. Her fingers closed around something round and cold. A coin. She brushed away the soil with her thumb, revealing the profile of a Roman emperor pressed into ancient gold.

Her breath caught in her throat. She should report this, should put it back, should—

Movement caught her eye. She lifted her phone, its beam

cutting through the darkness to reveal... nothing. But then it appeared again. The massive form of a wolf, but not quite solid. Its outline shimmered, its paws making no impression on the muddy ground.

Nicole's grip tightened on the sword stick, but the spectral wolf showed no aggression. Instead, it padded a few steps away from her, then turned back, its eyes reflecting her phone's light with impossible intelligence. The wolf moved forward again, then turned once more, its intent unmistakable.

It wanted her to follow.

"This is madness," Nicole whispered, but her feet were already moving. The coin felt impossibly heavy in her hand as she followed the ghostly wolf away from the vault.

More ethereal shapes materialised from the darkness. More wolves, each one larger than any modern wolf could be. They formed a procession, leading her across the fields toward Tyne Green. The howls grew stronger now, no longer muffled by phantom walls but still carrying that strange, otherworldly quality.

Nicole found herself walking in a daze, surrounded by these impossible creatures. Her rational mind screamed at her to run back to the farmhouse, to the warmth and light and sanity of the kitchen, where Lillian and Badger sat. But something deeper, something about the magic in the air, kept her moving forward.

The wolves led her toward the ancient pool at Tyne Green, where flickering lights suggested another presence. As they drew closer, she could hear chanting, which set her teeth on edge. Something was happening by those dark waters. Something that the wolves — these ancient guardians of Britain's wild places — wanted her to see.

Nicole followed her spectral guides into the darkness, the sword stick steady in her hand, wondering if she'd crossed the line between curiosity and madness. And what would Mel say about this?

Lift the Barrier

"Apple!" Julius's shout echoed through the empty Iceni camp. His wounded leg buckled as he searched their sleeping area, finding only her abandoned blanket. The blood from Marcus's blade had soaked through his makeshift bandage, each step sending fresh agony through his body.

He found Gar by the fire. "She's gone. That devil has taken her. Where are they?"

Gar's face darkened. "The ancient pool where the old ones made their sacrifices."

Julius's heart seized. Sacrifice. The word he'd been dreading since he first saw the hunger in Iolo's eyes whenever he looked at Apple. Without her, how would he ever find his way back to Lillian?

They moved as fast as Julius's injury would allow, following tracks that only Gar could see in the darkness. The howling of wolves grew stronger as they approached the water, but the sound was distorted, as if it fought against Iolo's magic.

Then they saw a circle of rush lamps surrounding the ancient altar, their flames burning an unnatural blue. The barrier they created was visible in the air. And beyond it...

"No!" The cry tore from Julius's throat.

Apple lay bound on the altar, her white hair ghostly in the light. Iolo stood over her, a knife pressed against her throat, his chanting making the very air shiver with power.

Julius lurched forward, but hit the barrier like a physical wall. It felt like trying to run across the mudflats, each movement requiring impossible effort. "Iolo!" he shouted, but his voice was swallowed by the charged air.

"His magic... he's using the old ways. The very old ways," Gar grunted beside him, pressing his own hands against the invisible resistance.

Julius pushed harder, feeling the barrier bend but not break. Each step was agony, both from his wound and from the magical resistance. Blood ran fresh down his leg, but he couldn't stop. Apple was his link to Lillian; to everything that mattered.

Through the shimming air, he saw Iolo raise the knife higher. The druid's voice rose to a fever pitch, and the rush lights flared brighter, strengthening the barrier.

"The wolves," Gar cried. "Look at the wolves."

Around the circle, ghostly shapes materialised – more wolves, their forms flickering like bad memories. They hurled themselves against Iolo's barrier from the other side, making it ripple and weaken.

But would they break through in time? Julius watched helplessly as the bronze blade began its descent toward Apple's throat, his own voice joining the wolves' howls in a cry of desperate rage.

"Did you hear the door?" Lillian asked, breaking off her conversation with Badger. They'd been so absorbed in discussing tomorrow's police interview that they'd almost missed the sound.

"Nicole?" Badger moved to the window. "What the hell is she doing out there? It's freezing."

They could just make out Nicole's figure moving across the field, her phone light bobbing in the darkness. The sound of howling echoed across the property, making Lillian's head throb with an eerily familiar pain.

"Nicole!" Badger called out, opening the kitchen door and pulling on his boots. "Come back!"

But Nicole showed no sign of hearing them. She moved as if in a trance, following something they couldn't see.

"Something's wrong." Lillian jammed her feet into her walking boots, not bothering with the laces. "Come on, we have to stop her."

They hurried after her, their shouts dying in the frigid air. The howls seemed to come from everywhere and nowhere, and Lillian's headache intensified with each step. Reality felt thin here, like worn fabric about to tear.

"Nicole, stop!" Badger tried again, but she continued her eerily purposeful walk away from Ithaca Farm.

Lillian's vision began to blur, the landscape seeming to shift and overlap with itself. She could see the modern fields, but also ancient trackways, ghostly walls that had crumbled centuries ago. Her head felt like it would split open. Now Badger was having to support her as they stumbled across the uneven ground, trying to keep up with Nicole.

Then suddenly Nicole stopped walking. She stood motionless in the darkness, the sword raised in front of her. As Lillian and Badger caught up to her, Lillian reached out and grabbed Nicole's arm.

Nicole's skin was ice cold, but that wasn't what made Lillian gasp. The moment she touched Nicole, everything changed. The world split open, past and present existing simultaneously. She could see what Nicole was seeing — the spectral wolves, their forms flickering like candlelight. They were gathered around something in the distance, by the water's edge...

"Oh god," Lillian whispered, her grip tightening on Nicole's arm. "I can see them. I can see Apple. And... Julius?"

Through the layers of time, she saw a familiar figure standing by while Apple was tied to an ancient stone altar while the ragged man from her nightmares sliced into her friend's neck.

Lillian moved without thinking. Her fingers closed around the sword stick's handle, the silver wolf's head cold and solid against her palm. Nicole released it without resistance, still lost in her trance.

Time fractured around her as she ran.

Each step carried her through different ages, through modern grass and across ancient stones, along paths that had existed and paths that never would. The rush lights flickered like dying stars, their barrier tangible even to her.

A war cry tore from her throat as she plunged through the magical barrier. It felt like pushing through a wall of thorns, but her momentum and the purity of her purpose carried her through.

The druid never saw her coming. His attention was fixed on Apple, on the blood already trickling from the shallow cut he'd made.

Lillian's sword stick found the spot between the druid's shoulders with surgical precision, and she felt the moment it severed his spine, and the resistance of flesh and bone gave way.

Iolo's scream existed in multiple times at once as the rush lights exploded in a cascade of blue sparks. The ghostly wolves surged forward as the barrier collapsed, their forms becoming more solid with each step.

"Lillian!" Julius's voice reached her through the chaos. He was limping towards her, his leg dark with blood.

Lillian ignored him. Apple was still bound to the altar, bleeding from her neck. Lillian yanked the sword free from Iolo's falling body and slashed at the leather straps holding Apple down. Behind her, she could hear Badger shouting, but his words made no sense — he was seeing only shadows, only pieces of what was happening.

"The coin!" Nicole's voice cut through. "Use the coin!"

Lillian turned to see Nicole on her knees in the mud, one hand stretched out toward them. A Roman coin fell from her fingers and bounced on the stones.

"Choose," the wind seemed to whisper. And in her heart, she knew that the coin would only be enough to save one of them.

Lillian's heart tore in her chest as she looked between them – Julius, the man she loved across centuries, and Apple, young and vulnerable and so far from her own time. She could only save one.

Julius met her eyes, and she saw in them that he

understood. They were from different times, different worlds. Any future between them would be borrowed, stolen. But Apple... Apple should have a real life here, in her own time.

"Apple," Lillian whispered, the word feeling like glass in her throat. Julius smiled, sad but proud, as if he'd known all along what she would choose.

And then the moment began to fade. The worlds were separating again, the barriers between times reasserting themselves. Julius grew less substantial with each breath.

"No," Lillian reached for him, her hand passed through Julius like smoke. "Please, not yet..."

The last thing she saw was Julius's sad smile. Then he was gone, leaving only the moonlight, the winter's air, and Apple's very real body bleeding on the ground beside the water.

Nicole remained on her knees, shaking. Badger stood frozen, trying to process the fragments he'd witnessed. And Lillian still gripped the bloody sword stick, its silver wolf's head warm now against her palm.

"What do we do now?" Badger's voice seemed to come from very far away.

Lillian looked down at the weapon in her hand, and then at the very ordinary English field, which had just hosted an impossible convergence of times.

"Now," she said, "we go home. And we forget all about this. It's over."

The tears came then, falling onto the silver wolf's head of the sword stick still clutched in her hand. She'd chosen right — she knew she had, but it hurt. Like a thousand cuts with a sword, it hurt. Some sacrifices left wounds that would never truly heal.

The Last Journey

Neumegen stood alone at the site where the ancient altar had once been, before its stones were carted away to build Hexham Abbey. He could feel the power of time thrumming beneath his feet, the resonance of centuries of ritual.

Lillian's coin glinted in the mud where it had fallen. He picked it up, turning it over in his hands, feeling its weight. A piece of time itself. Like all the objects that allowed them to travel – his watch and sovereigns, and Pramod's various treasures. Lillian's coin held the power to breach the walls between years.

Lillian had called him an hour ago. Her voice had been shaky but determined as she explained what had happened at Tyne Green. Apple was at the hospital now, getting stitches for the cut on her neck. "Deep, but not life threatening," Lillian had assured him. "She'll be fine." She didn't mention Julius, but she didn't need to. The catch in her voice had said everything. Neumegen had listened, offered what comfort he could, and then made his way to where it had all happened. He knew what he had to do.

From his pocket, he withdrew a small carved wolf he'd found among Pramod's belongings in the library.

His friend's precise workmanship was evident in every detail, from the curve of the creature's spine to its watchful eyes. The mere existence of the carved wolf supported his feeling that Pramod would return to Britain, but not to this time. Pramod would return to Britannia. Neumegen felt it in his bones. There was a reason which would lead Pramod back. And although Neumegen couldn't quite grasp the why, he now knew it wasn't his place to disrupt what time had in store for his friend.

He could go to Rome now. Neumegen knew the exact date, and he knew he could find Pramod easily enough. But how many journeys did he have left? Each trip took its toll, ageing him in ways that normal means couldn't measure. And his heart... his heart was in Auckland, in his shop. In a place without the internet, or televisions. Without tele-evangelists and without billionaires destroying the planet.

He dug a small hole where the altar had stood, placing Lillian's coin and Pramod's wolf inside, before covering them with soil. A message through time for his friend to find when the moment was right.

Neumegen pulled out his 18-carat gold half hunter Russells of Liverpool pocket watch. The case caught the weak winter sunlight, its engravings as crisp as the day it was made. From his waistcoat pocket, he retrieved a gold half sovereign, dated 1863, and struck by the Sydney Mint, his ticket home.

His fingers found the watch's winding crown, its ridged surface familiar as an old friend. The small cabochon-cut sapphire adorning the crown pulsed with an inner light, deep blue and perfect. He turned it counterclockwise, watching the slender hands move across the dial, aligning to his chosen hour.

Wars were coming. And wars had already been. But he'd had enough of being witness to time's pivotal points. He wanted the comfort of his ledger books, the sound of horses' hooves on Queen Street, the chatter of dockworkers and the hammering from the shipyards, and the silent reading of books by lamplight.

With practiced precision, he pushed the crown back into place. Then, with one last look at the place where past and present had collided, he flicked the half sovereign onto the sacred ground.

The world realigned, and Henry Neumegen returned home.

Epilogue

THE HEXHAM HERALD
February 28, 2025

MISSING MAYOR LINKED TO MUSEUM
THEFT AND LOCAL DEATH
By Jasper Fletcher

Police have confirmed that Jane Badrick, Hexham's
former mayor and centre of recent investigations, is
believed to have fled to mainland Europe following her
alleged involvement in both the theft of Roman
artefacts from Caernarfon Castle and the death of
local archaeologist, Anson Darby.
Speaking at yesterday's press conference, Detective
Sergeant Bishop stated that evidence suggests Darby
stumbled upon Badrick's illegal activities at Ithaca
Farm, leading to a fatal confrontation. "We believe
Jane Badrick was using her political connections and
professional credentials to facilitate the sale of
antiquities," Bishop explained. "Mr Darby appears to
have been in the wrong place at the wrong time."
The Roman coins stolen during the 1969 investiture of
Prince Charles at Caernarfon Castle, and subsequently
taken by Badrick, have been returned to the museum,
thanks to the efforts of the Art Loss Register working

with an unnamed informant. How the coins made their way to Hexham remains unclear, though investigators suggest they may have passed through multiple hands over the decades.

In a related development, the recently discovered Roman altars at Ithaca Farm have been authenticated by experts and cleared of any connection to illegal activities. Initial concerns about their provenance have been dismissed, with farm owner Lillian Arlosh receiving praise for her "exemplary cooperation" with heritage authorities.

Despite attempts by the British Museum to acquire the altars, they will remain in the region, finding a permanent home at the Roman Army Museum. This arrangement has been made possible through an unexpected source — a substantial endowment from the publishers of Loretta Hambly's bestselling series of knitting books. When asked about this unusual partnership, museum curator Dr Martha Andrews commented, "We're delighted to keep these important artefacts in their historical context, regardless of how the funding materialised."

The altars will go on display next month, accompanied by a new exhibition about Roman religious practices along Hadrian's Wall. A special section will be dedicated to the memory of Anson Darby. As for Jane Badrick, international warrants have been issued, though authorities admit the trail has gone cold. "Some mysteries," DS Bishop concluded in a statement that seemed to encompass more than just the case at hand, "may never be solved."

[Continued on Page 4]

Review

Dear Reader,

Thank you for making it to the end of a long journey!

If you enjoyed reading *Ithaca Found*, could you please leave a review or a rating on your favourite digital platform?

And if you are ready for more time travel, try *The Deadly Life of Diana Penn*, a collaboration between myself and Shawn Inmon.

Thank you

Kirsten McKenzie x

Book Club Discussion Questions

1. What was your favourite part of *Ithaca Found*?
2. Which part of history would you want to change?
3. Which scene would you like to rewrite?
4. What surprised you the most about the book?
5. *Ithaca Lost* goes back 1,900 years. Where and when would you like to time travel to?
6. What is one question you have for the author?
7. Soldier, Politician, or Publican? Who would you want to be in Roman Britain?
8. If you had to trade places with one character, who would it be and why?
9. What one piece of historical knowledge would you want to take with you if you went back in time 1,900 years?
10. Will you read another book by Kirsten McKenzie?

Cast Of Players

THE ITHACA SERIES

Lillian Arlosh, owner of Ithaca Farm

Andy 'Badger' Badrick, Friend of Lillian
Matthew Badrick, Badger's Father, Archaeologist
Jane Badrick, Badger's Mother, Mayor
Raymond Lamont, Jane Badger's assistant

John Revell, Editor, Hexham Herald
Gail Revell, wife of John Revell
Jasper Fletcher, Reporter, Hexham Herald
Sue, Receptionist, Hexham Herald
Tom, Print Manager, Hexham Herald
Damien and Jan, Advertising team, Hexham Herald
Rhema Patel, Classifieds Intern, Hexham Herald
Lorna Milroy, BBC London Reporter
Charley Scott, Newcastle Reporter

Darren Saunders, Lawyer
Seb Arlosh, Friend of Badger's
William Arlosh, Seb's Grandfather
James Losh*, 18th century ancestor of William Arlosh
Lola Cassidy, Councillor
Jesha Martin, Friend
Apple Collings, Friend

Holly Corben, Girlfriend of Badger
Paige Spencer, Bellingham Tea Rooms Proprietor
Anson Darby, Archaeologist, Tyne River University
Ayla Raposo, Portable Antiquities Scheme
Constable Robson, Hexham Police
Sergeant Gavin Bishop, Hexham Sergeant
Chief Inspector Kevin Readdie, Newcastle Inspector
Clifton Beaufort, Hadrian's Heroes Metal Detecting Club
Graham Ryan, Hadrian's Heroes Metal Detecting Club
Pete Savin*, Photographer

Nicole Pilcher, Antiques Dealer
Pramod Sharma, Librarian
Henry Neumegen, Pawnbroker
Ryan Francis, Art Loss Register
Gemma Dance, Art Loss Register
Emma Humphreys, Royal Mint
Dafydd Wynne, Retired Curator
Loretta Hambly Wynne, Dafydd's Wife
Joyce Wynne, Dafydd's Daughter

Julius Stertinius Carpus, Roman Soldier
Marcus Aurelius Julianus, Roman Soldier
Darius, Roman Soldier
Gaius Cossutius Saturninus, Roman Soldier
Titus Caelius Castus, Commander of Ithaca Fort
Claudia, Castus' Wife
Metella, Brothel Keeper
Carmella, Metella's Servant
Silas, Metella's Manservant
Gattus, Healer
Caelius Apicius*, Roman Recipe Book Author
Decimus Clodius Albinus*, Governor of Britain
Publius Septimius Aper, Father of Metella
Quintus Valerius, Innkeeper

Gar, Iceni Chieftain
Bricius, Iceni Warrior

Iolo, Druid
Diviciacus*, Druid

Satiada, Celtic Goddess worshipped in Roman Britain
Meditrina, Roman goddess of health, longevity and wine
*Genuine historical figures

312

About the Author

Kirsten McKenzie spent 14 years fighting international crime as a Customs Officer in England and New Zealand before joining the family antique business. Now a full-time author, she writes time travel trilogies and thrillers from her home in New Zealand, where she lives with her husband, two daughters, and a rescue cat.

Her historical time travel trilogy, *The Old Curiosity Shop* series, has been called "*Antiques Roadshow* gone viral". Her latest collaboration is the Cheviot Hills Time Travel series with author Shawn Inmon. Book #1 is titled *The Deadly Life of Diana Penn*, with book #2 - *The Helpful Life of Gris Morley*, out in early 2026.

Kirsten's bestselling gothic thriller *Painted* almost made it to Netflix. Her latest thriller, *The Vampires of York Tower*, adds a dark twist to her body of work.

When not writing, she organises author events and speaks at literary festivals worldwide.

Join her newsletter at:
www.kirstenmckenzie.com/newsletter